DEADBEAT

MAKES YOU STRONGER

Also by Guy Adams and available from Titan Books

Sherlock Holmes: The Breath of God
Sherlock Holmes: The Army of Dr Moreau

Coming soon

Deadbeat: Dogs of Waugh

DEADBEAT

MAKES YOU STRONGER

GUY ADAMS

TITAN BOOKS

Deadbeat: Makes You Stronger
Print edition ISBN: 9781781162514
E-book edition ISBN: 9781781162521

Published by Titan Books
A division of Titan Publishing Group Ltd
144 Southwark Street, London SE1 0UP

First edition: June 2013
1 3 5 7 9 10 8 6 4 2

Did you enjoy this book? We love to hear from our readers.
Please email us at readerfeedback@titanemail.com or write to us at
Reader Feedback at the above address.

To receive advance information, news, competitions, and exclusive
offers online, please sign up for the Titan newsletter on our website:
www.titanbooks.com

PART ONE

MAX

1.

There comes a time in everyone's life when you become aware of a very real and urgent need to look at what you've become. That moment when you see yourself with agonising clarity and realise it might be time to make some changes.

Speaking personally, that moment had arrived. Typically, the timing wasn't good. Hanging from a church bell-tower by my fingers, there seemed little I could do to act on it. I could open up to one of the many pigeons that shared the ledge, staring at me in their peculiar dead-eyed manner. Their counselling skills were no doubt limited, but preferable to the only other option. Call me churlish, but I wasn't inclined to discuss matters with the bastard that threw me out here in the first place. Childish, perhaps, but he was in my bad books and I was determined to give him the silent treatment.

My left hand slipped in a slick spray of pigeon shit, and I gripped at the iron railing even tighter with my right. That was the pigeons off my Christmas card list as well.

Hanging there one-handed, doing my best to lodge my toes into the crack between bricks, a thought struck me. I could turn my mono-dextrous situation to my advantage if I was careful.

I rummaged in my jacket pocket with my free hand. It was entirely possible – if not expected given my current run of luck – that what I was hunting for was in the other pocket and out of reach. Still, you've got to catch a break occasionally and, as my fingers closed around the small packet, it seemed things were on the up. I fumbled open the packet and drew out the object I was after, holding it between my lips as I searched the pocket again. No. Empty. Somewhere in the distance God was heard to laugh.

What a bastard he is.

I was out of options. Time to swallow my pride and talk to my attacker. Straightening the cigarette in my mouth, I sighed and shouted up to him.

"Don't suppose you've got a light?"

In hindsight I'm assuming he was one of those evangelical non-smokers. Otherwise, kicking at the one hand that was keeping me attached to this soot-stained tower when a simple "no" would have sufficed would have no justification at all.

I wondered on this sort of intolerance of others as I toppled backwards, if only to take my mind off the immutable facts of gravity.

2.

The air in the memorial garden was thick with black smoke, so I saw no problem adding more. "Smoking harms you and others around you" the pack assured me as I shoved it back into my jacket pocket. Without wanting to be presumptuous, the gravestone I was leaning on insisted that its occupant had been in the ground since '74, so it was a safe bet that health issues were a low priority. He might chuckle if a few worms developed tumours though, so I puffed a cloud of smoke towards the earth and wished him well.

I loosened the black tie at my throat, letting some air in. It had been insufferably hot inside the church, the typical muggy air of a city summer hugging old stone. I'd sat at the back, feigning polite distance from the family and close friends but frankly just desperate for the draught from the open doors. Even in that slight breeze it had been sickeningly close; much hotter and I felt I'd be joining the deceased in their urns. The priest had been suffering too, wafting his surplice during the hymns, desperate for updraught. After the third or fourth time it occurred to me that he could have been naked underneath, and the thought disturbed me for the rest of the service. It seemed a touch sacrilegious somehow; surely trousers were a prerequisite when in the presence of the dead?

Little would surprise me as far as he was concerned: the thin red veins that spread across his cheeks and nose reminded me of a summer hiking with an Ordnance Survey map when I was still young enough to think it might be fun. Careful analysis of his face would probably lead to many hidden treasures; maybe that large eruption to the left of his mottled beak was the final resting place of the Grail? Or, more likely, his secret stash of appropriated altar wine. Judging by the accelerated speed of the service, he was clearly eager to get the body burned and return to his bottle. I egged him on.

We took our cue for the final hymn and, feeling I'd done my duty, I used the distraction to get out in the fresh air and sneak a fag.

Not that it was much cooler outside; a haze clung to the gravestones like syrup. The buzzing of a lawnmower that had hung under the words of the service had stopped, the gardener sitting down in the shade of a tree to pick at limp sandwiches from his plastic lunchbox.

Embers were floating from the mouth of the chimney above the crematorium, wafting their way towards civilisation. I wondered whether it was supposed to do that: a goodly quantity of her ashes were being spread whether she'd wanted it or not. Thinking about it, she would probably have been pleased. I'd barely known the woman, but had heard as many stories of her exploits as there were to be told. The "doyenne" of theatre had been self-proclaimed, as comfortable with the image of eccentric dame as she was skilled at portraying it. A faded folk icon to the glitter-and-camp brigade, destined to be remembered with trilled speeches and raised gin. Why they had chosen this dreary suburb to send her on her way was a mystery, but certainly she would have felt a touch of pride at being smeared across its dirty red brick and concrete. It was a streak of glamour on a mundane backcloth, scarlet lipstick on the mouth of a corpse.

People were beginning to appear at the chapel exit, black-clad mourners parading their grief in so overt and grotesque a manner that I fought the urge to applaud. One final drama to end them all.

"Bloody awful, isn't it?"

Tom Harris' ability to sneak up on me was one of his

most redeeming features. Don't get me wrong, it pisses me off something rotten, but it was undoubtedly the nicest of his bad qualities. The way he always managed to convince me to do something, for example, now that was really irritating.

"Come on, I'll let you buy me a drink."

"Yeah, all right."

See? Infuriating.

I'd known Tom for more years than I care to count. One of the first theatre directors to put work my way – and indeed, keep offering it over the years – I felt I should class him as friend rather than employer. For his part we worked on a similar wavelength. He knew he could rely on me to do the job he was asking without the need for extensive direction – we just tended to look at characters in the same way. That and the fact I bought him wine when asked.

There's a little more to it than that, but I don't intend to get caught up in that story if at all possible. Suffice it to say we had considerable shared history.

We hit the pub a good round or so ahead of the other mourners, who had, no doubt, been delayed by a few days' or so mutual backslapping. I bought Tom his preferred large glass of Cabernet and a pint of lager for myself – not that I don't like wine, but I am very much the sort that feels a bit of a ponce ordering it in a pub. Pathetic? Certainly, but with the twenty or so years between us, Tom and I straddled that peculiar age barrier: he was just old enough to realise it was all nonsense, I still had sufficient youth to believe it important.

We hid away in a corner snug. While Tom and I could never quite resist attending events like this, we made a point of avoiding the company that inevitably came with them. We keep ourselves to ourselves.

"God, but I hate these old theatre bashes," Tom sighed, scratching absently at the cropped beard he calls "silver" but a more uncharitable person might call grey.

"You love it, reminds you of 'the old days'."

"'The old days'? Dear Lord… when did I get so bloody old that I possess eras?"

"Ages ago."

"I suppose there's a dreadful pleasure to be found in counting the empty seats around the tables, mentally ticking off those who've pegged it since the last get-together."

"You're a sick old bastard, you know that?"

Tom smiled.

"And you, Max, are a terrible hypocrite."

Truth was, both of us liked hovering on the edges of the old circle; it was nostalgic. Tom and I did little theatre work these days, general circumstance having nudged us in a different direction. We both liked to keep a creative hand in now and then, writing the occasional review just to prove that we could. Generally though, we had other things on our minds.

First round sunk. Tom replaced it, and the cycle for the next few hours was set. By the time we left the pub it was dark and our rather self-conscious swagger had been replaced with a jaunty stumble that took out several of the coats hanging by the door and saw Tom nearly impale himself on a fibreglass guide dog that stood by the door hoping for charity donations.

"Down boy," he said and we tumbled onto the pavement with limited physical injury but further wounding to our reputations.

Strolling along the street in the direction of the church and the hope of a taxi rank, we laughed at things without humour and tripped over absent stumbling blocks.

Just another patented Harris/Jackson skinful.

"It's no good," Tom muttered.

"What?" I replied, laughing inanely for some reason I can no longer recall.

"I'm going to have to pay a visit to a darkened corner."

He scrabbled over the church wall, unzipping his jeans as he went, in that drunken sense of preparation, or perhaps just making sure he did so while he remembered it was necessary.

I sighed, chuckled again and attempted a nonchalant vault over the wall that resulted in nothing less than a grass-stained cheek and a bent cigarette. Getting quickly to my feet, I checked if Tom had noticed and was relieved to see that he had his back to me and was apologising to the deceased residents as he emptied his bladder.

I replaced my cigarette and strolled through the tombstones in his general direction, gazing up at the dark church building. It looked better at night, lit by spaced-out floodlights that gave it a fine dressing of gothic shadow but hid the dirt stains of years of traffic and industry. Once upon a time this would have been a focal building at the centre of a small village. Then suburbia came, ploughing through the countryside, subsuming all the smaller outposts it came to. One day the cities will eat everything.

A movement caught my eye by the church door. Darting behind the closest stone, I watched a group of people carrying a coffin. Tom was beginning to hum Miles Davis, something he has a habit of doing when he forgets not to.

I enjoyed a nice fruity curse and dashed towards him, trying my best to keep to the shadows of the far wall.

He was, thankfully, zipping himself up as I drew up behind him.

"What?" he said in a manner that was both indignant and too loud for my liking.

"Keep your mouth shut, we've got company," I said, pointing towards the group of people a few hundred feet away.

They had a large Transit van. One of them was opening the doors as the others carried the coffin over.

"Hardly the most salubrious form of transport. Not to mention the wrong direction," Tom whispered, and began tiptoeing towards them.

"Where do you think you're going?" I asked, trying to keep up.

"I'm being nosey," he replied, crouching rather unsteadily behind a gravestone no more than a healthy spit away from the front of the church.

I decided that giving him a good kicking was likely to draw attention so, pencilling it in for ten minutes' time, I resigned myself to hiding behind the stone next door to his.

It wasn't even as if they were up to anything particularly exciting. I mean, true, a Transit isn't a preferred transport for coffins, not full ones anyway. That said, for all I knew, it happened all the time, leaving the hearse for more ceremonial occasions. What the family didn't know was hardly likely to concern them. Then I realised what he'd meant about direction – why would you take a corpse *away* from a graveyard?

At that moment one of the men stumbled, twisting his

ankle on a large stone that sat out of place on the gravel driveway. One of the others gave a panicked shout as the coffin slipped out of his grip, and I fought the instinctual urge to dash towards them as I watched the coffin drop to the ground.

The lid cracked open and a satin-wrapped body fell out. The men stared at the body for a moment, as if uncertain whether it might suddenly sit up and shout at them for being so clumsy. The man by the van, clearly the boss, marched over and clipped one of them across the shoulder.

"Pick her up, you clumsy bastards!"

The spell broke and, as one, they lifted her back into the coffin.

"Come on!" the boss said, shoving them towards the open back doors of the van.

They hoisted the coffin in, all concerns of gentility gone, shoving it towards the back with a clang of heavy wood against metal.

Two of the men jogged back to close the church doors while the boss walked around to the passenger door, climbing in as the driver started the engine.

Church closed, the others clambered into the back of the van, slamming the doors shut behind them as the driver reversed out and then drove off through the church gates. Both Tom and I ducked as the headlamps swept across the front of the stones we were hiding behind.

After a few moments we stood up.

"Well that was interesting," Tom said.

"Worrying, certainly. You can't get good staff these days, can you?"

Tom looked bemused.

"I think you're missing something. What did you notice about the woman in the coffin?"

"Never seen her before in my life."

"That's not what I was asking, there was something particular about her."

I leaned on the tombstone and lit a cigarette, to buy me a little time more than anything else.

"Other than the fact that she was being manhandled into the back of Transit van by the most thug-like undertakers operating in the Greater London area? Not much… She was in her thirties, blonde hair, about five and a half foot…" I took a drag of my cigarette while trying to think of something else. "Wrapped in a red satin sheet…"

Tom sighed.

"All true, but you've missed one rather obvious point."

"Really?"

"Yes." Tom put his hands in his pockets and strolled out onto the gravel drive. He was scanning the ground for something. "Aha!" he shouted and dropped to his haunches.

"What?" I was getting a touch impatient. Much more of this and I might have to call my secretary and have the Tom-kicking moved forward.

"A set of keys," Tom replied, holding them up. "They came off that man's belt when he fell over."

"About the body, you infuriating git!"

"Oh." Tom nodded, popping the keys in his pocket. "Well, you managed to describe what she looked like well enough, but there was one obvious feature you didn't catch."

He moved over to join me.

"She was breathing. Not a common habit among the dead."

3.

After all the running around, hiding, and being generally weirded out, Tom and I were pretty much on our way towards sober (say somewhere in its suburbs following the "city centre" signs and keeping our eyes peeled for car parks), which seems ironic to me because any action or event capable of sobering me up at preternatural speed tends to be exactly the sort of thing where I need a stiff drink after. It's good that Tom had the foresight to buy a nightclub a few years ago; it meant that – after a bit more stumbling around looking for a taxi – we had somewhere to go.

It wasn't a big place: about thirty tables and a stage filled it to capacity. He could have fitted a few more punters in if he'd had a smaller bar, but Tom didn't like to skimp on the important stuff. There was live music most nights, jazz and blues as a rule, although Tom could occasionally be caught unawares and end up with a little variety slipped onto the schedule behind his back. Generally though, if it didn't have a horn section it wasn't going to set foot on his stage. Tom was nothing if not a man of principle. His attitude had certainly paid off: the place was extremely popular and, as a result, he was hardly short of a shilling. Not that he had much hand in the day to day running of the place; he left that to Len Horowitz, his manager – a man with a wit so dry it would give a lizard cottonmouth. He was good at his job though, and the club's reputation was strong enough to bear the occasional rude comment towards the clientele. I think most of them rather liked it. There is a universal rule among such establishments:

get it right and the customers will do all the hard work, keep clear of fashionability and they'll come to you. "Deadbeat" – something of an in-joke between Tom and I – was a place to go.

"Ah," Len sighed, twitching his thick moustache in disgust as we leaned on the bar. "The only two regulars I haven't the authority to bar. What'll it be?"

"A brace of sturdy caipirinhas, I think. Don't you, Max?"

"It would be exceedingly rude not to, Tom. Smash those limes, Len, show 'em who's boss."

"Oh they know, Mr Jackson. It's Mr Harris here that sometimes get confused on that score."

He went on the hunt for cachaça and we for a corner booth.

"So," Tom said as we sat down out of the way of the few diehards that were still loitering near the stage, "that was all very intriguing wasn't it?"

"One word for it."

He pulled the keys he'd found out of his pocket and began to examine them.

"Fascinating… there's so much you can tell from the objects people carry around with them every day, little clues to their lives and habits. Even with only a cursory examination, in far from perfect lighting, I can make a number of insightful assumptions about the owner of these keys. He has money." He held up a car key. "The car that belongs to this doesn't come cheap. He keeps himself fit and works in a job that requires a uniform: there are two locker keys, you see?"

I nodded, just to keep him happy.

"He's either a drinker or extremely short-sighted: there

are a number of scratches and dents that suggest repeated misaligning of key and lock."

He held the keys up to his nose and sniffed, raised an eyebrow, then sniffed again.

"Very distinctive odour." He put on his best "ruminating" face and then slammed the keys on the table. "Embalming fluid. He works in an undertakers."

He'd timed it perfectly; Len placed the caipirinhas in front of us right on the full stop.

"Very impressive, Holmes," I said, taking a sip of my drink, "to be able to tell all of that from just a 'cursory examination'. I would be in awe of your deductive abilities, were it not for the fact that I too can read." I held up the leather key fob with the name and address of an undertaking firm on it.

"Oh, you saw that, did you?"

"Yes, you theatrical old queen. That and the fact they were pissing about with coffins led me to believe they weren't fishmongers. Where did you get the rest from?"

"Made it up, can't see a thing in this light. How was my delivery though?"

"So ham it would unnerve Jewish people. Congratulations."

"Thank you." He performed a half bow.

We drank our cocktails for a few moments, Tom waiting for me to suggest we investigate further, me refusing to give him the satisfaction. I knew impatience would force him do it himself eventually.

"So," he said, "you reckon we should look into it?"

"Why? Nothing to do with us."

"Don't tell me you're not interested."

"Not particularly."

A blatant lie, but I was damned if I was going to roll over straight away.

"What else have we got to do? It would pass the time, if nothing else."

Which was true. Both Tom and I had been in a considerable rut of late. Deadbeat ran itself; in fact whenever Tom tried to get too proactive he ended up getting in the way. I wasn't working. The days were starting to get a little monotonous for both of us. "Why don't they just go to the police?" you ask. Well… suffice it to say that we couldn't. For personal reasons, talking to the police would be a Really Bad Idea.

I picked up the keys and made a show of sighing and rolling my eyes.

"All right then, we'll have a little nose around."

"Excellent!" Tom slapped the table with his palms and got to his feet.

"I'll get us more drinks by way of celebration."

Which, unsurprisingly, is exactly how all of our worst ideas start out.

4.

Start as you mean to go on. A couple of hours later and I had entered that state of mental shutdown that a night at the bar often brings, staring vacantly as a handful of ice cracked and melted in the tumbler in front of me, much like my brain.

As is always the way when I straddle that transient line

between consciousness and utter oblivion, my mind started to fart images at me: always the water, that slap of ice to the face, the roar deep inside the eardrums, the splitting pain in my chest as the heart fights to keep beating, the distant bellow of horns. And at that point more drink will only make them clearer, not blot them out completely. Still, you refresh your glass, work through it, keep running in the only direction you know: towards darkness and a lack of responsibility.

Right now even telling this story is too much work for my liking. You don't know who I am, not really. Sat there questioning my motivations and thoughts... wondering why... There's so much I could tell you, things unsaid... perhaps I should just let it all come out. No more secrets. But then, while some things would be clearer, the rest would be worse... If you knew everything about me you wouldn't still be here. You'd have started screaming long before now.

Christ, drink makes me waffle...

2

TOM

1.

Finley Peter Dunne, the American writer and humorist, was a fiercely wise chap. "Alcohol," he said, "is necessary for a man so that he can have a good opinion of himself, undisturbed by the facts." When the clock drags its heels towards the early hours of morning it's a thought that often rolls around my head. Sat there on one of the barstools watching the last soldiers fall from the assault of grape and grain, limping wounded onto the no-man's-land of Soho for a taxi to take them home, I wonder on the truth of his words. Do I drink to bolster low self-esteem? Do I drink to wear down the edges of memory? Is it a crutch that maintains my ability to walk through this life with some degree of efficacy?

The thoughts haunt me, so much so that I pound the hell out of them with a few stiff measures of brandy. Nobody needs that sort of depressing nonsense in their brain when they're trying to have a good night. Takes all the fun out of it.

That night it wasn't an issue. I had more than enough

to occupy the scant few grey cells I had mercifully spared from the booze. It had been some considerable time since anything had provided so much as a buzz of mental interest. Life can become interminably dull if you allow it.

Max, as per usual, passed out across the table we'd been sitting at and I had the boys bundle him home. There will come a time when I will have to insist that he move in upstairs, if only to save petrol.

Watching the hustle and bustle of the staff clearing down, sweeping up and generally turning the club back to its previous state, as if it were a crime scene that we wished to disguise, I decided to shut myself in my office and leave them to it. I'm hopeless with a dustpan and I'd only get in the way. Besides, the office is where I keep most of my record collection and the speakers are wired up perfectly. It is the best place to lose myself in music that I know. I have been assured by Len that it would also be an ideal place for any clerical work involving the club, accounts and general paperwork, but I've seen no reason to prove that as yet. In my mind, offices lose some of their charm if you start working in them.

I slipped Oliver Nelson's *Swiss Suite* onto the turntable and turned the volume up enough to dissuade anyone from knocking on the door and interfering with my mood. Thus assured of not losing my reputation by being observed, I brewed a cafetière of strong coffee and turned my little laptop on.

People assume I can't operate a computer. I must have a Luddite air to me. It's true enough that they baffle me frequently and many's the time when I have had an extremely strong urge to hurl the thing across the room.

But that's technology for you, you take the rough with the smooth. I wouldn't be without it and – keep it under your hat – I actually write a couple of music blogs (one on classical and one on jazz) under a pseudonym. It pays very little but then I don't do it for the money, it's just fun to waffle about one's passions…

I checked my emails – offers of penis enlargement and cash-rich Nigerians for the most part; my correspondence is never less than scintillating – and then wandered aimlessly online while sipping my coffee. After a ten-minute stroll through the sites I usually frequent, by way of asserting to myself that what I was hunting for was most probably nothing of interest and therefore not worth rushing over, I tapped "Lloyd & Bryson Undertakers" into a search engine and glanced at the page of results. It assured me that the "and" had been unnecessary as it searched all phrases by default, which was all well and good if it could have shown me the fruit of such confidence by way of a useful link. As it was, there was a list of funeral homes in America, none of which could be of the slightest relevance.

I couldn't help but think that I was letting the spirit of Philip Marlowe down.

Bringing up the phone directory page, I managed to pin the office of the undertakers to an address in Kentish Town. Not far from the church then. That was something – at least we now knew where it was.

I made a new search: Kentish Town undertakers… plenty of those – they're dropping like flies in Camden. I hit upon a link to a message board where posters were sharing their grief in the cosy anonymity of the Internet. One woman's message contained a list of agonies regarding her husband, who had clearly been struck fatally ill and had gone from fit as a fiddle to dead and buried within a matter of weeks. She made a reference to an undertaker that had been recommended to her via the health insurance company she had a policy with, but it could have been anyone. She had nothing but praise for them and made no reference to Transit vans or midnight flits.

This really was getting us nowhere.

To hell with the Internet, we needed to expend shoe leather.

I dialled Max's number and left a message on his answer machine telling him to meet me at the church in the morning. I suggested a not-so-distant time that I knew he would deeply disapprove of. I also knew that the persistent beeping of his machine would ensure he woke up to meet the appointment. His answer machine takes no prisoners – I know, I bought it for him.

Poor Max, so easily led…

I should tell the story of how we first met, if only because I know it would irritate him hugely.

Max often tells people that he and I worked together in theatre, which is not entirely true. Well… it's not true at all, actually, but I know why he says it. Certainly we both have a history as far as the stage is concerned, and that shared background added to the ease with which we hit it off and grew close. I was a child in Stratford-upon-Avon; I grew up on Shakespeare and sonnets (as well as Hemingway and pulp war novels – my literary upbringing was a field of highs and lows). I was there in the sixties when Peter Hall kicked The Bard up the arse and gave the Royal Shakespeare Company the birth it needed. Shakespeare was as cool as

Miles Davis, and they were my poster idols as I surfed adolescence. I worked as a writer and director in theatre for many years, in between more lucrative employment. Max has the handicap of being younger than me, but nonetheless found himself on a similar path: a trained actor hacking out a living in profit-share theatre, the sort of shows that have larger casts than audiences, occasionally paying for food with the odd appearance on television.

By the time we crossed paths it was a lifestyle that had pretty much been squeezed out of both of us. I had recently bought the club and Max… Well, Max had been drifting.

He wasn't always the well-adjusted gentleman you see today (yes, I'm being sarcastic). When I first clapped eyes on him he was a ragged and weary young man. He had all the confidence of a whipped dog, carrying himself as if he expected to be jumped upon and beaten at any moment. Nervous then, yes, but it was more than that. His awkwardness and perpetually twitching sense of imminent danger was not a temporary fixture, this was how he was. A man scared to exist in his own skin.

I was attending a fringe show in the dingy top room of a pub in Camden, all black painted walls and the fug of tobacco and old beer. I knew one of the cast, and out of a misguided sense of loyalty I had decided to turn up and show a little support.

After an hour or so of watching *Romeo and Juliet* restaged as a lesbian love tryst (with the nurse a jaded transsexual replete in goatee and Laura Ashley) I was losing the will to live, and determined to bail out of this creative death-pit the moment the lights went up for the interval. I spotted Max in the row just in front of mine.

Like me he was loitering in the back seats, keeping his head down (in my case I had no wish to announce myself, even less now it was clear that I would be incapable of surviving the whole performance). His hair was a good deal longer than he favours these days, curly and spiked in a manner that suggested lack of treatment rather than the swirling fringe sculptures that seem popular today. He was wearing a long overcoat that he tugged around himself like a blanket, as if desperate to lose himself in one of its pockets. His attention to the stage was minimal. He glanced at it now and then in a rather dutiful manner but he wasn't even giving it enough attention to loathe it. It was something that just happened to be going on in the same room. He spent more time looking around, ignoring the mangled verse and histrionics in favour of analysing the chipped plaster walls and the frayed set dressing. He was a man gripped by discomfort. There were a few momentary exceptions whenever one of the female cast entered. Then, and only then, his attention was total. I assumed he was there out of a sense of duty, much like me. That aside, his discomfort was so pronounced I couldn't help but watch him closely.

When the interval finally raised its slovenly head and the house lights revealed the small gathering of bewildered audience – friends and mothers all, no doubt – I found myself following him down the stairs into the bar. I was intrigued by him and wanted to know more.

Rather than take a place at the bar as most of the audience did (hoping to drink enough to make the second half tolerable), he walked straight out onto the street. I did the same and put a little spurt on so as to draw level with him.

"Two theatre lovers, alike in dignity," I said, mangling poor old Bill Shakespeare no more than the actors had. "I take it you hated it as much as me?"

He flinched, that sense of unease and fearfulness given full rein for just a moment before he snapped it back down and smiled. "I heard Shakespeare screaming in agony five minutes in."

"Apparently they try and up the ante in the second half with a naked love scene. The papers were full of it."

"Romeo could fire ping-pong balls into the crowd with all the skill of a Bangkok stripper and it still wouldn't stop me from falling asleep."

He didn't stop walking – that would have meant embracing the conversation, which he was clearly still unwilling to do – but he was polite enough to slow down a little so that walking and talking were easier.

"I know one of the cast," I said, eager to keep the conversation moving, "otherwise I wouldn't have bothered chancing it."

"Not one of the leads?" he asked.

"No, thank God, I wouldn't have admitted it if I did. The nurse."

He laughed. "He looks cracking in a frock."

"Yes, one of the prouder lines on his CV I'm sure." I had hoped he was going to admit knowing the woman he had been so drawn to. No such luck. Perhaps he needed lubricating. "Fancy a drink?"

I nodded towards a pub across the road. That worried look returned to his face; no doubt he thought I was trying to pull him, arrogant bugger. He need hardly have worried on that score.

"Er... no, thanks though, I need to be getting home really."

He started walking a little quicker and I realised I needed to play dirty in order to keep him from vanishing. The thing is, I had a hunch what it was about him that had drawn my attention – beyond his bizarre mannerisms – and the only way I could think of to stop him was to trust my instincts and use it. There was something else the two of us shared beyond an appreciation of what made truly awful theatre and, if I was right, the realisation that it was a mutual affliction would be enough for him to stop for a second and hear me out.

Now, this is tricky. You see, there is indeed something unusual about Max, and I was right when I thought I sensed it in him on that first meeting. Still, it is hardly my place to announce it. You'll just have to trust me when I say that there is a reason he drew my eye and that it would be of benefit to both of us to sit down over some finely chilled alcohol and discuss it. You will have to accept that, for now at least, you do not need to know what that is.

It's enough to say that my gut instincts about him had been right and, after a panicked moment when I thought he might run anyway – so concerned was he that he had been so easily discovered – he relaxed and we headed over the road for a drink.

Secrets. My entire life is complicated by secrets.

We talked about lots of things. He told me about his theatrical past. He also admitted he'd been there to watch the young woman forced into Mercutio's doublet and hose. I got the impression their relationship had been a little more than just having worked together, but he refused to be drawn on the details. What was clear was that he had no intention of being seen by her and would have done a runner in the interval whether the play had been good or not.

He talked about his background in Yorkshire, his childhood, how he had come to be in London… He talked about everything. It is always the way with someone so tensed up, someone who has become so nervously clenched as to be almost physically deformed by it: when they are given the chance to unwind they do so with such violence that one is advised to just sit back and allow it, adding more alcohol and the odd supportive nod or grunt as and when it seems required. We got heroically drunk. Drunk enough in fact that we decided the only way forward, after groaning at the depressive death-knell of the bell behind the bar, was to make our way to the club and drink some more.

I am only too aware, thinking back on the two of us stumbling through the streets, how the template was set for so many of our nights to come. We are creatures of habit, Max and I, and that was the night that formed it all.

Back at the club, I marvelled at how the terrified young man I had first spotted hours earlier had become transformed into this whirling dervish, dancing on his own to the sound of Dixieland. Fists raised in the air and face grimly set into a frown of deep concentration as he moved like Cab Calloway.

It goes without saying that Len had his reservations. It is an awkward conflict of interests for a bar manager when the one individual that could be defined as worthy of removal is there at the owner's invitation, and therefore above the law.

"That bastard's making eyes at me!" Max shouted at

one point (though the band were between tunes and he
didn't need to raise his voice to be heard).

"Len is a man of infinite intolerance," I assured him,
"don't let it bother you."

Max grinned, necked the gin and tonic he had been
working on and spiralled back onto the dance floor as the
band picked up again. He came to a halt in the centre of the
room – regressed to the showy little performer he had been
so many years ago, before financial failure and perpetual
joblessness had started to knock it out of him – held up
his hands and prepared to make a speech. Before he could
so much as utter a syllable though, his face drooped on its
bones and a look of absolute confusion poured itself into
his eyes. He spun around and, in an act of pure abandon
that makes him cringe heartily whenever I mention it –
which, of course, means I mention it frequently – he threw
up into the bell of the bass saxophone behind him. The
mortified saxophonist – a pale and timid man who had been
muscling up to lead into "Sweet Georgia Brown" – gave a
roar of disgust and dropped the slopping horn. Max caught
it, face still pressed against the brass rim of its bell, and fell
back on the floor. He sat, legs splayed, saxophone hugged
to his belly as the now-silent club fixed its attention on him.

That's how I first met Max Jackson.

||||3

MAX
1.

I live in a small place in Wood Green. What it lacks in size, charm, comfort and class it makes up for in tube connections and quantity of grocery stores with twenty-four hour opening. I am a man who frequently buys milk and chocolate at four o'clock in the morning, so the facility to do so is a great comfort. Shopping at that time of day is a dreamlike experience, shuffling under the bright neon lights with a handful of other lost souls. We try and focus on shelves of tinned meat, fighting to keep our balance and not step on each other.

Wood Green's not a bad spot. It has plenty of coffee shops and two cinemas, so combine that with twenty-four-hour food shopping and my needs are fulfilled. It's far enough out that people in the city look at you funny when you mention it, as if you've just admitted that the Piccadilly Line reaches as far as the moon. There's a part of me that likes that too.

The opinion felt more accurate than normal that morning, as I headed to meet Tom at the church. No doubt this was more to do with the fact that the Piccadilly Line was feeling more hostile towards the people travelling inside it than usual. I wasn't alone in my suffering, the train filled with all the sorts of people I normally don't see: people in suits, people that compose emails on phones and work their way through their copies of the *Metro* newspaper as if it's a timeworn duty.

I met fresh air in Kentish Town and walked towards the church we had visited yesterday.

Tom was sat at a bus stop a short way away from the main gate. He was having an in-depth conversation with a Jamaican woman about the benefits of owning a cat. She was all for the idea whereas he took the view that sharing a home with felines was a recipe for mutual disappointment.

"Cats," he explained, "are like women. They're far too sensible to put up with a man's ways."

"What a stupid thing to say," she replied.

"Proving my point," he sighed, getting up and moving over to me.

"New girlfriend?" I asked.

"I suspect not, she already knows me too well."

We walked the last few yards to the church.

"So," I asked, "other than staring at the place, what do we hope to achieve by coming back here then?"

"Oh, I don't know, think like a private investigator. I'm sure something clever will occur to us."

He began looking at the gravel beneath our feet as we entered the graveyard.

"Maybe," I suggested, "as well as dropping his keys he dropped his diary. Or perhaps a signed statement explaining the night's events."

"At least Watson wasn't so sarcastic," he said. "I bet Holmes would never have founded a career if he'd been straddled with an impatient swine like you."

"Nor if he'd been an alcoholic, serial husband and jazz freak like you."

"Can I help you at all?"

We looked up to see the vicar from the service we'd attended the day before. He had the look of a man who had occupied himself with a thirsty evening. I felt a bond with him. Maybe we could all go on the hunt for a fried breakfast and a strong coffee.

"I dropped my keys here yesterday," said Tom. "I don't suppose anyone's handed them in?"

"Not that I know of," the vicar replied, the slight look of concern he had been wearing fading into one of apathy. After a moment he obviously decided he could do better by his flock. "I could check with the cleaner," he suggested.

"That would be so kind," said Tom, taking the man's hand and holding it in a manner he no doubt thought conveyed reverence. It made the vicar incredibly uncomfortable, but Tom was not a man interested in observing others so he held on for a few more moments.

"She's inside," the vicar said, pulling his hand away and leading us down the path towards the church.

"So nice to see," said Tom, gesturing to the wide-open doors. "They lock some churches up these days, don't they? I don't think that's right. The House of God should always be open to the public."

The vicar looked at him as if he were quite mad. It's something Tom gets a lot.

"The doors are only open because I'm here," he

explained. "We could hardly leave the place wide open all the hours."

"What a terrible symptom of a broken society," Tom replied, "that we cannot trust people to respect the sanctity of our churches."

"Quite," said the vicar, moving ahead beyond the altar, where an old woman was working her methodical way across the carved wood of the choir stalls with a cloth.

"Valerie," he called, "this gentleman lost some keys here yesterday. He was wondering if anyone had found them."

She paused in her dusting to give the two of us a long appraisal. It was the sort of look that nobody could fail to wither under. It was a wonder she didn't clean the church simply by glowering at it.

"Keys?" she asked, as if they were singularly unusual objects to carry or lose.

"Yes," said Tom. "My house keys. To be honest it's the fob I'm more worried about. A gift from my wife. In fact…" he raised his hand to his mouth, "it was the last thing she gave me before…"

Oh God. Any excuse. Tom can't pass a mirror without performing in front of it. Which would be less grotesque if he were any good at it. He stifled a sob and I did my best to look sympathetic, as if his performance could be improved by at least one of us appearing to be moved. If things went badly I could always beat him senseless with the altar cross and make a run for it. Imagine my surprise when the withered old cleaner wilted before our eyes.

"Oh, my poor love," she said. "You never get over it, do you?"

He offered her a damp-eyed look and then shook his

head. "Like a part of you has been torn away."

"The better part of you."

She took him in her arms, and I glimpsed Tom's face crumple into disagreement that any of his wives had been the better part of him. He controlled it by burying his face into her dusty cardigan.

The vicar and I looked at one another, feeling awkward. I considered suggesting we pop to the pub and leave them to it. He looked as thirsty as he had the day before. I'm sure he would have gone for it, despite the early hour.

"What was it?" Valerie asked. "Not the cancer like my poor Ted?"

Oh God… could this situation get more awful?

Tom shook his head. "She fell under a bus on the Strand. If nothing else it was quick, though I believe the driver is still receiving counselling."

That's it, Tom, I thought. Black humour, that's what this situation needs to make it much more palatable. Tosser.

The world just passes Tom by. He's the kind of man you cringe at when you meet them at parties. The sort of insensitive idiot who jokes about infidelity to the man whose wife has just left him or dances around people in wheelchairs. He's not evil – well, I'm pretty sure he's not – just so blindingly unaware of the feelings of those around him that he never notices when he's treading all over them. I had no doubt that while I was squirming at this tasteless mockery of a woman's grief he was having the time of his life.

"How awful," Valerie replied, clearly happy to believe his story. After all, who would be so horrid as to lie about that sort of thing?

"I would hate to think I've lost it," said Tom, "it means such a lot to me."

"Of course it does, my poor love," Valerie replied. "Though I'm afraid nobody's handed anything in to me."

Tom wailed like a cat auditioning for *The X Factor*.

Valerie looked startled.

The vicar looked as if someone had kicked him right up the apse.

I considered buying a gun, if only to avoid such future embarrassments.

"Perhaps someone from the funeral after us found it?" Tom suggested after he had got his breath back. "The funeral for that young lady… I forget her name."

"Oh that was sad," Valerie agreed, "I saw the notices. That was no age at all to die, was it?"

"So young…" Tom agreed.

"Natalie something wasn't it, vicar?" Valerie asked.

"I'm not sure we should really be discussing that," he said, a look of palpable concern on his face.

"Oh don't be silly," Valerie replied, "hardly secret is it? Campbell. That was it. Like the soup. Natalie Campbell."

"I don't suppose you would have a contact number for one of the family?" I asked, having seen where Tom was going with all of this. "We could maybe ask if someone had passed it on?"

"I can't give out that sort of information," the vicar said.

"I'm sure they wouldn't mind," said Valerie, "not in the circumstances. Her husband was beside himself, he would understand."

"No." The vicar was quite insistent on this point. "I can't just hand out people's phone numbers."

Valerie looked at him with brazen disgust. Returning her gaze to Tom, she gave him a damp kiss on the forehead and hugged him as tightly as a mother packing her son off to war.

When they disengaged, he took my arm and headed towards the door.

"Thank you, father," he said to the vicar as we passed.

"Isn't that just for Catholics?" I whispered as we stepped back outside.

"No idea," he admitted, "they're all the same to me. All cassocks and flannel."

"You're a fine one to talk. I've never heard such flannel in all my life."

"Worked though."

"We have a name. There's no guarantee it's even the same woman. Besides, how many Natalie Campbells will there be in London?"

"One less now, in theory. Besides, I did a little better than that." He led me towards the pub we had retired to the day before. He ordered a pair of drinks and checked his watch. "My new best friend, Valerie, will be here in about half an hour to give me the contact number."

"Really?"

"She whispered as much in my ear. Women never can resist me."

"You terrible shit, she's doing it because she thinks you're a widower."

"Widower? Divorcee? What's the difference bar a smaller bill and a less enthusiastic party?"

"Evil."

"No. Experienced."

We sat a table in the window so we could keep an eye on the street.

"What did we think of the vicar?" Tom asked.

"Not much. But then, I never do."

I'll admit I have something of an attitude problem towards the church. A handful of good moral messages doesn't outweigh a history of bigotry and unpleasantness. Don't get me started on the subject at parties or I'll turn the air blue. It's not just a matter of opinion, either, some of the things I've experienced in life give me a solid perspective from which to rant.

"I meant in general rather than as a point of philosophical argument."

"Drinker."

"As are we. Currently sat in a pub at ten o'clock in the morning. Can't hold that one against him."

"True. He wasn't really interested in helping."

"I'd go as far as to say he was actively trying not to."

"He didn't have to take us to meet the lovely Valerie."

"No. And I get the impression that he regretted having done so."

"Probably thought he'd have to officiate at your wedding."

"We know that the church should have been locked last night," Tom added. "Not that I imagined anything else. Still, it confirms our reverend is involved."

"Or that they possess a set of keys."

"True," he sighed.

Feeling that I should at least shoulder some of the detective work, I had taken out my phone and put "Natalie Campbell dead London" into Google. I scanned through a local news item:

"Natalie Campbell, thirty-six, collapsed yesterday in the Hackney branch of Beech's Supermarket. Witnesses commented on her symptoms, the severity of which led a number of fellow shoppers to suspect she had been attacked. Medical assistance was quick to arrive but sadly Mrs Campbell died in the ambulance. She leaves a husband, Laurence."

"How horrible," said Tom, "fancy shopping at Beech's. Aisles of microwave dinners and cheap bottled cider."

"We haven't all got your bank balance," I reminded him, switching to an image search. The first page was useless but the second offered a familiar face. It was the woman we had seen, a smiling, rosy-cheeked shot taken on a chilly English beach.

"She was on Facebook," I said. "Her profile picture ring a bell?"

"Definitely her." Tom dropped the gallows humour. "But if the newspaper insists she was dead, how come she was breathing when we saw her?"

We looked at one another, an idea bubbling unspoken between us on the table.

"She couldn't be..." I said, "could she?"

Couldn't be what? you wonder. Well, wonder on. I already warned you I didn't intend to go into everything. At least I think I did... Well, if I didn't, consider yourself warned. This is my story and I'll tell as much, or as little, of it as I like.

"Whatever was going on, the undertakers were involved. They were rushing her out of there, don't forget."

I took a sip of my drink. "You know, this seemed funny and intriguing last night. Today it just feels horrible. She could be in terrible trouble."

He nodded, looking again at the smiling photograph.

"Here you are my lovelies," said Valerie, appearing at our table in the sort of genteel manner adopted by Ladies of a Certain Age and nation-destroying weather events. "Mine's a small sherry."

I went to the bar, abandoning Tom to her advances. I wasn't in the mood for playacting any more. I couldn't shake the image of Natalie Campbell on the beach, a cold wind turning her face pink. The smile had been heartfelt, offered freely to the camera, or more likely the man holding it – her husband? "He was beside himself," Valerie had told us in the church. Yes. I'm quite sure he was. What would he think if he'd known we'd seen her alive and not told anybody? We needed to pack Valerie off and then think of a way of getting the police involved.

But Valerie wasn't interested in being packed off. She drained the sherry the minute it hit the table, the dark liquid vanishing into her mouth as speedily as if she had simply inhaled it.

"Would you like another?" I asked, not even bothering to sit down.

"Keeps the cold out," she said, sipping at her second drink. Neither of us bothered to mention the perpetual hot spell we were enduring.

She reached into the pocket of her cardigan and pulled out a scrap of paper. "The husband's name is Laurence," she said. "I had a hell of time finding his number as the whole thing was organised by the undertakers."

"Oh yes?" said Tom. "Who did he use?"

"Lloyd & Bryson." Her mouth twisted into a slight

frown. "I can't say I like them much, but we get a lot of their business."

"I'd heard they were very good," said Tom.

"Oh I'm sure they're fine," she replied, "but the staff… well, I wouldn't want them manhandling me, that's for sure."

An image that was hard to shake once it had bedded in.

"Why?" I asked once it was clear she didn't intend to elaborate.

"They're a rough lot," she said, "they look more like they're hoisting around bags of potatoes rather than loved ones. I know that's not always uncommon, not these days. People are so insensitive now, aren't they? Still, I don't like them… There's something about them that sets my teeth on edge."

"At least she was cremated," said Tom, though I knew he was taking a guess. "I dread to think how they might have handled an interment if they're as bad as you say."

"Oh it hardly bears thinking about," she agreed, "bad enough to think of them shovelling away at the ashes, like cats in a litter tray."

"You just can't get quality people these days, can you?" agreed Tom.

"You can't. It's like the ruffians that delivered my fridge the other day, you'd think they were doing their single best to smash the thing to pieces, the way they kept dropping it. I said to them…"

Valerie was like an old motor car, cold to start but once the engine was in full flow it just ran on and on. I did my best to change gear:

"What does the vicar think of them?"

She looked slightly put out that I had interrupted her

but not so much that it kept her quiet.

"Oh he's getting worse by the day. I shouldn't speak ill of the cloth but I'd be surprised if he lasts the year, the way he's been drinking. I mean, we all love a drop now and then, don't we? It's positively medicinal. Father Gibbons though, you rarely see him without his hipflask in hand. That man is an accident waiting to happen."

She then proceeded to list examples of his misbehaviour during services, signs of forgetfulness, mispronunciation and one particularly grotesque moment when he had proceeded to recite a ritual for exorcism at a christening.

It was all wonderfully comic but hardly helped, and Tom and I were relieved to finally escape about an hour later, claiming a prior appointment.

"We need to be serious about this," I insisted as we walked back past the church. "What if Natalie's in trouble and we don't tell anyone?"

"I'll speak to Thackeray," Tom promised. "Leave it with me for a few hours and I'll see what I can do.

2.

We went our separate ways on the Tube and I arrived back home feeling panicked.

I'll admit this isn't altogether unusual. Life seems to wash off Tom with no lasting effects. Not me. I'm the sort of man who can't quite shake the idea that it's all a bit too much. This had seemed a harmless game yesterday, silly and intriguing. Now it felt mammoth, a situation that had already overwhelmed us and could only grow larger. I just hoped that Tom managed to get the authorities involved.

Jamie, the boundless idiot that is my dog, was clearly more cheerful than me. He proved as much by jumping on me the minute I opened the door and punching me in the stomach with his front paws. If asked by anyone – other than Jamie, naturally, I'm not a complete bastard – whether I preferred cats or dogs, I would always say cats. You can leave cats to it. They are flat-mates not children. Flat-mates that complain about the way you chose to live and leave scathing notes pointing out precisely where you keep going wrong. Living with them can be terrible for the self-esteem but at least you're not burdened with responsibility. Jamie was a buffoon. If it wasn't for me he'd be utterly lost. Any creature relying on a Max Jackson to provide stability and common sense is, by definition, a very silly creature indeed.

If only to stop the swine beating me up further, I decided to take him for a walk. It might even do me a little good, get my thoughts in order and let me calm down a little. We headed out towards Alexandra Palace, where Jamie could exercise his obsession with tennis balls and I could try and think things through.

The problem I kept coming back to was that the only evidence we had was that of our own eyes. As I've made clear, going to the police was not an option for either of us. The only way we could get them involved would be to anonymously present sufficient evidence that they were forced to investigate. Try as I might, I couldn't see how that was going to happen. We knew nothing. If we called in an anonymous tip that someone had seen Natalie Campbell alive after her funeral, it would be laughed out of the police station. As much as I wanted to run away from the whole situation I was fast realising that, right now, we were probably Natalie Campbell's only hope.

Which meant she was in a great deal of trouble.

I rang Tom, hoping he would be able to tell me that I was wrong and that he had achieved miracles.

"Thackeray is looking into it," he said, "but you're right. There's nothing to build any kind of investigation. Either we keep going or we walk away and leave Natalie Campbell to whatever fate it is that has befallen her."

Of course, he knew I couldn't do that, however much I might want to.

"So what do we do next?" I asked.

"I've found Laurence Campbell's address," he said. "What say we offer our condolences?"

4

TOM

1.

Has Max told you about Jeffery Thackeray? I doubt it. That boy could never tell a story properly.

Jeffery is a doctor – though he keeps a limited practice, spending as much time on research as he does the day-to-day curing of ills. He is also a man of influential friends. I counted myself one of them, although in truth there was little that our friendship afforded him except a free bar and all the live jazz he could endure. As Jeffery is a light drinker and a man who considered music to have stopped worthy production with the death of Mahler, I was under no illusion that either meant a great deal to him. Still, we went back a long way and he had never been shy of affording me favours.

There is a class of gentlemen, commonly found in corduroy and tweed, who think nothing of exercising their influence in the assistance of their social circle. I suppose it becomes a form of currency. When you have all the money you need, it loses its purpose, and you're left with favours and negotiations, the mutual scratching of backs. Jeffery is not a man I imagine to have ever suffered an itch.

I had promised Max that I would have Jeffery take the matter off our hands. In truth I knew that wouldn't be possible, but it's often best to let one's friends come to their own distasteful conclusions. That way they don't tend to blame you for them.

That said, I was only too happy to call him and share what we had discovered so far.

"Intriguing," he admitted, his voice as rich and fruity as Christmas cake. "And what do you plan on doing about it?"

"If we can keep digging," I said, "we might uncover enough to get the authorities involved."

"If there is anything that merits their involvement."

Jeffery was too polite to come out and say it, but I knew what he was thinking. Both Max and I had drunk more than our fair share, could we really be sure what we – no, I – had seen?

"She was breathing, Jeffery, I'm certain of it."

"Then of course you must look into it, though it baffles me as to what you may have stumbled on. A false insurance claim, perhaps? It happens. People faking their death in order to claim. Usually they have the common sense to simply go missing, of course. I can't say I've ever heard of something being organised on this scale. It's a possibility though, I suppose…"

"One that might best be judged by paying the husband a visit," I suggested. "After all, he would have to be involved."

"Indeed. Though do be careful, old chap, if he truly is a grieving widower he may not take kindly to you riding rough-shod over his grief."

"I shall be sensitivity itself," I promised, gleefully ignoring Jeffery's incredulous chuckle.

"I shall look into the undertakers," he promised, "just run a few checks, see what I can find. There certainly won't be any mileage in investigating the remains. If they claim to have cremated her then getting a DNA result would be problematic to say the least. While I have known crematoria to be slack enough in their work to leave viable bone fragments, I wouldn't like to swear whose bone fragments they were."

"Fancy meeting up for tea soon to swap notes?"

"Sounds lovely. Of course there's only really one way to investigate the undertakers thoroughly. One of us needs to get in there."

An idea had occurred to me. Oh but it was a naughty one, no question. Very naughty. Max would hate me for it too. Still, I'd never let a small thing like that bother me…

I suggested it to Jeffery.

He had the breeding to neither laugh nor swear like a trooper at the unorthodoxy of my request.

"That's a tall order, old chap, but I may be able to pull a few strings. Call me in a few hours and I'll see what I've managed to come up with."

"Thanks, Jeffery, you're a scholar and a gent."

"True on both counts."

2.

Max called. Predictable as ever, he had realised that we didn't have enough to go on to hand matters over to the police. I was relieved that he had come to the conclusion on his own. Now, when things got more difficult I would have the pleasure of reminding him it had been his idea to keep sticking our noses in. I told him to put on a suit and clamber aboard a train.

Laurence Campbell lived in Hackney, that much-maligned borough. Once it was a rural village, popular among London's more affluent populace for home and recreation. Green fields, manor houses and horse-riding aplenty. It was an old joke – so old in fact that Daniel Defoe once uttered it – that Hackney contained more coaches than Christians. Then the Victorians put the boot in and built it up with cheap housing and industry. Some would say it's never recovered and it's frequently cited as an excellent place to go for a lively evening of getting your head kicked in. Personally I'm not one to be put off by the sort of skewed crime figures oft reported by bastions of fair journalism such as the *Daily Mail*.

Besides, how can anyone dislike somewhere that contains the Hackney Empire? In its music-hall days it saw the likes of Charlie Chaplin and W.C. Fields on its stage. It saved comedy from the doldrums in the eighties and, as someone who thought he might die if forced to endure another moment of Bernard Manning or his ilk, I considered that a life-changing event. One can only hear so many jokes about black people or beaten wives before they have to take to the stage and thrash the comedian to death with his own microphone. Things like that tend to take the edge off a night out.

I met Max at Hackney Downs. He was wearing a deliciously grumpy expression which I took a moment to savour before we walked into Town Hall Square to grab a cup of coffee and plan the meeting ahead.

"Just promise me you won't start crying on him," insisted Max, harking back to my enthralling performance with Valerie that morning. He has always been jealous of my ability to immediately leap into character. He is one of those performers that have to slowly feel their way into a role, taking time to prepare, trying out movements and voices. I lean towards a more immediate, instinctual performance and the fact that I'm so terribly good at it drives the poor dear batty. Not that Max was ever a bad actor, I wouldn't want you thinking that. He was perfectly fine in that "natural and forgettable" sort of way. You can't litter your stage with diamonds after all, it would blind the audience.

"I thought we could take the life insurance route," I suggested, "two kindly souls just checking on the details so that the paperwork can be swiftly stamped and filed."

"Because everybody loves talking to insurance agents."

"If you have any better ideas, feel free to suggest them."

Naturally he didn't. I've always been the ideas man.

"That's why you wanted me wearing a suit," he complained, tugging at his tie like a dog complaining over its leash.

"One can't live one's life in T-shirts."

"It's hot. Hot is what T-shirts are for."

"Don't be such a drama queen. With your lousy circulation you should be just about equable in this weather."

Such banter was repeated ad nauseam until our coffees were drained. Fresh out of excuses for delay, we made our way out of the town centre and towards the home of Laurence Campbell.

3.

It only occurred to me once we were virtually on the fellow's doorstep that he might not even be in. This is the sort of irritating detail that never seems to trouble the detectives in novels. Presumably Laurence Campbell worked for a living – most people are forced to do so after all. I could only hope that he had been allowed a little time off given his circumstances. It's difficult enough to plod through an occupation without the spectre of grief making things even more intolerable. At least one assumes so; having never truly experienced either, I'm having to guess.

Arriving at his house, our thoughtlessness was rewarded by the sight of a small van in his driveway. "Laurence Campbell – Mechanic" was emblazoned on its side. God bless the freelancers of this world and their ability to work the hours they choose.

"I'll do the talking," I told Max.

"Of course you bloody will," he replied, as if he would have it any other way.

I rang the doorbell and tried on my most reassuring, affable smile.

Laurence appeared behind the ripple-effect glass of his front door, a pale, blonde head cut into distorted strips.

"Yes?" he asked, opening the door. I had expected suspicion, perhaps even hostility. Laurence had neither. His manner was vague, dreamy and ethereal. I knew then and there that this was not a man who could be complicit in the false death of a loved one. He was a man in shock. A man brought so low that he was no longer entirely in control of himself. He was on autopilot, drifting and lost.

I'll admit I felt somewhat uncomfortable in what we were about to do.

"Mr Campbell?" I asked.

"Yes."

"So sorry to disturb you. We're from the insurance company. Nothing to worry about, just a couple of details we need to iron out."

"Couldn't you have rung?"

I took a gamble on this one. "Apparently someone from the office tried but they couldn't get an answer. My colleague and I were at a conference in the area and the boss asked if we could just pop by on the off chance. I know it's far from ideal, I can only apologise and promise we'll take up as little of your time as possible."

He shook his head but stepped back from the door and beckoned us in. I had no doubt that his state of mind was very much to our advantage. If he had been thinking straight he would never have let us in so easily. He didn't even ask to see any ID, which was fortunate as we didn't have any.

"I thought everything was sorted," he said, leading us through into the kitchen. The room had become a waste-ground through lack of care. Washing-up was piled high on the worktop and a couple of grocery bags sat, unpacked, in the corner. None of it registered with him. He had taken up residence inside his own head and no doubt it would be some time before he rejoined the rest of the world. He sat down at the kitchen table and stared out of the window. "The girl from the office said everything was taken care of."

"I'm sure it's fine," I assured him, catching a warning

glance from Max. "They didn't say there was a problem. I think they just wanted to make sure it all went through quickly. Can I ask who it was you spoke to?"

"I can't remember her name."

"Local office?"

"Just the number on the card."

I pulled out the small Moleskine notebook I affect to carry, if only so I have somewhere to file away lost appointments. "0845 303 0495?" I asked, making the number up on the spot.

"Don't know." He sighed, got up, moved over to a set of drawers, opened one and pulled out a card folder filled with papers. A cartoon sun shone on the name of the company: Sure Future. He tossed it over. "It was the number on the back."

I nodded and handed the folder to Max, tapping the number. "Central office, that's fine." Max got the idea, standing just behind Laurence so that he could tap the number into his phone to save it.

"I'm genuinely sorry to have to intrude," I said again. "I know how difficult it can be at times like this."

"Do you?" he said, making eye contact for the first time.

I considered lying but I couldn't quite brazen it out. I decided to be as honest as I could. "No, not really. Sorry. I can't imagine how awful it must feel."

He nodded. "Everybody's sorry. They ring you up on the phone to tell you. As if that helps. As if you want to hear it. As if it makes it better."

"I don't imagine anyone knows what to say. When something happens so suddenly…"

"Suddenly." I had been taking a punt on that, I admit.

"She was fine. We were fine. Then… Suddenly. Yes."

He went back to looking out of the window, and Max caught my eye.

"I don't think we should do this now," he said. "It's obvious Mr Campbell would rather be left in peace."

"Of course," I agreed. We moved towards the door. "Oh," I said, "just one thing. Was everything all right with Lloyd & Bryson?"

He looked at me in confusion. "Who?"

"The funeral directors. Was their service acceptable?"

He shrugged. "Fine. I didn't have anything to do with them, really. You organised it all."

"Naturally, just wanting to make sure they conducted themselves with suitable respect. We'll leave you in peace."

We let ourselves out, Max virtually running for the front gate.

"God, that was horrible," he said as we marched up the street. "If I believed in a hell I would certainly expect to end up in it."

"At least we can rule out his involvement," I said. "There was no way he was playacting. He's certain his wife is dead."

"Doesn't help us much."

"It narrows things down a little. And we have a bit more information than we did: she died suddenly. And we have another company to look into, they may even be able to give us more information."

"You can't just ring up an insurance company and say 'Hello, could you tell me the personal details of one of your dead clients? Only I'm playing at being a private detective, you see, and it would be terribly useful.'"

"I admit I had assumed we would have to be a little more cunning than that."

Max is such a whining ninny. But I was hoping he would hit upon the next logical step so that I wouldn't have to suggest it.

"Besides," he continued, "who cares about the insurance company? It's the undertakers we need to investigate."

"And how do you propose we do that?"

"I don't know… Ask around a little?"

"By which you mean pop on to Google. Already done that. There's nothing."

"We need to get in there, I suppose."

Bingo.

"Yes, you're probably right. The question is… how?"

"Well," he lit a cigarette and smiled, "I can't think of everything! I'll leave that up to you!"

Mission accomplished.

4.

I returned to the club to enjoy that industrious few hours pre-opening where everyone seems to have lots of jobs to do. I find it quite fascinating to sit back and watch. Len has made it infinitely clear that I shouldn't get involved. He has a system and he views me as anathema to such a thing, grit in the camera lens of productivity.

I wasn't alone in my casual observance. Deadbeat gathers its children to it in the afternoons, eager to drink my coffee and leech my Wi-Fi. I took a table with Douggie and Steve to catch up on gossip and bathe my lips in cappuccino froth.

Douggie handles security. I've known him for nearly twenty years. I first met him in a small club in Edinburgh where I had been trying to make ends meet directing a play in one of the smaller festival venues. Douggie hails from a particularly rough Glaswegian background and has the violent red hair and grey skin to prove it. He's built like a municipal car park and, despite being the rather tiresome sort of chap who uses his sexuality to start fights, he has a heart of gold ç even if some of his connections and hobbies make the Kray twins look like Hinge and Bracket.

On that first encounter I narrowly avoided being thrashed to death by an irate skinhead wielding a barstool, and it's to Douggie's credit that I escaped unscathed. Mind you, as he had started the bar fight in question – by walking up to group of thugs my attacker swore allegiance to and asking if they might be interested in following him outside for some vigorous sex – I suppose it was only fair.

I imagine it must have been difficult growing up in the grim world of his youth as a young gay man but, certainly in today's more open-minded society, I do feel he can afford to stop grinding his axe on occasion. I think he sees the regular fights he creates as a cost-effective workout method.

I bumped into him shortly after opening the club, and was only too happy to give him a legitimate vent for his itching knuckles, and he's good enough not to pick fights with my customers unless they're really asking for it.

He lives with Steve, who does something in computers. I assume he does something in Douggie too. Steve is almost Douggie's exact opposite. Slender and refined. The sort of man who can discuss moisturising cream and doesn't skip past the fashion spreads in men's magazines.

He is as precise and delicate as the gossamer frames of his designer spectacles – as unexpectedly strong, too. For all his gentility Steve has a titanium core.

"Now then, Tom, laddie," said Douggie as I sat down. "How's your fanny for spots?"

This is the sort of greeting Douggie offers frequently. Crude and meaningless, something you could no more interact with than you could a thorny pot plant.

"Fine, thank you," always does the job as well as can be expected.

Steve just nodded and smiled before returning to rub at his iPad with his manicured fingers.

"Did you know," he said after a moment, "that seven thousand Americans die and more than one and a half million are injured due to the illegible handwriting of their doctors?"

With this pearl of Internet-reaped wisdom dispensed, he returned to browsing and sipping at his coffee. Steve does this a lot. He treats obscure facts as currency. It pleases me immensely.

"It's for a very similar reason that we don't let Mr Harris anywhere near the paperwork," said Len on a fly-past of our table. Poisonous old git.

"So what are you up to at the moment?" Douggie asked, ignoring Len's comment.

I told him the events of the last few days. There are no secrets between me and the boys. I think it's important in life to gather people to you with whom you can discuss anything. People who will guard your truths as if they were their own. The freedom to do that allows you to lie atrociously to everyone else.

"The fear of being buried alive," said Steve, "is known as taphephobia. Taken from the Greek word for grave: 'taphos'."

"Ignore Stephen frigging Fry over there," suggested Douggie. "So what are you planning to do about it?"

I told him the plan I had hatched when talking to Jeffery the night before. They both laughed heartily.

"Poor Max," said Steve, "one of these days he'll have the common sense to run away from you and never come back."

"Never," I said, "he'd be lost without me."

"He'd have a more boring existence," said Douggie, "that's for sure."

"The worst fate of all to endure."

"You may be right there," Douggie agreed. "Well, if you get yourself in trouble – and knowing you it's only a matter of time – you know who to call."

"Count on it."

Len was shouting at the tables and chairs. Apparently they were refusing to accommodate his expansion of the stage space and he'd had just about enough of their unruly ways. Poor Len. Everything does seem to take against him so.

I left them all to it, retiring to my office. I called Thackeray to make sure he had arranged everything and then sent Max an email telling him where to meet me the following morning. You just can't argue with an email.

5

MAX
1.

The next morning found me sat outside a little coffee shop nursing a triple espresso with enough caffeine content to make a tortoise dance. It was your basic morning thing. I subscribe to the belief that the human race is divided on this subject: some of us like mornings, and some of us recognise them for the insidious little bastards they are and treat them as a vile flaw in existence to be suffered but never truly accepted, much like colds or screaming babies. It's not a matter of laziness, let me make that quite clear, in fact I loathe lying around in bed. I'm just more of a night person, I feel more energised when the sun goes down. Plus, people that really like mornings are the sort that tend to needle at your very soul with incessant chirping about "the best part of the day", the sort of people that call freezing cold days "fresh", the sort of people that sit next to you while you're smoking outside and cough at you like an old man with tuberculosis. You know, really irritating bastards.

I had one now, wheezing away and waving at her face as if someone had just taken a dump on her hirsute top lip.

Again, nothing inherently wrong with non-smokers, they're making an intelligent decision, no doubt about it. There are just a few who seem determined to fill their healthy longevity with unreasonable attacks on people exhibiting free will in areas specifically designated for the purpose.

Maybe they're bored with all that lease of life they've found and are just hoping an irate smoker will put them out of their misery if they goad them long enough. I've always been a "pleaser" and was just picking up my teaspoon to insert it in her eye when Tom appeared, putting me off my stroke. He gave the woman a cheery smile and sat down.

"Morning, dear, and how are we?" he said.

"Just getting over the discovery that they have two eight o'clocks in every day," I replied, sipping at my coffee.

"Thrilling isn't it?" He grinned widely and waggled his fingers at the waitress, who was staring into space, no doubt imagining how wonderful life could be were she anywhere but here. "You didn't mind another early start, then?"

"Of course not, who would ever wish for more than four or five hours of sleep every night?"

The waitress slouched over and Tom fixed her with his biggest grin.

"Hello, dear. A cappuccino and something sweet and sticky, please."

I sighed and tried to hide behind my cup. Tricky with espresso, but at least my nose remained unembarrassed.

"You what?" she replied, with all of the charm and wit of a root vegetable. She had been working on her first significant thought of the day and Tom was screwing with her synapses. She chewed her gum faster, stoking the engine of her mind.

"Some sort of Danish pastry," Tom continued, showing her no mercy. "I'd even settle for a muffin."

"Low-fat carrot and poppy seed?"

"Except that sort of muffin." Tom sighed and glanced through the large window towards the counter inside. "What are those to the left there?"

"Pain au chocolat." She pronounced it "payne".

"What a way to suffer. I'll have one of those please."

"Do you want skinny, soya or semi in your cappuccino?"

"Cow, please."

She looked bemused and irritated.

He sighed. "Semi-skimmed will be fine."

"Make that two," I added.

She scribbled on her little pad and shuffled off in silence.

"Charming girl," Tom said. "She might be a waitress one day."

"You're excessively cheerful this morning," I said, finishing my lovely black mud.

"I know, dreadful isn't it? I do apologise."

"Accepted. Just mind your manners, we don't want to get thrown out. We've got the perfect spot here." I pointed to where Lloyd & Bryson – Funeral Directors could be seen just along the road.

"Casing the joint," Tom chuckled in a passable Bronx accent. "Seen anything?"

"Not one soul has crossed the threshold. Possibly due to the fact that it's still the middle of the night."

Annoyingly, someone chose that moment to open the shop door and flip the small card sign from "CLOSED" to "OPEN".

"It looks legitimate enough," said Tom.

It certainly did: small shop front, gold stencilling on the large plate-glass window, display of wreaths and headstones on the inside. Bizarre idea, I've always thought. Once upon a time all you saw were flowers; now these places offered window-shopping for the bereaved.

"What we need is a good snoop about inside," I said, "though don't ask me how we go about it. I certainly don't fancy trying to break in."

"Not really our forté, is it?"

"True, no gentlemen thieves at this table. So what then?"

"Well." Tom smiled. "I did have a bit of a thought. Bear with me a moment."

He got to his feet, left the café and dashed across the road. Our coffees arrived just as he stepped inside the undertakers. I stared at them for a moment, sighed, then lit another cigarette. The woman at the nearby table began to cough and mumble things under her breath. The coffees began to cool. The waitress turned on the radio inside and a group of tone-deaf, prepubescent boys started to sing about love, honour, faith… a whole host of things they were too young to know about. Tom was pacing to and fro behind the undertakers' window. The woman gave up coughing and just fixed me with the sort of stare reserved for child-killers and war criminals.

The coffees continued to cool. I finished my cigarette. The waitress picked at something underneath the index finger nail of her left hand with a disposable coffee stirrer. The DJ on the radio talked excitedly about things that meant nothing. A car drove by filled with baseball caps and noise, a speaker bigger than any single passenger pounding out from the confines of its cheap hatchback. Tom was nodding in agreement with a severe-looking man. I took another cigarette out of the pack but didn't light it – I wasn't in the mood. The waitress began to look at a glossy magazine filled with people on red carpets and beaches, sometimes both. The coffees cooled some more.

Tom came out of the undertakers and took his mobile from his pocket. Glancing over his shoulder at the shop front, he crossed the road and talked quickly to whoever was on the other end of the line. I lit the cigarette, if only to piss the woman off. Tom returned to the table, thanking the person on the other end of the phone profusely before hanging up. I took a sip of the coffee. It was cold.

"What was all that about then?" I asked. "You've been gone ages."

"All sorted, plan's hatched, schemes laid, that sort of thing." He sipped his coffee. "My drink's cold."

"Sod your drink, what plan?"

"Well," he said, "we agree that what we need is someone on the inside, yes?"

"Christ, you haven't got a job with them, have you?"

"Dear Lord, no. I'm hardly undertaker material, am I? Are we having another coffee? Mine's cold."

"What have you done, you terrible bastard?" I said, not really caring about the huff of disgust from the anti-smoker at my loud profanity.

"What are you up to tomorrow afternoon?" he asked, innocent as you please.

"Oh… you shit. You've got *me* a job there, haven't you?"

Tom laughed.

"Don't be silly, I wouldn't dream of doing that to you. No, it's far simpler than that. You won't have to do much at all. Very little. Barely lift a finger, really. You could do it in your sleep."

I stared at him for a good half a minute or so before the penny dropped.

"You must be fucking joking."

2.

"This isn't going to work," I said, shifting awkwardly.

Which was my subtle way of getting across to Tom that lying in a coffin propped up on my dining room table wasn't a preferred way of passing a quiet afternoon.

"Don't be such a whiner," Tom said, taking a sip of red wine and beating out a casual jazz paradiddle on the coffin lid. "After all the trouble I went to getting this arranged, the least you could do is hold up your end. Do you know how many favours I called in just to get the paperwork sorted?"

"About half as many as it'll take to have this bloody box removed from you by the time I've finished."

"Don't start getting all agitated. You're supposed to be a corpse, dear, think of your motivation."

"God but I want to hurt you." I sat up and hit my forehead on the lid.

"Easy now, you'll do yourself a mischief. Now shut up, they'll be here any minute. Remember what I told you, the catch opens here." He pointed at the metal latch on the inside of the coffin. "And don't knock it accidentally or they'll be able to open it from the outside."

He took another sip of his wine and checked his watch.

"As soon as you think the coast is clear, out you pop, have a quick look about, then get back inside and I'll collect you in the morning."

"In the morning!"

"Of course. We wouldn't want to raise suspicion, would we? I'll just tell them there's been some sort of complication, and Len and I'll have you out before you can say 'necrophilia'."

"At least give me my iPod or something."

"No chance, they might hear it."

"A book?"

"Too dark to read, silly."

"A torch then?"

"They might see the light filtering out, can't afford the risk."

"Well what the bloody hell am I supposed to do to pass the time?"

"Lie back and think of England."

The doorbell rang. Tom gave me a wink and that insufferable gap-tooth grin. Then he closed the lid.

3.

Have I ever told you how much I hate coffins? No, of course I haven't, why would I? It's not been relevant. Well, I'm telling you now. I hate them.

That faux opulence, all that dark wood luxury, it's all just so much bullshit. As if the idea of being packed into the wet earth can be mitigated by a critical mass of satin.

Plus I'm not all that good in confined spaces, they

remind me too much of… Well, of coffins, I suppose.

I heard Tom come back into the room, his voice a master-class of "grieving friend". I'd have clapped, but there wasn't room.

"Here he is," he said. "Dear old Max."

There was a pause, followed by the sound of sniffing. Dear God, he was only turning on the waterworks again, wasn't he? Such a bloody ham.

"I'm sorry," he continued. "We just miss him so much. It came as a terrible shock."

"It's all right, Mr Whitman, my colleague and I quite understand," said a new voice.

Mr Whitman? Typical Tom, he always wore his tastes on his sleeve. Still, could have been worse, I've heard him pretend to be called Beiderbecke, Krupa and – God help us all – Hemingway in his time.

"It's always a struggle, isn't it, Mr Ackroyd?" the undertaker was saying. His voice seemed familiar, though it was hard to be sure from the way it echoed inside the coffin.

"Yeah, Mr Lloyd," his colleague replied, without a great deal of sympathy, in my opinion. "Struggle."

"That is, after all, why we're here," Lloyd continued. "To take the physical burden from you. Once the sadly departed is taken into our care, you can move on to the important process of remembering your friend and the many happy times I'm sure you enjoyed together."

Yeah, like that great time when he locked me in a pissing coffin… Happy times.

I was pretty convinced this Lloyd guy was the same man we'd seen outside the church, the one that had been in charge. There was a hint of Welsh to his accent which struck a chord.

"That is a great relief," Tom said. "I would rest so much easier knowing that he was in your capable hands."

"Oh capable indeed, is that not so, Mr Ackroyd?"

"Capable. Yes."

"Our firm has a long tradition, Mr Whitman, and, we like to think, a noble one. If we might hurry through the loathsome business of the red tape, we can get on with our accustomed task of your friend's welfare."

"Of course."

"Forgive me, Mr Whitman, but I must confess to a small degree of surprise to see you already possess a casket for the departed. May I ask where you purchased it?"

"Dear Max, such a worrier, a fine and noble young lad but – not to put too fine a point on it – something of a neurotic. He had a morbid fear of being, well, plundered after his passing. It was a frequent concern, something of an obsession in fact. He was convinced that his remains might be... interfered with."

"I can assure you, Mr Whitman, that our company is of the highest possible calibre, our testimonials unimpeachable!"

Lloyd was getting as theatrical as Tom.

"Oh, but of course, Mr Lloyd, I cast no aspersions on your good selves. It was nothing but the delirious fancy of a man only too prone to them. It was a phobia, an irrational concern, and one without the slightest shred of justifiable cause. Nonetheless it was real to him, poor soul. So much so that he had this coffin specially commissioned a number of years ago. It's locked from the inside, you see? Once sealed there's no way you – or I for that matter – could gain access. Like I say, the folly of a paranoiac."

There was a pause, perhaps the slight ruffle of papers.

"Well I must say, Mr Whitman," Lloyd continued, "this is most unorthodox, not to say legally questionable."

"You don't know the half of it, Mr Lloyd. It's caused no end of upset among both friends and family, particularly those with their hearts set on an open-coffin service. Not to mention some small financial irritation on my part. I had the misfortune of dropping a rather nice fountain pen in there when laying him to rest. I only noticed it had slipped from my jacket pocket after closing the lid which was, of course, far too late."

Dear God, this was typical Tom, over-elaborating to the point of nonsense. I found myself clenching my teeth. Push an act too far and it stops being believable.

"However, I have acted on his firm wishes and the coffin is now impervious to outside influence. If you note, the registrar's form does mention this small peculiarity, by way of legal endorsement so to speak."

Again the rustle of papers.

"So I see, Mr Whitman."

There was a further pause and I found myself hoping that Lloyd would stick to his guns and refuse to take me, at least that way I'd be out of here within the next few minutes and enjoying a glass of Tom's wine – preferably while bludgeoning him mercilessly with the empty bottle.

"Of course," Tom said, "I will insist on compensating you for the undoubted inconvenience it causes."

"Oh please, Mr Whitman, don't think it's a matter of money."

"Not all, my dear chap, but I wouldn't have it any other way. Your sensitivity in this matter shouldn't go unacknowledged. I should never rest easy. Shall we say…?"

I didn't hear the number; most likely he didn't say it out loud. I could just picture him folding a wad of notes with feigned awkwardness, tucking it into the man's waistcoat pocket or perhaps pressing it into his palm.

"Why, Mr Whitman, I couldn't accept all that. It will be donated to our chosen charity at the earliest possible convenience."

Liar.

"As you wish, Mr Lloyd. Now, if you please, might we have the matter at an end?"

"Of course, sir, you can leave everything to us. If you would be so kind as to sign the release forms here… and here."

"Certainly. Might I borrow a pen?"

I heard Tom slap the papers on the lid of the coffin, and the sound of his florid signature echoed inside the coffin.

No respect, that was Tom.

"Good bye, old chap, may you rest in peace," Tom said, patting the coffin lid. "If you'll forgive me, gentlemen, would you mind if I left you to it? I'm not sure I can bear to watch him carried out." The false sniffles had returned and I heard them retreat from the room as Tom exited stage left.

"Can't bear to help us lift it, more like," came the surly voice of Ackroyd.

"Keep your trap shut and cop your end," Lloyd replied, all trace of charm having vacated the room with Tom.

I tensed my body and waited for the inevitable. The coffin lifted, Ackroyd grunting with the effort.

"Fat bastard," he hissed.

Cheeky fucker, I thought.

With a little more gentility than I'd dared to expect, I felt myself move out of the room and along the passageway towards the front door. At least they could be grateful I had a downstairs flat. There was a brief shudder as the door was negotiated, and then I was outside.

It's fascinating how our senses adapt. Relying purely on noise, my ears had become markedly more sensitive. The sound of the traffic, birdsong, the distant chatter of a radio from somewhere up the street, all that plus the sound of exertion from the two men that were carrying me and the rubbing of their suits against the wood. All of it seemed so damned clear. There was a shudder as the man in front switched his grip and pulled his car keys from his pocket; I could hear the grating of the key in the lock, the hiss of the hydraulic hinges that opened the rear door. I surged forward with a slight jolt as I was dropped into the back, the coffin shaking as I was pushed all the way in. There was a grinding sound as everything was fixed in place, and then the door closed.

There was a brief pause before the driver and passenger doors opened, the suspension springs bouncing as they got in.

The car engine started up in that horribly quiet hearse way and we pulled out.

Which was about the time I remembered how prone I was to travel sickness.

4.

I zoned out for the length of the journey, trying to ignore the movements of the car – the notion of spending so many hours trapped in there was bad enough without the thought of sharing that space with a cooling puddle of sick. Besides, one of the men had turned on the radio, and if they were speaking, I couldn't hear them.

I thought about Natalie Campbell. The happy woman, smiling on a beach. Who knows what had become of her by now? It was three days since she had been bundled into the back of a van. Three days is a long time. A lot of bad can happen to a person in three days.

I sometimes worried about being responsible for a dog. Now I was responsible for a woman's wellbeing. There's a reason I've never really managed to sustain a viable relationship. Responsibility does not sit well with me. Why hadn't we just marched up to that van on the night and demanded to know what was going on? Well, because only one of us thought something strange was going on, I suppose. Yes. It was all Tom's fault. As per fucking usual.

The point was simple: however ill-prepared I might think myself for what I was doing, I had no choice. I couldn't ignore the possibility that Natalie needed all the help she could get.

The car stopped.

They got out.

The boot opened.

Ah well, I thought, Max Jackson – gumshoe – is on the case.

Whether he likes it or not.

5.

After a few minutes of the predictable grunting and cursing, I was dropped onto some form of plinth and all went quiet on the outside.

I reached into my jacket pocket, which in itself took some doing, and pulled out my mobile phone. I pressed a button to light it up and looked at the time. Quarter to four. Then it occurred to me that maybe I ought to switch it to "silent". Which, I like to think, is just the sort of thing that proves I wasn't cut out for this line of work. It's not as if I receive many calls, but I really should have thought to do it earlier.

Just for japes, I sent Tom a text message using words that the built-in dictionary had never heard of. Then I played *Angry Birds*. Because I am a simpleton. After beating my highest score and just remembering not to shout "Who's the Daddy?" at the top of my voice, I decided to quit while I was ahead and checked the time again.

Five to four.

God, but it was going to be a long night.

I lay back and closed my eyes, trying to zone out again, get lost in my own thoughts for a bit. Maybe I could use this time to make some good plans, start to build towards a productive future, one that didn't involve coffin work.

After all, if you'd asked me ten years ago what I would do if I didn't have to worry about work and money, all of that vital stuff, if I had no commitments whatsoever and could fill my days and nights with whatever I damn well chose, I could have written you a whole list of projects. They'd have been good projects too, worthwhile, the sort of things you could really be proud of. Now that I had that lifestyle, all I seemed to do was mess about and drink far too much. Which either says something profound about human nature or something shallow about me.

Not that it was too late. I could take this opportunity to turn over a new leaf. I had hours of private reflection ahead of me; in a way, Tom had done me a favour. Come the morning I could have a whole new life mapped out, a life filled with desire, energy and enthusiasm.

But what would it be?

I let my mind wander...

A while later I checked the time again.

Four o'clock.

I played another game of *Angry Birds*.

After a bit of this I noticed my phone battery was getting low; it's given long service and doesn't hold its charge like it used to. Deciding that knowing the time was something I couldn't do without, I stopped playing.

I closed my eyes and tried to relax, which isn't easy in a coffin. They don't tend to think of providing comfortable head and neck support when designing them. Can't think why...

Despite the discomfort, I eventually fell asleep.

||||6

TOM
1.

I watched Max being loaded into the rear of the hearse through his living room window and spent a brief moment feeling concern for what lay ahead. Then I got distracted by his book collection... Dear Lord, but he's a fan of the more pulp end of literature. Deciding that anyone possessing a complete set of James Herbert novels deserved everything he got, I went through to the kitchen to do his washing-up. Let him moan all he liked about being stuck with the dirty work; after that, I could point at his housework and tell him to count himself lucky.

That done, I walked his dog, Jamie (don't ask, who knows how the poor fool's mind works), then returned him to a full food and water bowl and advised him to urinate on Daddy's paperbacks should the long night get tough.

I rang Douggie, arranging to borrow a couple of boys for the evening (whatever Max might think, I had no intention of leaving him high and dry at the undertakers. I would park up outside and keep an eye on things just in case), and then called Jeffery to thank him for his efforts.

"No problem at all, old chap," he replied with his usual good grace. I had no doubt that my requests had caused all manner of problems, but Jeffery was far too "old school" to admit such a thing. The matter was done and that was that. "We still on for tea at the clubhouse?"

When Jeffery referred to "the clubhouse" he meant the Athenaeum Club on Pall Mall. Like many gentlemen languishing in the rarefied air of the upper echelons of class, it pleased him to give it a colloquial, inconsequential air. He talked about the place as if it were a tatty Legion club or Scout hut. In reality, of course, it was one of the most select clubs in London.

"Absolutely," I replied, always eager to chuckle at the gentry. "I shall be there in half an hour or so. Have them slaughtering cucumbers and eviscerating Battenberg in anticipation."

"Will do. See you soon."

I left Max's flat to its dust, questionable library and godawful CD collection (barely a trumpet or saxophone to be found) and strolled out to the Tube station. Once upon a time the Wood Green Empire had opened its doors here, broadcasting its innocent fare to those lucky enough to have a TV set. I'd seen Arthur Haynes there once, with Kenny Ball and his Jazzmen playing "Midnight in Moscow" to the happy crowds. Now they've knocked it all down of course, and dumped a shopping arcade on its grave. Progress be damned.

Switching from the Piccadilly Line to the Victoria Line at Finsbury Park, I sandwiched myself in a corner and lost myself in the hot smell of the bullfight with the copy of Hemingway's *Death in the Afternoon* that I had shoved in my jacket pocket for emergencies.

A quarter of an hour later I emerged into Piccadilly Circus with a head full of the bravery of Juan Belmonte and a sadness at the bullet to the brain he would give himself a year after Hemingway. Why did all my heroes blow their brains out? It must say something singularly unhealthy about me.

Heading down Pall Mall, a few minutes later I drew up in front of the impressive Athenaeum and smiled, not for the first time, at the frieze that encircled it. Instead of giving in to the many requests for cold storage from the members, obstinate co-founder John Croker forced young Decimus Burton to include a duplication of the Elgin Marbles in his architectural designs. "I'm John Wilson Croker, I do as I please; instead of an ice house I give you – a frieze!" as the witticism goes. I'm sure they have fridges these days, so maybe he made the right choice after all.

The entrance hall is a cool combination of white pillars and tile with just enough gold and red to take the edge off its austerity. These days the gentlemen's club has had its day really, the phrase more likely to conjure images of jiggling breasts and sequin thongs than it is smoking jackets and the rustle of broadsheets. Perhaps that was only natural. Just as Marks & Spencer had replaced Arthur Haynes in Wood Green, so interests waned here. Still, as was always the way when I met Jeffery here, I paused at the foot of the staircase and listened out for the ghosts of Churchill, Dickens, Darwin, Kipling and, of course, Conan Doyle, a man who might even have had some sympathy with my current interests.

Jeffery was waiting for me in the dining room, a large

pot of tea and a tower of sandwiches and cakes in front of him.

"Sit down, Tom, help me work through some of this." He made it sound like it was a hardship.

I took a seat and began foraging through the salmon and cucumber sandwiches.

"So," Jeffery said, dabbing a stray breadcrumb from the corner of his lips with his napkin. "Lloyd & Bryson. Despite its rather gothic-sounding name, the company has only been in operation for the last four years. That, on its own, is unusual." I had a mouthful of sandwich so I raised an eyebrow by way of query. "How many people do you think go into business as funeral directors these days?" he asked. "Almost all of the little independent firms are family businesses that go back generations. Despite the common habit of the human race of popping their clogs, it's not exactly a growth industry. The big groups expand, but, like all trades, the day of the little independent is as deceased as most of their clients."

"Okay, so it's unusual, but hardly cause for panic in itself."

"No. It just makes my palms itch a little more. There's definitely something afoot here. They're not registered with any trade organisations – the National Association of Funeral Directors or the British Institute of Embalmers, for example – again, not a legal issue but unusual. They are, however, affiliated with a small life-insurance company, Sure Future, although finding that out took some digging on my part."

I decided that I had done my bit for sandwich consumption and moved on to the cakes – a small French Fancy in particular had been winking at me ever since I'd sat down. That bit of business dealt with, I admitted that the Campbells had been customers of Sure Future, as Max and I had discovered when visiting the grieving Laurence.

"Is such an affiliation uncommon?" I asked.

"Not hugely. A lot of companies have a bank of tradesmen that they recommend to their clients, should the need arise. Still… it feels wrong." He smiled and topped up our tea. "Purely gut instinct if I'm honest, but there's something about it that doesn't sit right with me. I'll be interested in finding out what else you discover."

"You'll be the first to know," I promised, and started drawing my marksman's eye across the rest of the cakes.

2.

Afternoon tea consumed, I made my way back to the club to prepare for the night's vigil.

Douggie had made a few calls and was happy for me to borrow two of "his boys" for the night's jaunt: two brothers who regularly worked the door, Carl and Dave. Carl had brought his car, and we headed off to Kentish Town round about six.

Pulling into a space where we could keep an eye on Lloyd & Bryson's window while still maintaining a low profile, I gave Dave some money to avail us of a takeaway curry from a restaurant we'd passed a little way along the road. After all, there was no need for us to slum it too far.

A few minutes later we were wreathed in pungent steam and the car was filled with the crack of snapping poppadoms. You can't beat a good curry.

It became clear early on that while Carl and Dave were a pleasant pair of giants, their conversation was limited, so once I'd eaten, I excused myself to lie down on the back seat and flick through a few more pages of my book. Meanwhile the pair of them glanced around the streets for something to occupy them during what could be a very long night.

"I know," Carl said, in a voice like an elephant sighing, "I spy with my little eye, something beginning with…" He paused for a moment, clearly having peaked too soon and not chosen a subject before deciding on the game. I peered over the top of my book and watched as he looked at his brother in no small amount of confusion before smiling slowly as some form of cogent thought dripped into his forebrain like congealing gravy. "D," he said.

His brother nodded as if having just been informed of the latest in evolutionary thinking. His face showed a furrow of sincere gravity across the brow and he glanced around to see if he could solve this intricate conundrum.

"Dog…" he said after a few moments, though whether because he had just spotted one or was simply working from a really short list of alphabetical words in his brain, I couldn't tell.

"Nah…" Carl replied, finding it hard not to giggle at the cleverness of his little wheeze. "Want me to tell ya?"

Dave thought about this for a while, not wanting to give in too easily. Perhaps he checked his mental list again and found the sheet under "D" blank, perhaps he just wanted to cheer his brother up by letting him have his moment of victory. "Go on then."

"Dave!" Carl said, pointing at his brother and laughing like a loon.

Dave was still baffled for a second and then, as the penny dropped, he began to chuckle too and nodded. "Tha's bloody good, I'll give you that, never would have got that, mate, not in a million years…"

"Your turn then, innit?" Carl said, shuffling in his seat, presumably to find the position where his brain worked best.

Dave looked positively terrified for a moment, utterly bereft of the slightest inspiration. Then he smiled and methodically announced the magic words: "I spy with my little eye, something beginning with C."

Carl scratched at the slight growth on his chin (given the manliness of these two it was far from impossible that his beard wasn't growing at a rate fast enough to observe with the naked eye), then smiled and nodded. "Cat?"

I lay my book over my eyes and quietly hoped for the apocalypse or morning, whichever would come quicker.

7

MAX

1.

With sleep comes the sound of the distorted car horn, a bellowing, primeval noise such as you would expect from a bloated deep-sea creature. That lightness, a warm flush against the cold, rising up through me until it fizzes in my brain like Alka-Seltzer in an inch of water. I become two distinct people, one calm – almost sleeping – the other frantic and screaming, beating at the indifferent wall of my skull, begging to see some action. There is silence, silence that you can never imagine ending. It feels like a law that nothing would dare break.

But, break it did, in the end.

And it was so, so wrong…

2.

I knew I was awake by the way that my head rapped the lid of the coffin. As a method of consciousness it can be effective; do it too hard though, and it has a habit of sending you right back where you came from. I lay still for a few minutes, concerned that I had alerted someone to my presence by my thumping. The room was silent but for the pounding in my head. I was pretty sure nobody else could hear that though, so I risked checking the time. It was eight o'clock. Typical, it was too much to hope I had slept longer.

I was tempted to risk a peek outside. Surely everybody had left by now?

I convinced myself to be patient; there was no need to take unnecessary risks, after all.

At five past eight I flipped the catch. Enough was enough.

The room was completely dark, and I spent a few minutes hoping my eyes would adjust. It was no good – there was no light to adapt to – so I was forced to risk falling flat on my face climbing out.

I took it steady, reasoning that whatever the coffin was sat on must be fairly sturdy, otherwise they were hardly likely to go dumping heavy things like me in a big box on it. At one point I nearly sent the coffin tumbling as I put too much weight on the lid, shifting its point of balance. Eventually though, I managed to get to the floor with as little noise as possible.

I was feeling like a pro until I slammed my balls into the corner of another plinth across from mine. That brought me back down to earth.

It occurred to me that I could use the backlight on my phone as a torch. My testicles rebuked me for not having come up with the idea a little earlier.

I shone the phone around the room. The plinth I had bruised myself on was empty but a third carried another coffin. Only too aware that the odds of it containing a Natalie Campbell were insubstantial, I decided I had better check. It was empty.

I worked my way carefully over to the door.

I listened for a few seconds: silence.

There was nothing for it but to risk opening it a crack.

I turned the handle as gently as I could and peered outside. There was a light in the corridor and it took me a few seconds to stop wincing. There was nobody in the direction I could see through the gap, so I tensed up and swung my head around to look the other way.

Empty.

Right, now came the really hard bit.

I stepped into the corridor. All was still quiet.

There was little of the typical funereal opulence here; it was all cheap beige carpet and ceiling tiles. Obviously I was outside the public area, which seemed to me a good thing. Just ahead the corridor led around to the right, while behind me there were another three doors as well as the one I'd just stepped out of: one in the middle, one on either side.

Deciding to work up a bit of courage investigating close to home before wandering off around the building, I tiptoed past my open door to the next one on the same side.

I put my ear to it: absolute silence. I was about to open the door when I decided it might be better to check the other doors for noise too, so I padded across and listened again. All clear. I went to the one in the middle – same again.

Due, no doubt, to an emotion I can best describe as arse-shattering fear – not something that had ever been covered in the many detective novels I'd read – I had a very strong urge to consider that an end to the night's investigating. Maybe grab a few threads of carpet, a fleck or two of paint from the door, you know, just to show willing, and then head back to my nice safe coffin and wait it out until morning.

I thought of Natalie again and told myself not to be such a bloody coward.

It was a toss-up between the three doors so, figuring it made little difference, I went for the one I stood by first. It was locked. Great. Brilliant. Wonderful.

I moved to my right and tried again. Not locked. Better. Opening it carefully, I stuck my head around the door. It was pitch black. I ran my fingers along the inside wall by the door, found the light switch and, biting at my lower lip, flicked it on.

I was in a cleaning cupboard.

The Case of the Stolen Mop Bucket had just got hot.

I switched the light off and tried the other door.

My first impression was that I was in another cleaning cupboard. It was a tiny room, decked out with shelves filled to the brim with pots and jars. On closer inspection though, they were all pharmaceuticals. Which, I have to say, struck me as a little odd. You shouldn't have much need for pills and such in the undertaking business, I felt, most of your clients being far beyond the help of antibiotics.

I checked the corridor again (though what I would have done if there had been someone heading in my direction I couldn't tell you – run away screaming, probably), and then stepped inside for a closer look. Much good it did me: all I could see was a blur of Latin names that meant as little to me now as they did then. I took a couple of small phials of liquid and a pot of pills, shoving them in my pockets in case they were important.

Stepping back into the corridor, I closed the cupboard behind me.

The locked door. If she was likely to be anywhere it would be behind a locked door.

In movies, spies and detectives have clever gadgets to get them around the problem of locks. Either that or they achieve miracles with hairpins or credit cards. I was lacking the former and the latter was useless as I discovered, snapping an off-licence loyalty card in half in the attempt. Maybe the keys were somewhere else in the building?

All I had to do was pluck up enough courage to go for a stroll. I risked whispering a few really foul words under my breath, purely because they made me feel better, and began to move along.

Turning around the end of the corridor, I found another couple of doors to my right and a large double pair to my left. Deciding the double doors were probably the way out, I opted for the first door on my right. I found myself in an office.

"Bingo!" was the word that sprung to mind.

I closed the door behind me and sat down at the small desk. It had a medical feel to it again, lots of white Formica and box files. Maybe an embalmer with ideas above his station?

As well as the desk there were three filing cabinets, a large sliding door to what I assumed was a walk-in cupboard (it was closed but I'd got the geography well enough by now to realise there couldn't be a room of any size beyond it), and a small row of shelves where the box files lived.

Feeling absurdly brave for some reason, I booted

up the computer and started to forage through the desk drawers while waiting for the PC to do its thing. The lack of keys was pronounced. Aside from the usual staples, rubber bands, biros and the like, I found a medium-sized appointment book.

I had started to have a quick flick through when the computer suddenly came to life with a fanfare, blasting Bill Gates' pride to the world, and in all honesty I dropped the book in a fit of absolute panic.

I sat still for a minute, but nobody burst out of anywhere and threatened mind-numbing violence, so I figured I was safe, and had a browse through the computer desktop.

There were a bunch of files that, by now, I was feeling a little too tense to concentrate on. So I hunted for a blank disc in one of the drawers; that way it could be someone else's problem once I got out of there. I struck gold in the third drawer down, slapped it into the drive and dragged the "My Documents" folder to copy onto the disc.

In movies this would be a work of mere seconds, files flashing to and fro accompanied by cool screen graphics. In the real world, of course, computers aren't so competent. The disc drive farted and a tiny graphic of files flinging themselves at a silver disc popped up, as well as the warning that it would be just short of an eternity until the task was done. While I waited, I opened the Internet browser and checked its history. There was a web-based email provider and a random selection of pages that weren't familiar.

Honestly. I couldn't tell you what "Hot Pink Sluts" was about. At all. Not even a guess.

So I checked the email account.

No use, password needed, and, forget what you see on

telly, it's extremely unlikely that anyone could just glance idly around the room and hit on the answer with cool smugness. So I copied the address down in the hope that I could pass it on to someone who knew how to go about that sort of thing.

The disc drive was still whirring and grinding, so I was killing time browsing one of the other web pages when I heard another noise. A deep mechanical sound. In fact, if you want a spot-on description, I would say it was the sort of sound a lift makes. It was coming from what I had assumed was a cupboard, but wasn't. It was a lift. Hence the lift-like noise it was making. Fuck.

The disc popped out of the machine right on cue. I grabbed it, shoved the drawer closed and switched the computer power off, not really caring if I did any damage.

Grabbing the appointment book off the floor, I dashed out of the door just as the whining of the lift motor stopped.

I ran down the corridor, not worried about what lay ahead this time, the pair of voices behind me quite enough to be terrified about for now.

I stepped inside the room my coffin was in, closing the door as quietly as possible and leaning against it to listen.

"I can't believe you took someone in!" said the first voice in a gentle Scottish accent.

"What was I supposed to do? I can't keep turning customers away. People complain, they get vocal, they draw attention. That's something neither of us want." I recognised that voice: Lloyd the noble tradesman.

"You say he died recently?"

"Yesterday."

"And he was young?"

"Apparently."

"He's worth checking then."

A whole host of thoughts occurred to me at that point, as I realised they were heading towards this room.

Oh shit sums them up at their most succinct.

I did my best to remember where my coffin was, waddling at high speed towards the plinth it sat on. I found the open edge and rolled myself up and over, catching the falling lid just as the door opened. I drew it down gently as the light turned on.

The latch didn't snap shut, just rested on the mechanism.

Oh shit turned into *Oh fuck* as the two men walked into the room.

I lay on my back and waited for the inevitable, book and disc beneath me, medical bottles digging into my hip.

The coffin lid opened. I stayed absolutely still and hoped for the best. I forced myself not to move as a rogue pair of hands peeled back my eyelids.

What can I say? I'm an actor. A damn good one as well. I'm method, I become my role. The stranger looking down at me didn't suspect a thing.

"That's not possible," he said.

"What?" Lloyd replied. "He too dead for you?"

He gave a bizarre laugh at that.

"You say this man died yesterday?"

"Yes. What are you saying?"

I thought inanimate corpse, I thought cold flesh, I thought death…

"Well, he's dead…"

Which shows you what a good actor I am, don't you think?

"… but that discolouration around the pupil and iris is caused by increased potassium levels post mortem, and to be visually recognisable to this level he must have been dead for a number of weeks."

Yes, well, that might have helped my performance a bit…

PART TWO

||||8

MAX
1.

All of which rather merits explanation, I suppose. I should have just cleared this up at the start, but you get used to keeping details of this nature under your hat. It's not the sort of thing you blurt out to everyone you meet, say, at one of the many social functions, galas, fêtes, that dead people rarely get invited to. People look at you funny.

Firstly let me assure you that the medical type with his index finger on my cyeball is not altogether correct. Obviously I haven't been dead for a matter of weeks. That would be ridiculous.

It's more like four years.

No, really.

Perhaps it's best just to tell the story from the beginning…

2.

It doesn't matter how far down the theatrical chain you are, there is a buzz at the end of a performance, a high, that just can't be bettered. There are those who swear that the applause, the reviews, all of that, means nothing. This is bullshit. I have never yet met a performer who doesn't feed off that stuff. That doesn't make them arrogant, often the reverse. They need that constant applause and praise just to maintain a baseline of self-respect. Acting's a funny business: it's for those who are good at pretending to be anyone but themselves. Let's not kid ourselves that we're dealing with the psychologically secure here – the profession attracts more than its fair share of broken people.

It was the last night of the tour. A comedy about a mental-health clinic in California. You can imagine the sort of thing: therapists all kookier than the patients, blah blah… Nothing special, but it paid a small wage and had managed to pack the odd handful of bored pensioners into village halls and clubs as it limped its way around Yorkshire in the back of a hire van. It was never going to make me rich and it certainly didn't make me proud, but it had been work and there was a simple pleasure in hamming it up for the crowds, soaking up the laughter. And, of course, even more importantly, there was Stella.

We'd met a couple of times at auditions, enough that we'd got to chatting. I'd walk into yet another casting call and smile to see her there, we'd sit together, give each other a boost before our names were called, then walk away at the end and console ourselves in our mutual failure. Nothing ever came of it. Not really. While always comfortable in the presence of women and a natural at flirting, I always drew up short when it came to taking it seriously. I would be hit by a sudden crash of nerves that would knock any intention to pursue things squarely on the head. Still, I began to have a bit of a thing for Stella. Acting's a lonely business at times and a bastard on relationships – most especially when your partner doesn't share your trade. There was something about Stella that made me imagine nice things. A future, for example. Don't mind that sudden noise, that would just be the gods of fate laughing – they know how things worked out, you see.

The audition for the comedy tour had been in a small civic centre in Manchester. A bit of a trip from London for the promise of little at the end of it, but when scanning the casting sheets left you with that or dressing up as a bear in Hamleys for Christmas, you stumped up the train fare and hoped for the best.

Stella had come too. I bumped into her in the buffet car and immediately ditched the extra two Kit Kats I'd been buying for fear of looking like a porky bastard. When you do things like that, you just know it's getting serious.

Long story short: we both got the job. It was an eight-week tour, staying in a rented farmhouse and travelling to and fro to perform a couple of shows a day. It was hard work and the sort of job that took its cast and rammed it tightly together. We were either squeezed up against one another in the hire van or piled high in the farmhouse – which had only three rooms split between the six of us. I can assure you this was the sort of theatrical venture where every financial corner was cut; they would have made us sleep in the van if they thought they could have got away with it. Stella and I got together and it was great. You know when you first get naked with someone you've spent far too long imagining, and everything turns out to be just so right? It takes every single ounce of self-control you have in you just to stop yourself jumping up and down in child-like hysteria singing about how great everything is.

It was the best gig ever. Right up until that last night.

The buzz was there, the applause, the relief of eight long weeks done, of a job finished and something new ahead.

Being actors, we had planned the last-night party long and hard. We'd stocked the house up with booze and – how unprofessional – all agreed to play a fast run so that we could get packed up and on the road as soon as possible. Chunks of script were cut as we ran through the scenes, sprinting towards drunken oblivion and the long trip home of the morning after.

It was still nearly midnight before we got back to the house, but the buzz held and we had the music on and the first round of beers cracked open within seconds of crossing the threshold.

Jason, a young man of ambiguous sexuality, was dancing around the living room in his overcoat, holding the tails as if they were the hem of a large dress. He was like a reincarnation of Olivier: plummy voice, Garrick Club tie and a fondness for soliloquising when drunk. I once had to calm down a taxi driver whom Jason had attempted to pay by way of recitations from Shakespeare. "He owes me ten quid!" the taxi driver kept shouting, while Jason pranced in the ad hoc stage of the car's headlights performing monologues from *Hamlet*.

"Do you not know who I am?" Jason had hissed when it became clear his audience of one was uninterested. I had ended up paying the taxi driver.

On the tour he had paired up with a rather hyper girl called Sue, much to our considerable surprise: he was as

camp as a poodle doing the backstroke in a lake of glitter
and gin, and we had never dreamed for one moment he
might be straight. At the party, she was chugging down a
bottle of cheap Chardonnay and egging him on. There was
a look in her eyes that made it clear he wouldn't be dancing
for long. She had a voracious sexual appetite and a fondness
for rough stuff that had had Stella and me in giggles as we
heard their misadventures through the old walls ("Harder!
Harder!" "Dear Christ, woman... let me breathe!"). It had
been testing his endurance, certainly. I think he looked at
his time on stage as a well-earned chance to relax.

Jamie, our charmer of a leading man, was tuning up
his guitar and playing along to the CD, all fiddly finger-
work interspersed with deep mouthfuls from the Amstel
bottle he would also use as a slide for the fret board when
the mood took him. I believe he runs a live music agency
now... People move on.

Angela, who had taken to acting after a particularly
unpleasant divorce – running into a new life in a need to
eradicate the old – drank a glass of wine and looked on. She
always seemed happiest not to be involved, content just to
be there, to watch and encourage. Good old Angela... I
often wonder what became of her.

Stella and I drank and laughed along with the rest of
them, but I could tell there was something up. She was
being false – not unusual for an actor I grant you, but
with her it stood out a mile, her natural openness having
been one of the most alluring things about her. There
was something on her mind and I began to squirm with
discomfort, my smile fixed and painful enough to wedge
the neck of a beer bottle into.

Sue, as had been predicted, gave it an hour or so, then grabbed Jason by his tie and yanked him in the direction of the bedroom they had earmarked as their own. Jamie continued to play even as we heard the initial sounds of sexual battle commence, lost in a world of his own. Angela finished her wine and slipped quietly off to her bed, sad that it had all come to an end. Tomorrow it was back to real life, a place she liked not one bit.

Which left Stella and me. I suggested we pop outside for a cigarette. She nodded and we strolled out onto the gravel drive and stood in silence for a while under an insipid winter moon. The atmosphere between us became even more awkward now that there was no noise from the others to cover it.

"I've got a boyfriend," she said. Quiet and disposable, something that fell from her mouth only to be brushed away from her lips as speedily as possible, an unwanted thing.

I knew it to be true as soon as she said it. Even found myself acknowledging the evidence of it earlier in some of the things she'd mentioned while we had lain cooling in our bed. It wasn't a surprise. Still, it gutted me more than I feel comfortable admitting.

"Oh," I said, feeling I was expected to form some sort of response, but having not the first idea as to what it should be.

"I'm not leaving him."

Again, I couldn't think of a reply. This wasn't a conversation, however much she wanted to play it as one. This was her getting the truth out at the last minute.

"I'm sorry," she added, after the pause had grown too fat to be tolerated. Those useless two words, so often said. They're never any fucking use. "I really like you," she continued, "and I've thought about it… really thought about it. We've been having problems."

"Problems?" For a second I thought she had meant the two of us. Of course she didn't.

"He doesn't like me going off all the time, he gets jealous. He's pretty insecure."

With good reason, it seemed to me.

"I guess I just felt hemmed in," she said. "We're getting married in the summer."

I lit another cigarette. I didn't want it but it filled my mouth for a moment, stopped it saying things I felt it shouldn't say.

She carried on speaking, there was no stopping her now. "When we ended up getting this job together I just wanted to… pretend, you know? To be free again. You're fun and…" She looked at me with a small and brittle smile. "… you made me laugh."

The sudden realisation that I'd never be part of her body again rammed into me right there. It wasn't shallowness, whatever you might think. I'd just got used to being able to share her skin, to be intimate, to be inside. Now I was a stranger again. Evicted. There was a part of me that wanted to beg one more time, one more night to appreciate and savour it. I didn't say it. I kept that small piece of pride.

She turned away again. "But I owe it to him to give it one last shot, try and make it work. I…"

She was about to tell me she loved him. It was as predictable as that line about "owing it to one another" like a relationship is a business agreement and that you're only fighting on through some perceived notion of debt. I wasn't in the mood to hear any more.

"It's fine," I said, letting her off the hook, however much I didn't feel it. "Don't worry, I understand."

I didn't of course, not at all. I wanted to yell and scream, to hurt her, to savage her for building up my stupid pissing hopes and then leaving me exposed. But I really needed her to shut up and it was the quickest way to do it.

"Thanks," she replied, giving another one of those smiles. I didn't like those smiles. I liked the real ones, plenty of teeth; they reached the eyes. I would never see them again.

"I'll sleep on the sofa," she said before shifting slightly, not knowing how to break away. She touched my arm and then walked inside. I stood there and tried to quiet the fleet of things I wished I'd said. Another cigarette. I felt so stupid, it was only eight weeks and yet I was feeling like I had just broken up from a relationship that had been my whole life. I suppose for those weeks it had been. That, and the promise of what was to come. So stupid…

"Christ!" Jason shouted from the doorway before stomping out in his underpants and overcoat. In his left hand he was carrying his belt, in his right he was lighting one of his menthol cigarettes. "Hit me, she says! Hit me harder!" He sighed and leaned next to me. "It's like working in a fuck factory, too much like hard bloody work."

3.

Which is when I did something really stupid. I still had the van keys in my pocket – being the driver put an extra twenty quid on those crappy weekly wages – and I walked away from the house, got in and drove off. I just couldn't bear the idea of talking to them. Any of them. I wanted to cry but I wouldn't share that with those people, I didn't know them well enough. I wanted to rant and moan, to demand sympathy and assurance. I wanted to vent. I just couldn't bear the idea of doing it in that company.

I was drunk of course, but that was so far off my radar that it didn't even begin to register. I just wanted to run, as fast and as angry as I could.

It was a few moments before I even thought to turn the headlights on. I wasn't thinking about my driving, it was as though someone else had taken over as I swerved around the tight country corners, barely touching the gears.

In my head the conversation was happening all over again, only this time it was playing the way I wanted it to. It was angry and violent, it was a conversation of clenched teeth and fists, of words that cut right into the flesh, leaving blood and bruises that would heal long after mine.

The lake that ran alongside the road was large and beautiful. We often passed people fishing along its banks as we headed out to a performance. It was good for fishing, so the owner of the local convenience shop had told us, steep banks… "Like a bloomin' swimming pool, it is… straight drop… packed full of fish… jump on the hook they do…" Stella and I had fancied strolling around it but there hadn't been the time. I would appreciate it for myself soon enough.

The fox's eyes burned in its rough, amber head as my headlights hit it. It stood, sideways on, in the middle of the road, as transfixed by me as I, for a moment, was by it.

I wrenched the steering wheel to the left and slammed on the brakes, glimpsing it running away in the opposite direction just as the van vaulted the grass verge and flew straight towards the water. A low branch beat through the windscreen as I sailed past, showering me in crystals of glass. There was a moment as the sensation of it lingered… cubes of thick glass in my mouth… the cold of the air against my face… the taste of blood… then I hit the water.

I was thrown back then forward (I wasn't wearing my seatbelt, of course. That would have required a rational thought, and they had been sparse for the last half hour or so), slamming against the steering wheel and sounding the horn in one long bellow as the van sank into the water. The water flooded in through the smashed screen, pushing me back again from the wheel (but still the horn seemed to be sounding in my head, the sound of emergency, the sound of disaster…).

I lost consciousness, the water swallowing me down into the dark.

And that was it.

For a while.

4.

Scenes from a dead man's dreaming head:

Floating through a spinning soup of cold water with broken-glass fishes throwing borrowed starlight from their smooth scales as they headed towards the weeds below.

Spread-eagled on the water's surface, the currents of the outflow river tickling at my body and beckoning me to follow, like a Soho hooker. The long fronds of the rushes beneath attempting to discourage me by pulling at my ankles.

The roar of water breaking itself in frothing suicide over rocks as the first fragile signs of dawn crept into a winter sky.

Tumbling, flung in all directions before plunging once more, like the ghost of the crash.

Cold, the roar of water, the feel of soft, slimy rock. Darkness.

A sun, refracted through a curtain of white water, rises and then falls, rises and then falls…

Sometimes there are voices, but who knows if they're outside or inside the dripping cave of my skull?

5.

The first solid piece of consciousness was a long time in coming. I was lodged in a rocky hollow behind a small waterfall, the cold so entrenched in my grey limbs I felt burning hot. I tried to move but my body had locked into position, and for a few scary minutes I was convinced I was a cripple. I spent a while imagining a life ahead of wheelchairs and strangers with awkward smiles and fistfuls of toilet paper, before managing to roll over and fall back into the water. Beaten every which way by the flow of the waterfall, I found myself moving and clawed my way out of the rush and towards the manageable flow of the river beyond. Coughing and spluttering, I fought my way towards the river bank. Despite the intense cold, the mud along the bank was slick and came away in clumps as I tried to get a grip. I fell back into the water several times and had to keep moving along a few feet to stand a chance at getting any kind of a firm hold. Finally, managing to dig my nails into the gnarled root of a tree that was stretching itself towards the water, I dragged myself out of the river. Having decided that was more than enough physical exercise for the day, I stayed flat on my face for a while. I'd make the rest of the journey when in better spirits, say in a couple of weeks. Maybe when spring had warmed things up a bit.

The winter sun had as much warmth in it as a candle, but I soaked it all up. I became aware of having passed out as I was startled awake by a King Charles spaniel giving my ear a chew. I rolled over and backed away from the lank-eared bugger. It stared at me, maybe wondering whether it might effectively eat my face off without getting in any major trouble, then barked a couple of times and sat down to watch what I was going to do next.

"Are you all right?" someone had the good grace to ask. Being as I was soaking wet and covered in mud, I can only assume this was a polite way of broaching the "What the fuck happened to you?" subject with me. He was dressed in a wax coat, rubber boots and flat tweed cap. I put his appearance and taste in pet together and came up with Lord Hawtytawty of Pilesofcash Manor and immediately decided to make friends with him.

"Fell in," I managed to stutter between wobbling jaw, before suddenly finding my mind blank as to exactly how I'd managed to get there in the first place.

6.

Human beings are amazing. Beyond the fact that we suck at relationships and fuck our world up with all the enthusiasm of a drunk clown with a pneumatic drill, we're built well and our bodies are stunning things (even if most of them look like an embarrassing, pink, shit-mountain when naked). I was in danger. I had no idea of it at the time, I was just a shivering mess in need of a shower and shave, but I was a hair's breadth away from glistening scalpels and headlines. So, while my brain didn't cough up the information I needed, it did clamp down on what I shouldn't say or do.

At that moment I had no memory of the accident or my previous life… nothing beyond coming to on a cold river bank with mud in my hair and a dribbling dog in my face. Alongside that though, there was an overwhelming sense of calm, none of the panic or confusion one would expect. I had no idea who I was, but I did know that that was okay and all I had to do was work my way through the immediate, pressing concerns. I needed warmth and I needed dry clothes. Alongside that directive, there was a gentle yet insistent urge to keep my head down, keep my mouth shut and not raise any suspicion. Basic animal survival instinct.

"Fell in?" the dog owner said.

"Yeah… slipped on the mud like an idiot and went for a swim." I stood up, which, with my frozen legs still quivering, was hard work, but I managed it, resting against the tree for support. "I thought I'd never get out again! The bank's so slippery. I imagine I look a bit of a state." The actor's gift for reflection was creeping subconsciously through me, my natural accent becoming more clipped and upper class to match his. If you want someone to do something, then make them think you're like them.

"I've seen worse."

For a moment, I thought he meant washed up on the river bank.

"I doubt that," I said with what I hoped was a suitably self-critical air.

I became aware that I needed to get rid of this man. That gentle sense of self-preservation was insisting as much.

"Anyway," I said, "no need to hold you up on your walk, I shall be perfectly fine."

"Nonsense," he said. "I wouldn't dream of leaving you in such a state. Come back to the house with me and I'll get you fixed up."

Kind. Or so I thought at the time. But awkward. Inevitably, such help would come with questions. And when the answers to those questions were either not forthcoming or just plain wrong, then things would get difficult.

"I wouldn't want to put you out," I said.

"No problem at all, in fact I insist." He smiled and held out his hand to shake. I looked at him, weighing him up. He was somewhere in his late forties, early fifties. A light-brown moustache so thick one could swear he came from another century entirely. He was the very epitome of gentility and surely nothing to fear. Still, how to persuade him that all was fine and that he didn't need to pry further?

"Derek Farmer," he said, and already we were in trouble. Try as I might, I couldn't even remember my own damn name.

I took his hand and shook it, smiling as effusively as a man wearing half a river and suffering from amnesia brought on by major shock can. "Pleased to meet you, Mr Farmer," I said, as if that was all that was expected of me.

While our hands shook Derek Farmer smiled and silence fell. A silence as deep and unpleasant as the river I'd just climbed out of.

Eventually he decided to once more take the initiative. After all, it clearly wasn't coming from me. "And you are?" he asked.

"Max Jackson," I replied instantly, the name popping into my head. At the time I assumed it was the truth, whereas it's actually the name of the character I'd been playing in that godawful play about psychiatrists. Yes, that means I haven't told you my real name either. Don't worry about it, I've used Max Jackson for so long even I need to check my birth certificate to correct myself.

"How do you do?" he asked, as if there had been no social awkwardness at all. Say what you like about the upper classes, but little fazes them. I knew a baronet once who managed to hold a civil conversation with a man he'd caught exposing himself in the public gardens of his stately home. "Of course," he had said, "you must be pleased with how mild it's been this spring."

"Is your car nearby?" Farmer continued, automatically assuming I must have one. Had my memory been more reliable, I might have pointed him towards a hire van that by then would likely have a glove box full of fishes. As it was I simply shook my head.

"I wasn't driving," I said, "just walking."

Here in this lofty vantage point of hindsight, I should have been suspicious of how accepting Farmer was of what could only be utter bullshit. At the time, of course, I was just glad to find myself in the company of someone who was willing to help. It never occurred to me that Farmer might have reasons of his own to be grateful that he was in questionable company.

God, but I wish I hadn't started telling you all this. It's none of your business, after all. Maybe we should just leave it there…

I just don't want to talk about what came next.

7.

He laid a blanket on the passenger seat of his Land Rover (what else?) and we drove to his home with the persistent snout of his spaniel, Dudley, bobbing between us.

He didn't push for conversation – no doubt, as I now know, because he had thoughts as weighty as mine to occupy him – so I sat and stared out of the window trying to get my head straight.

I have discussed that strange period post-reanimation with everyone else I know who has been through the experience (which is not many, naturally, though we instinctively club together – we reanimates are rare). It really does make one question one's psychology, the natural, automatic way in which our subconscious seems to take over, guiding us through the confused time before our previous memories reassert themselves.

Thackeray has done a great deal of research into it, though freely admits it must be the province of the psychiatrist as much as the physician. "The brain certainly produces a chemical that makes us relax," he later told me, "something that stops us from screaming our heads off and alerting the rest of the world to the freak in its midst." I will always remember the look on his face when he leaned forward to emphasise his point, because it was so alien to his normally relaxed features. "Because if there's one thing nature will not abide, it's a freak. Despite the frequency with which it throws them up, it's always quick to stamp them out."

Brain dope aside, I am fascinated by the way that information comes so quickly to the blank slate that is the rest of us. I appreciate it may seem far-fetched to someone who hasn't experienced the sensation, but it really does feel as if there is a back-seat driver in control, someone who just nudges you in the right direction when needed.

Again, it's something Thackeray is quick to have an opinion on: "It's not that unusual," he told me once. "There are countless examples of the subconscious taking over on important decisions, everything from mountain climbers finding the dexterity and reflexes to keep them from falling, to the parents who share a bed with their newborn but never roll on the child during their sleep. We like to pretend we're not creatures of instinct; we like to pretend we're always in control. In truth though, we are just as reliant on automatic function as any other animal."

I have gone on to prove this time and time again; no matter how much alcohol I drink I always end up tucked up in my own bed. I am a boon to science.

Back then, however, misting up the car windows as the heating system turned my damp clothes to warm, steaming flannels, all I could do was wonder as to the basics: who was I and what the hell had I been doing floating down the river? My lack of memory didn't hamper my imagination: was I an escapee from an institution? Or had I been running in fear of my life from some unknown attacker? Nothing, no matter how absurd, could have led me towards the truth, of course. That realisation was still a long way off.

Farmer worked his way along the sort of narrow roads that only the country can pull off, the sort of winding affairs that can't possibly have been premeditated. I swear traffic planning in the countryside is a hobby involving strong cider and a load of tarmac. The fact that you ever reach a destination can only be luck. Or perhaps the roads came first, a spaghetti of hard-core and potholes on which the unfortunate yokels had to place their front gates.

Farmer's was wrought iron and led on to a driveway that was of a far-superior build than the road had been. The crunch of gravel, the grind of a handbrake and we were looking up at what I shall charitably call a small mansion. Don't get me wrong, you couldn't have charged pensioners to walk around it, it wasn't that big, but it was certainly more space than this middle-aged man needed and yet it was obvious the minute we stepped through the door that he shared it with nobody else. Loneliness can seep into the bricks of a house just as surely as it can the bones of a man. It shows itself in the way the furniture lies, the trail of a single person moving through their habitat and leaving everything else to gather dust. Nothing looks right aesthetically, it just becomes a functional place of the well worn and the ignored, a place that isn't so much lived in but endured.

"Nice place," I lied, loitering on the welcome mat so as not to stain the carpet with any part of myself.

"It does the job," he said, as much a liar as me. "Let me take you straight through to the bathroom, where you can get those wet clothes off and warm up under a shower."

I was about to insist that there was no need – I may be dead but I am also English and we don't know how to respond to kindness in any way other than denial – when the thought of a hot shower shut my stupid mouth. Unsurprisingly I was freezing cold, and the idea of raising the heat a little didn't feel so much welcome as vitally bloody necessary.

I followed him up stairs so dusty they betrayed footprints like dance patterns all the way up to the first floor. A long landing was lined with the sort of artwork you expect to see in old village pubs: county maps and red-coated twats being mean to foxes.

"Here you go," he said, opening the door to a large bathroom. "There are towels in the cupboard to the left of the bath. Throw your dirty clothes out here and I'll put them in the wash."

"Honestly," I insisted, "there's no need for you to do that."

"No problem in the least," he said. "I shall find you a change of clothes in the meantime. I'm sure I have something that will fit."

He retreated back into the hallway and closed the door behind him.

For the first time since coming to on the river bank I was alone. My clothes felt like they were beginning to set on my body so I followed his sensible advice, stripping them off and dumping them in a pointlessly folded pile outside the bathroom door.

I was so cold. My skin had that pale, almost blue tinge that you only really get by swimming in the North Sea on misguided childhood holidays. I looked at myself in the mirror and tried to convince myself that I was more than just a familiar face, someone who I would glance at twice in a crowd. I leaned in close and found myself despairing at the puffy, unhealthy face that looked right back. Whoever this man was, he was no looker.

My skin was unsurprisingly clammy. Pressing my fingers to my chest, the flesh felt like a loaded sponge, waterlogged and funky. It seemed mad to add more water, but I turned the shower on anyway and spent the necessary five minutes trying to work out the controls. One day, shower manufacturers will agree a simple, obvious global standard and that will be the day that we evolve as a species.

Hmm... or perhaps we already have.

Don't get me wrong, I'm not putting myself forward as an improvement on you, the living, but when nature takes a wild leap like this you have to wonder, don't you? In a world that's getting increasingly fucked-up, what next for evolution but curing death?

Back then, my thoughts were nowhere so deep. I stood under the jet of water and tried to scrub myself warm. It seemed that however high I turned the temperature, it only came out tepid. I stared down at the grey puddle between my feet as it slowly turned clear and soap-sud clean.

My head grew dreamy beneath the flow from the shower-head and as much as I tried to force it to fix on the problems in hand, all it would do was doze. A couple of times I had to hold my hands out to steady myself as I began to topple. Exhaustion? I wondered, or perhaps shock. Maybe I would do well to fight against the strange urge for secrecy and get myself properly checked out. After all, I was clearly not fighting fit: memory loss, extreme coldness, dizziness...

However much I thought about it, I knew I couldn't act on it. That subconscious insistence on secrecy was far stronger than anything my conscious mind could come up with. The conflict between the two of them was beginning to make me feel sick, and I switched off the shower and sat on the edge of the bathtub. The nausea rose quickly and I stumbled out of the bath and over to the toilet just in time to regurgitate a gutful of river water into the pan. I stared down at the brown slime that had just bubbled out of me and found I was looking at a large, slick oak leaf. That seemed disgusting beyond all words, and in no time at all I was throwing up again and again.

"Are you all right in there?" Farmer asked.

Clearly not, I thought.

"Fine," I lied, because that's what you do to strangers.

The sickness seemed to have stopped for a moment, and I sank back against the bathtub, splayed out on the linoleum floor, empty, wasted and confused.

I found I actually did feel better. More importantly, if I didn't start acting better then Farmer would most certainly be on the phone to someone. If he hadn't been already.

"I'll be out in a minute," I said, hoping to forestall his thoughts in that regard.

I heard him step away from the door and move off down the hallway.

Getting to my feet, it occurred to me – for the first time, I am not a deep thinker – that I was stark naked in a stranger's house. This was not a position of extreme comfort; I am not the sort of man who wanders around the world shedding his clothes with abandon. If I had a better body then no doubt I could be, but as it stands I treat my physique like a guilty secret, something to be hidden away and denied at every opportunity.

I wrapped a towel around my waist and draped another across my shoulders. Tugging at both, I decided this was as dressed as one could possibly be when only able to use bath linen.

I flushed the toilet, making sure I had left no evidence of my sickness.

At the sink I washed my mouth out several times, never quite able to get rid of the taste of earth. Giving up, I checked my reflection and decided I looked as presentable as a man can wrapped in white cotton.

I opened the bathroom door and stepped back out into the hallway, noticing that my pile of wet clothes had disappeared.

"Hello?" I called. "All done."

There was no immediate reply so I found myself standing awkwardly between the bland countryside prints trying to decide what to do. I looked at the pictures and noticed the dust on them. Like the rest of the place they hadn't been looked after for quite some time. They had been hung here to go off, like the game they frequently represented running through the bracken awaiting the hunter's shot.

Eventually I decided to head downstairs. I wasn't about to start knocking on bedroom doors.

I made my way through the entrance hall and lounge, really seeing how bad everything looked now that my attention was drawn to it. The whole house didn't appear to be lived in. It was a run-down, grotty ghost of a home. Everything felt sticky with dust. There was a smell of damp, and worse, a rotten odour, perhaps of unfinished meals long past? Farmer may have given the impression of affluence and civility, but his house contradicted him. Something bad had happened here.

I found him in the kitchen, the sort of big, country room that looks like it might once have had staff, full of cast-iron pans and those big, heavy wooden tables that would be perfect for slaughtering pigs on.

"There you are," I said, rather stupidly.

He was drinking, which seemed out of place to me. Wasn't it early morning? Not that I've always been known to keep my alcohol intake to socially acceptable times of the day, but I expected more from Farmer. He was normal. Upstanding. Respectable.

He wasn't.

"Here I am," he agreed, draining his glass and putting it down on the sideboard. He made a slight improvement to his demeanour, as if only just noticing me now that he had spoken. Was it the drink making him slow, or something else? I had a feeling the drink was a symptom not a cause.

There was a horrible moment of silence, me stood there in his towels, him staring at me. Then the polite face of Derek Farmer clicked back into place.

"Better?" he asked with a smile that was perhaps a touch too drunken.

"Much," I replied, wondering how to broach the subject of clothes as he hadn't. In the end I decided to keep it simple. "Did you find anything I might wear?"

He shook his head. "Sorry, I forgot."

He was lying. Badly. And with that I realised that, far from finding help, I had in fact got myself in even worse trouble.

"That's okay," I said. "Maybe I could just borrow something and send it back? Only I really do need to get going."

"Do you?" he asked.

"Yes. I'm late as it is, obviously. Not that I don't appreciate everything you've done, but I really should get moving."

"Where?"

These short answers were worrying and I was clearly floundering to reply, try as I might to conjure up a believable story.

"I was due to meet some friends." It suddenly occurred to me that I didn't even know where I was. No idea. None. The nausea was returning.

"Where?" he asked again, reaching for a bottle behind him on the worktop and pouring a little into his glass. Whatever he was drinking was dark and thick. It made me think of the regurgitated river water, and for one horrible moment I was sure I was going to have to throw up in his sink.

"Just in town," I said, hoping that this was a suitably nondescript reply. "We're renting a place near here. I was a little early so I was taking a walk. You know, killing time."

"But you don't have a car. You told me so. How were you going to get to town?"

"Well, it's not far, is it? I thought I'd walk it. I'd been dropped off on the main road and thought I'd just cut across…"

He shook his head. "You're lying." He took a drink. "In fact I think you've been lying ever since I found you."

I didn't know what to say, after all it was true, and with my memory the way it was, this conversation was like playing poker with no cards.

"You were miles away from anywhere," he continued, "floating down the river. You gave me a name that I know isn't your own." He looked at me and smiled. "You're not a good liar and nobody has to think for a moment before saying their name."

"Try falling into a river and nearly choking to death. You might be surprised."

"No. I don't think that's it. When I first saw you I thought... well, I thought you were dead. There was an accident upriver a few weeks ago, some idiot drove their van off the road. They never found the body. So when I saw you there... so still..."

And the minute he said that my head began to spin.

The crash of broken glass. The bellow of the horn. The punch of ice-cold water.

I had to grab hold of the sideboard as a wave of dizziness swept over me.

"Interesting," he said. "That actually means something to you, doesn't it?"

"Of course not, I just felt... Look, it's been a difficult morning, but I just want to get some clothes and be on my way."

I made to walk away, though God knows where I expected to go.

"No," he said, taking a firm hold of my arm, "I don't think so."

Thinking back – and I often do – I wonder why I didn't just clock him one and then do a runner. Certainly that would have been better than what came later, but at the time it felt beyond me. I was weak, confused, and Farmer, for all his own weaknesses, felt stronger.

"You're on the run," he said, "that's the only possible explanation I can think of. You're hiding from someone, the police maybe? Escaped from somewhere?"

"If I was then don't you think you should be being a little more careful in dealing with me? I might be dangerous." I didn't feel it.

He let go of my arm and walked past me over to a large sideboard in the corner of the kitchen, the sort of place where well-to-do sorts display their selection of crockery. And keep their rifles, it seemed. He pointed the barrel at me.

"More careful?" he said.

"Much," I agreed.

"Nobody bats an eyelid to owning one of these in the country," he said. "It's one of the fun things about being out here. They expect you to shoot things, birds, rabbits..." he looked at me meaningfully, "intruders."

I held up my hands, desperate to pull this situation back if I could. "Look," I insisted, "this is ridiculous. There's really no need to–"

"What's your name?" he asked.

"Max Jackson." He raised the shotgun. "Okay! I don't know... all right? I came to on the riverside there and I couldn't remember." It seemed obvious that the truth couldn't make matters much worse than they already were. "I couldn't remember anything, in fact. My name, how I got there..."

"You can do better than that."

"I really can't! I wake up with your dog licking my face and the rest of it – all of it – is a blank..."

And that wasn't quite true, because even as the words came out of my mouth I felt that rush of nausea again, the sensation of falling, the car horn… I clenched the sideboard as tightly as I could, closing my eyes, though that could hardly block the things I was seeing. The darkness inside the van as the water came up to meet me, a hard wall in the darkness with only the slight reflection of moonlight on its surface to differentiate it from anything else.

"Maybe," I said, aware that Farmer was coming closer, "maybe that was me in the van, maybe I did crash…"

"Weeks ago? Don't be an idiot. You can't have been floating there all that time. Why are you lying?"

"I'm not! I really don't know!"

I looked up then, startled by the fact that he was starting to laugh.

"I'm glad you're finding this funny," I said, thankful at least that the distraction had sent the dizziness and recollection away.

"Oh," he said, "I've just come to a decision, that's all."

"A good decision?" I replied, trying to smile.

"That's a matter of perspective." He leaned back against the central butcher's block, the rifle still pointing at me. "Take off that towel."

I hadn't expected that. I had no idea what I had been expecting but… that?

"What?"

"You heard me."

I just stared at him, this smiling bastard who was pointing a gun at me like it was the happiest, best day of the year. Probably it was.

"No."

"I would. Honestly I would. Because, you see, that's the decision I've made. I can do anything to you, can't I?

Whoever you are. Whatever your real story is. I can do anything. Nobody knows you're here. I can do absolutely anything."

"But…"

"Take off the towel."

I tugged the towel off my shoulders and threw it at him, running behind it, desperately hoping it would be enough to throw him. It wasn't.

He darted to one side, turning the rifle and clubbed me hard in the hip with the butt. The blow knocked me a couple of feet to my right, and before I could compensate he hit me again, this time in the stomach. I dropped to the floor.

The towel fell off but I was too busy clutching at my stomach to care.

"There," he said, dragging the towel away with his foot before moving a few steps out of my reach, "that was stupid and pointless, wasn't it? Now get up."

I did so. There seemed little point in doing anything else.

Stepping a little closer, he raised the barrel of the rifle to my face and…

8.

No. No more.

I died and came back. The old me was destroyed and Max Jackson, your happy-go-lucky narrator, entered the world, making it a new and brighter place.

What? I told you. There are some things I don't want to go into. This is my story and I'll tell it the way I want. If you wanted an unbiased overview of my life then you needed a third-person narrator. As it is you have me, so you'll get what I choose to give for as long as I choose to give it. Which will be for a while yet, have no fear. I'm talking to you, aren't I? So obviously I got away from Farmer; that's the other thing with a first-person narrator, you always know that they lived at least until the next sentence.

I got away. That's all you need to know.

9.

So. Yes, I'm dead. But not.

Let's clear up some myths: I don't eat brains, shuffle around shopping malls or turn up in dodgy Italian Gut Munching pictures alongside actors on their uppers. I don't dribble, moan or walk around with my arms stretched out. Unless it has been a really bad night. In fact, you so much as mention the "Z" word and I'll stove your head in.

I am "reanimated". That's the polite word.

My body retains most of its vital functions, albeit in a very retarded manner. Healing is a very slow process – if it occurs at all. This last is the real kicker; it means you have to watch yourself a bit. There are options, there are a few medical stiffs in the dead community that are a dab hand at pinning and reconstructive surgery (Thackeray, for example), but as a basic rule – you break it, you bought it. The only way out is a patch job. We do suffer from a degree of decomposition, but again, there are ways to deal with it. Drugs, regular baths, make-up in extreme cases.

There's enough "life" pumping in the veins to keep the

worst effects away, but you do have to keep tidy. I've met some old-timers who've really let themselves go. They stink like a maggot's arse and leave stains on all your furniture. It's depressing.

So, yeah, I'm one of the Living Dead, part of a growing community in fact. You know what they say, there's one born every minute.

Tom, me, a small bunch of others.

And no, I don't know how it's possible. I'm an actor not a scientist.

I've heard theories; none of them ring particularly true to my mind. I find that, like most of the really important mysteries in the world, it's best to forget about it and just get on with things.

If you're the sort of person who needs full explanations then may I suggest making one up.

Try that old chestnut about a meteor passing close to Earth.

After all, it's worked before…

9

TOM
1.

I couldn't sleep.

Not least because Carl and Dave were making enough noise to wake the dead.

Joke.

In all honesty though, a good deal of my head was taken up with thinking about Max. He's a dear friend and a splendid chap, but far too easily led. I very much hoped he wasn't going to end up in trouble.

That's the thing with Max, trouble does seem to gravitate towards him. Only Max could get dumped, crash a car, drown, die, come back to life and then… well, things didn't work out too well for him after his reanimation. He met a rather bad fellow and he had to do bad things in order to deal with him. He doesn't like to talk about it, not so much because of what the man did to him, but rather because of what he did in return. Personally I don't know what he worries about; standing up for yourself is nothing to be ashamed of. Not that I know the details, I'll admit, but I've known him long enough to be able to read between the lines. He was hurt and then he did what he had to do in order to protect himself. I see no problem and in my opinion neither should he. I told him as much when I first met him.

Oh dear, but that was a very different Max back then. I've told you of that first night, haven't I? When he threw up in the horn section? I'm sure I have, I've told most people at one time or another. Well, it soon became clear that he had nowhere to go. He'd been wandering since his accident, spending the money he had managed to steal from Derek Farmer, but not willing to stay in any one place too long. He was too scared, too convinced that his condition would be obvious to anyone who looked at him. It was common enough for someone who had just reanimated. It takes a while to settle into being a new subspecies – a subspecies that would be herded up and burned in a medical furnace should its presence ever become known. Yes. Not just a subspecies, an underclass. But then I've always extolled the virtues of Miles Davis' latter albums so it's a position I'm used to.

Max though, Max is fragile, he's a man who always feels like he could fall off solid ground and tumble God knows where. That's why he needed looking after.

2.

When Max woke up on my office sofa the morning after that first, apocalyptic night, I think the only thing he was truly aware of was his safety. Everything else, from his whereabouts to the owner of the dinner jacket he was using as a blanket, was a mystery.

"Morning," I said, once he had finally braved his way out of the office and found me sat with Len in the bar.

"You have a stray," Len sighed, in that usual charitable manner of his. "Shall I drown it in the bottle-wash before it sprays its scent everywhere?"

"The cleaning staff would say he already had," I replied, because I never met a joke I couldn't add a punch-line to. I think any one of my ex-wives would point to my humour as the straw that broke the marriage vow. One day I'll find a woman who can take a joke – you would have thought it would have been a given after our first night in bed.

"All the more reason to kill it," Len replied. "Good cleaners are hard to find, drunks are ten-a-penny."

"True, but I think this one's a keeper."

Len is not a reanimate, though he knows that I am. He's one of the very few in my social circle without a tombstone who does, because I trust him implicitly. Still, not being a member of the subspecies, he doesn't understand the absolute need to look after your own. I would say that, at that point, Len didn't know Max was a reanimate, but I wouldn't want to assume; Len is terrifyingly astute and I suspect he knew damn well. That may even have been one of the reasons he was so eager to get shot of him – he knew how high-maintenance the living dead could be.

"I have a feeling," Max said, "that I may have had a little too much to drink last night."

"Well now," I replied, "that's a subjective opinion, isn't it? Who's to say how much is too much?"

"And there we get to the nub of your problem in one sentence," Len said. "I'm going to go and do some actual work."

He left us to it.

"The last time I woke up this confused," Max said, "I'd died."

"I don't think you were as lucky this time."

"Lucky?" He shook his head gently and settled to staring at the table. "I'm not sure that describes anything that's happened to me lately."

I couldn't let that one go. "Come on," I said, "there's something I want to show you."

"I've heard that before too," he muttered, but gave me a weak smile and followed me out of the club.

I led him around the side of the building where I park the little Morgan that gets used so infrequently it's a wonder I can remember how to drive it.

Londoners get out of the habit of cars and, for the most part, this is a good thing. We have underground trains, buses and – if needs really must – our feet. Adding another option only makes things confusing. Still, if you're lucky enough to find an open road and a clear summer's day to drive on, there's nothing quite like it.

Unfortunately it was February and the entirety of London seemed to be on the roads. Maybe it was only me that had heard about all those alternatives.

"Nice car," Max said, slumped in the passenger seat like a murder victim on his way to be dumped.

"It is," I agreed. "It belonged to my third wife but I kept it after the divorce."

"Harsh."

"I liked it more than I liked her, and I let her keep everything else."

"How many times have you been married then?"

"Too many, clearly. But I survived most of them."

He didn't seem to pick up on that but I didn't mind. The story of my passing shall be told one day, but it's far too good a tale to squander on a car journey.

"I don't suppose I ever will be now," he said, becoming more morose by the second.

"Never say never," I told him. "You have no idea what the future holds."

"I can make an educated guess that I'm not going to bump into a beautiful woman who has a thing for dead guys."

"Or a fellow reanimate looking for a partner? There's more of us than you think."

"The people at the club… are most of them…?"

"Not at all. Most of our customers are alive and kicking and so are all of the staff. Len knows about my condition…"

"You make it sound like Irritable Bowel Syndrome."

"I'm used to it, that's all. I've accepted it. So will you in time."

He grunted. "So, Len, that's the miserable bugger behind the moustache? He knows…"

"He does, as does Douggie, my head of security. The rest of the staff and the majority of the clientele just think I'm Tom Harris, playboy and *bon viveur*."

"Playboy?" He chuckled. "I think you have to be under fifty to claim that title."

"How do you know I'm not?"

He just looked at me, a slightly awkward look on his face, concerned that he'd gone too far and hurt my feelings. I grinned. "Actually, given my unusual lifestyle of the last few years, I'm knocking eighty, so I can hardly take offence."

"Eighty?"

"Fifty-nine when I died and a careful life ever since then. Once you're a reanimate, age really does start to become an irrelevance. It's not so much how old you are, as how long you've been post-coffin."

"You're looking good on it."

"A friend of mine, Jeffery Thackeray, has me on injections, some sort of preservation junk, embalming fluid probably." .

"Brilliant, can I have some?"

"He's reassuringly expensive, but I'm sure we can come to some arrangement or another. He's a reasonable chap and you look after your own, now you're a reanimate."

"Maybe I could get a job in your bar?" he said. "I'm an actor, my training in the service industries is extensive."

"Of course it is." I laughed. "We'll see. As I said, we look after our own."

I headed out of the city, working south-west towards Surrey. We sailed under the M25, just to teach it a lesson.

"So how many reanimates do you know?" he asked.

"A few," I admitted. "I'll introduce you soon enough."

"Are they all like you?"

"In what way?"

"Relentlessly bloody cheerful."

"Oh. No, they're not, but they should be."

"Why?"

"That's what I'm showing you."

We whisked past Woking and Horsell Common where Herbert George Wells had decided his terrible Martians would first land, working their slow way out of their capsule before turning their deadly heat rays towards the populace. A left at the golf course and we were where I had wanted to take him.

"Subtle," he said, taking in the acres and acres of tombstones.

"Brookwood Cemetery," I explained, "set up by the London Necropolis Company in the middle of the nineteenth century as a place to house London's dead. Five hundred acres, over two hundred and thirty thousand residents. For many years it was the biggest cemetery in the world. If there's one thing Londoners have always been good at, it's dying."

"Okay," he said, "I get it, it could be worse…"

"Certainly it could," I replied, pulling up and turning off the car engine, "but not just in the way you think. How many people do you think this happens to?"

"Reanimation? No idea… obviously…"

"Nobody does, but what we do know is that it only happens some time after the original death, yes?"

"Obviously, you couldn't reanimate otherwise…"

"No, I mean it doesn't take place right away. How long were you lying there, wedged behind a waterfall, dead, before something happened and you came back?"

"I'm not sure, a while…"

"A long while. And what happens to most people when they die?" I pointed around us. Slowly he got the point.

"So most reanimates would wake up after they'd been put in the ground…"

"Absolutely. The vast majority must do. There's not many people who end up lying around for days after they've died. So unless that's part of the process… but I don't think it is… the majority of reanimates regain their sentience when it's no use to them whatsoever."

"Horrible."

"Isn't it? Because one thing we do know: you only get one crack at death. If, like us, you get beyond it, then there's no more off switch. We're permanent, at least for as long as we have flesh to hold us. Even then, who's to say what happens? Is 'life' something experienced through the flesh? A sparking of impulses in the meat of the brain? Or is it more? A soul, something that could continue to be aware even after the flesh has rotted away, an unanchored sentience adrift in the world."

"What a nasty thought."

"Oh, I don't know, I imagine it would be quite restful. Anyway, the point is: you beat impossible odds just to be stood there, so don't tell me you're unlucky."

"All right, I'm the luckiest man alive. Or not."

"Ah… what's death? That's the great lesson, isn't it? Death is the thing that scares people the most; most of them spend their entire life being terrified of it. It hangs over everything. But not for us, not any more… We've shed our greatest fear, now we can really start living!"

"Did you make your money in self-help? I ask because you do go on…"

I turned the ignition key and begin to drive back towards Woking. "I'll buy you a ploughman's lunch. If my talking bothers you so much, put the pickles in your ears."

He didn't, though I think I nearly had him while discussing Benny Goodman; I can remove the oxygen from the room talking about him and Krupa. Luckily I changed the subject at the last minute, just before his face fell into the butter dish.

Which pretty much sums up the last few years really.

PART THREE

|||||/10

MAX
1.

So, where were we? Oh yes…

"I don't get it," Lloyd said, while his colleague continued to give my devilishly handsome, and quite dead, body a once-over.

"This 'Mr Whitman' lied to you."

"But why?"

"That's just one of the things we need to find out, isn't it?" He finally took his damned finger off my eye and walked back towards the main door. "Stay here, I won't be a moment."

I lay there, eyes closed, listening as Lloyd came closer. I was aware of him leaning over me, the shadow blocking out some of the light, the smell of his breath in my face.

The other man came back in.

"You might want to step back for a minute," he said, and I felt his hands pulling roughly at my shirt. He tore it open, buttons bouncing off the padded sides of the coffin. That really pissed me off: shirts are not as disposable as Hollywood insists, and I really liked that one. After all, you don't bury yourself in any old crap, do you? Still, I had more important things to panic about so I tried to stay calm and figure out what he was about to do.

It was difficult, not being able to see. Still, as I said before, it's amazing what the other senses can tell you. When blind, your hearing becomes incredibly acute. I could hear every rumple of the man's suit as he leaned over me. My sense of smell was also sharp, picking up an odour of old aftershave that didn't disguise the waft of chemicals. This was a man who spent a lot of time around test tubes.

Above all, it was my sense of touch that really swung into overdrive. I may not have been able to see the scalpel he stuck in my chest, but I certainly fucking felt it.

2.

This is not how it happened:

"Damn you!" Max Jackson snarled, fixing them with the hard eye. He swung a size twelve slice of quality shoe leather into Lloyd's jaw, chuckling at the lovely popping sound it made. With one swift move he struck the sawbones with a vicious hand-slice to the side of the neck – a move he had picked up during his time in Asia – and vaulted from the coffin. Landing steadily, he turned to face the screaming man-mass called Lloyd who was, even now, hurtling towards him with murder on his mind.

"You guys just don't know when to quit," Jackson whispered, in that really manly and sexy way of his. He pulled the scalpel from his chest and, with an almost casual air, threw it towards Lloyd, landing square in the creep's left eye. He was kissing carpet before you could so much as think "bullseye".

"By God, but you're good," said the voluptuous dame that had appeared from nowhere. "You make me feel all, gee... I don't know... gooey."

"Easy, sweet cakes." Jackson smiled, grabbing her manfully by the arse.

"Oooh..." she said. "You feel stiff."

"Damn right, sister, the stiffest in town."

He always liked the touch of a woman after the frisson of death. It washed the stench of the grave away somehow, made him feel more pure...

So he nailed her one on the lid of a coffin and was really, really good at it and she liked it loads.

It was much more like this:

"Jesus!" Max Jackson shouted, before screaming like a big girl and thrashing around uncontrollably. His left foot caught Lloyd a lucky blow to the chin. The doctor, finding the sight of a dead body screeching and wailing while trying to pull a scalpel out of its chest just a little bit more than his brain was happy with, crumpled in a faint to the floor.

With all of its occupant's panicked shaking, the coffin rolled over, the lid catching Lloyd – who was dashing towards it in an attempt to restrain the suddenly active corpse – square between the eyes, knocking him out instantly.

Falling face first to the floor, Jackson gave an almighty wail as the scalpel was forced even deeper into his chest.

He got slowly to his feet and gave both of the prone

bodies a damn good kicking just out of malice.

Trying to calm down, he got a grip on the stub of the scalpel handle and wrenched it out with a yell. He dropped it to the floor and ran out of the room.

A few seconds later he dashed back in and picked up the appointment book and computer disc which he had forgotten about the first time.

So let's have no more about truth being better than fiction, all right?

3.

Whichever way you cut it, I ended up running through the large double doors along the corridor and into what I took to be the public viewing room on account of the fact that there were too many dried flowers and red velvet curtains for it to be the bathroom. There was another pair of double doors in the corner that led to a short corridor with a couple of offices off it and, at its end, the shop floor itself.

The shop doors were, of course, firmly locked, so I used a little lateral thinking and put one of the showpiece tombstones through the window, stumbling onto the street outside a few moments later to the sound of shattered glass and a blaring burglar alarm.

"When hell is full, the dead shall walk the Earth," shouted Tom, who was getting out of his car a little way up the road.

"And they shall be in a right bloody mood due to the frankly horrid evening they've had."

"What do you know? Lying there having a nice quiet

rest, I had to listen to the world's first existential I-Spy championship."

"What's existential mean, Mr Harris?" Carl asked.

"Who knows?" he replied, ushering me into the car.

He climbed in the other side just as the angry face of Lloyd appeared at the broken window.

"He looks cross," Tom said. "Drive away, boys, quickly."

"Sure thing, Mr Harris," Carl said, turning the key in the ignition and driving away. He narrowly missed Lloyd, who had climbed out onto the street with the apparent intention of kicking our car over. Obviously this was over-ambitious on his part – and he was lucky Carl didn't just mow him down, I have no doubt he would have done so quite blithely had Lloyd been a few seconds quicker – but I'll give him the benefit of the doubt; he was angry and angry people do stupid things. Just to prove it, I tried to give Tom a dead arm. This is hard to achieve on a dead man, what with their retarded circulation. I will admit to enjoying trying.

"There's no need for that, is there?" he asked, rubbing his upper arm. "Most especially after I turned up to keep an eye on you."

"I've been poked, prodded and stabbed with a scalpel," I replied. "It has not been a good night."

"Sounds thrilling. What have you got there then?" he asked, looking at the appointment book and disc.

"You don't care one jot, do you?" I asked, handing them to him.

"On the contrary," he said, "I care a great deal. They look fascinating."

"About me, I mean."

"God, Max," he sighed, rifling through the address book, "you're so egocentric sometimes."

Which is when I thought about Natalie and that locked door. I had been so desperate to escape I had forgotten all about why I had been there in the first place.

4.

A little while later I was huddled in a corner booth with a drink in my hand and, to give him his due, a rather concerned-looking Tom sat facing me.

"So," he said after I had filled him in, "our first covert mission went well then?"

"Roaring success. Can't fault it. I singularly failed to save any kidnapped women and got myself stabbed in the chest."

I took a sip of my drink and pointed at the small pile of "evidence" I'd managed to purloin. "Anything there to have made it worthwhile?"

"I've been on to Jeffery about the drugs, said we'd pop them round later for him to have a look. Most of the computer files seem to be pretty bland: Word files, contracts, printouts… the sort of rubbish you save and then delete at a later date. There are a couple of encrypted database files which could be much more interesting, but it will take more than I know about computers to open them."

"Said as if you know anything."

"I turned the laptop on, what more do you want? I thought we could have a word with Charlie, see what he can dig up."

"Bloody hell, like I need a visit with that nutter."

"Knows what he's doing though."

"I suppose. Let's have another couple of drinks first though, eh? I don't think I could stand being utterly sober in that flat of his."

"Agreed." Tom raised his glass and gave me a wink.

"Well if it isn't the Deadbeat detectives." Len sauntered over to our table. "How's it going? Decided which one of you is going to wear the white suit and blow things up yet?"

"Thanks for your continued support, Len," I said.

"Please, it comes naturally. I take it you want another round?"

"Yes, please," said Tom. "Same again, but bigger."

"I'll have a tanker deliver it to your table."

"No, that would be dreadfully ostentatious, we'll stick to glasses."

"If you insist."

"With a cherry and umbrella," I added. "One must have a little decadence, after all."

"I wouldn't know, Mr Jackson, I've always been cursed with class."

He wandered off in the direction of the bar.

"Nice to know he cares," I muttered, once I was sure he was out of earshot.

"Believe it or not he was rather worried about you. I caught him slicing lemons in an absolute frenzy earlier, juice and pips everywhere."

"How sweet."

Tom smiled and leaned over.

"Sorry I got you into this, old chap. Didn't work out quite as planned, did it?"

"Don't worry about it," I said, draining the last of my drink. "Don't ask me why but, in hindsight, I rather enjoyed it."

Strange as it may seem, I wasn't lying either.

"Been a while since either of us felt alive, eh?" Tom replied, giving me a wink.

5.

We got to Charlie's place a little after eleven with what can only be described as a "spring in our step".

We'd ended up having a few more drinks than planned, initially to fuel our attempts at divining anything of use from the appointment book, then to drown our sorrows when we singularly failed to do so.

The entire book was filled with the most irritating collection of names and dates that could most accurately be described as "appointments".

I think it's the fact that this surprised us that upset me the most.

Anyway, we'd brought it with us in the vague hope that Charlie could run a search on a few of the names. Couldn't hurt to try.

He lived in a Victorian terrace not five minutes from my place. As we were so close I had intended on popping in to get a change of clothes but, as the night had dragged on, I'd grabbed a few spare things from the club instead, with the result that I cut something of a dashing figure on the streets of suburbia dressed as I was in an evening suit complete with white silk scarf. I did get the odd double take from passers-by but between the drink and an innate sense of theatricality, I couldn't care less and was jumping on and off the kerb as I pretended to be Gene Kelly.

Tom, in his ever-present blue jeans and jacket (which was just a little too pink to be purple), was trying to pretend he didn't know me.

I skipped up the steps to Charlie's front door and pressed the bell with a flourish.

The door opened and Charlie's wizened face popped out.

"Oh, it's you," he mumbled and stomped off into the house. "Time-wasters and scoundrels, as if I don't have enough of those close to hand."

Charlie Babbage was a long-term reanimate and something of a misery. A fun vampire of epic proportions, who used to complain in parliament about playing children and street entertainment. He also invented the computer. Well, a rudimentary version of it anyway. If you want to know any more, just ask him – he'll tell you in such intricate detail that eventually you'll die of it.

Given his age, he's also somewhat on the ripe side. He walks with a pair of canes and makes a squelching noise that I assume is his feet.

The years are not kind to reanimates, as I may have already mentioned, and Charlie had seen some years. He must have been clocking two hundred by now, and he died in an era when old meant old... Pensioners these days are all fashionable hipsters fighting off decrepitude with fine toiletries and designer drugs. Back in the nineteenth century, you knew someone was old because they left pieces of themselves behind on the carpet when they came to stay. He had the face of a howling ghost, wearing a chamois leather dipped in the chalk-dust shed during awful maths lessons. He was terrible. He gave me the heebie jeebies. I spent most of my time in his house choking back a scream.

But he knows his computers.

"The local kids been being a nuisance?" asked Tom as he led the way inside. "Do you want me to have words again?"

"What's the point?" Charlie asked. "The parents are as bad as their brood. Would you believe last summer they were cooking their meals over a fire in the back garden? I'm surrounded by savages."

"A barbecue," I said, my semi-drunken mind bubbling with self-approval having deciphered what Charlie was talking about.

"One step removed from barbarism," he replied. "Give them another twelve months and they'll be eating one another." He raised an eyebrow, as wrinkled and furry as a caterpillar's cock. "If they're not already, to mark them chewing on each other's faces when cluttering up the bus-stops, one can only wonder."

"Disgusting," Tom agreed, ever the politician. "We have descended into an era of slatterns and perverts."

"Indeed." Charlie nodded approvingly. He didn't fool me. He was the sort of prude that watched from windows with a bottle of hand lotion and a roll of kitchen roll within easy reach. There's nothing so quick to rise as a prude.

The place was a tip as always; everywhere you looked there was disposed packaging and tatty electrical components. At the top of the stairs I actually had to duck to get past a cat's cradle of wires that had got caught between the banister and the loft hatch.

"Come on through," he called.

Tom and I shared a look before we stepped into his office.

Inside was lit almost exclusively by neon and flashing "control panels" that I had every reason to believe did sod all except make you a bit dizzy after staring at them for too long. It was all part of Charlie's rather unusual attitude towards decoration.

"You're looking sartorially acceptable this evening, Mr Jackson," he said.

"Thanks, Charlie, didn't want to let you down."

Tom was trying to find somewhere to sit, finally opting for a turned-over packing case.

"It is such a hardship, making do without service," said Charlie. "I can't possibly be expected to maintain house and concentrate on my work."

"Indeed not," Tom agreed, knowing full well that you never get good favours from people when you criticise their decor. "And it's that work that brings us to your door."

"Of course it is," said Charlie, "I've never known you pay a social call."

Neither of us had much to say to that.

"Well come on!" said Charlie. "What is it?"

"A disc of files snatched off someone's computer," I said, offering it over. "We'd like you to try and open the couple of database files on there. They have passwords…"

Charlie waved his hand. "Passwords are nothing to me."

"Good, then you'll find it easy work. There's also an email address we'd like you to hack."

"And I have your word that this flagrant breach of the law is justified?"

Tom joined in. "We wouldn't ask were it not."

Charlie looked at us both for a moment and then nodded. "I shall do it." He put the disc in the drive and, after the Apple Mac equivalent of indigestion, a window popped up onscreen. "It all looks suitably mundane," he said, double-clicking a Word file to open it.

"'Dear Sir'," he read out, "'just a brief note to assure you that we are looking into sourcing options for the requisite component you have requested. Despite your understandable concerns regarding compatibility, we have high hopes of requisitioning something appropriate within the time window you mentioned.'"

"Sounds like computer parts or something," I said.

"Yes, it does rather," Tom said. "Or machinery. Either way, unusual for an undertaking firm." Tom scratched at his beard. "Unusual to be writing it in a letter rather than an email for that matter."

"Perhaps he's old-fashioned," I suggested.

"He wrote it on a computer," Tom replied, "and we know he was only too happy to use email."

"Sometimes businesses prefer hard copy," said Charlie, "as they need to show a paper trail."

Tom wasn't convinced by that. "A paper trail that goes out of its way to be unspecific?"

"Well, it shouldn't take me more than an hour or so to crack the encoded files," said Charlie. "Perhaps they will be more informative."

"Splendid." Tom got to his feet.

"You don't intend to wait?" asked Charlie, clearly put out.

I gave Tom a look, the sort of steely, no-nonsense look that can only be mustered by a drunk man in evening dress.

"I'm afraid we can't," he said, "but if you are able to

bring whatever you find around to Max's in a few hours?"

I rolled my eyes. Charlie would never set foot in the bar – he deemed it "an assault on the senses and an abomination against God" – but the last thing I wanted was him paying me a visit.

Charlie sighed. "I suppose so, though I do think you could show enough consideration to attend while I work."

"I'm afraid there are other avenues to investigate," insisted Tom, "and if we don't move quickly there will be countless deaths on our conscience."

Charlie narrowed his eyes. "As if there weren't already. Very well. I shall need no more than a couple of hours."

11

MAX

1.

We let ourselves out and sat on Charlie's wall to wait for a taxi. I smoked cigarettes and flicked the butts at the Starship *Enterprise* wind chime he keeps hanging in an arthritic apple tree. The tree looked miserable. Perhaps the weeds picked on it.

"The requisite component," said Tom, doing his best to seem wise and contemplative. I ignored him. If he was going to perform his detective routine again he could do it to passing suburbanites.

It often surprised me that Charlie chose to live out here. If you want to hide, the best place to do it is most certainly not suburbia. They were voracious for gossip, these people. Starved of any other stimulation, they stared out of their windows and traded stories over back fences. I wonder what they said about the crumbling dead man at number thirty-four? No doubt they had him pegged as a dirty old git and just tugged their children faster past his front gate.

The taxi pulled up and Tom gave the guy Thackeray's address. The driver grunted, though as a comment on the place we were departing from, or our planned destination, only the cleverest of urban translators could know. Perhaps he was afraid he didn't fit the dress code for Highbury.

Sitting in the back, Tom and I still didn't talk much. No doubt he was thinking up suitably oblique statements, pompous nonsense he could spout on street corners before dashing into the shadows. Like Sherlock Holmes if Sherlock Holmes was a bit of a twat.

Me? I was becoming quite convinced that everything I had thus far been through would turn out to be for nothing. Clearly not everything was right within the world of Lloyd & Bryson, but it was an act of insane overconfidence to think Tom and I could do anything about it. There is a reason policemen train to perform their duties: it takes more than half a bottle of gin and a hard-on for Agatha Christie to solve crimes. Tom and I had made a point of never knowing what we were doing in life. This had never previously been a problem because with fuck-all power comes no responsibility. Now we were sticking our noses into something we shouldn't. Something that probably should be investigated, but by someone with the faculties to do a proper job of it. I was feeling out of my depth and guilty.

2.

As you've no doubt already guessed, Thackeray's house was big. Medicine makes for good bricks and mortar, whichever side of the mortal coil you're sat on. The taxi crunched down the gravel drive and we could tell even the driver was impressed as we pulled up in front of the stone step. He threw a few extra quid on the meter just to prove it. Tom paid him and we trotted up to the doorbell trying to look as if we fitted in. It didn't work – even I felt under-dressed.

I glanced to my left and nearly knocked Tom over as I came face to face with a pair of glowing eyes. There was the sound of footsteps from behind the door and, as the porch light came on, I tried to look a little less relieved when I realised it was only a cat.

That's Thackeray's thing, you see. He loves cats. The place is filled with them; everywhere you go there's something furry and on the move.

Not that it bothers me particularly – bit of a cat fan myself. Still, it did get weird sometimes. He has hundreds of the things. He told me once that they just kind of gravitated towards the place. He started off with just a few and now he had an entire colony.

The door opened and Thackeray spread his arms wide in greeting.

"Good evening, my dear boys. Please do come in."

Boys? Tom was about Thackeray's age – at least in appearance; it gets a little difficult to keep track when you stop aging.

"Good evening, Jeffery. All well?" Tom was in his element now. This place was much more his style. Well, it would be if he could afford it and that says a lot – as I mentioned before, Tom can afford quite a bit.

"Oh, can't complain, Tom, can't complain. Yourself?"

"Fighting fit, thank you, old chap."

He led us into the entrance hall, all William Morris

wallpaper and polished wooden floorboards.

"Splendid. And you, Max? Haven't seen you for a while. How's that solution working out?"

He has me on regular doses of an embalming/plasma mix that he insists is good for me.

"Pretty good, thanks. Still don't like the needle bit, but I dare say I'll get used to it."

"Absolutely. Come through to the drawing room and I'll fix you both a sherry."

Sherry, good old Thackeray. One of the few people who didn't view it as just a trifle ingredient.

We wandered through, Tom and I keeping our eyes peeled for feline hurdles. There was an awkward moment when a particularly playful tortoiseshell grabbed at my scarf from its vantage point on a bookshelf, but I'm happy to say both the scarf and I survived, although I did suffer some slight scratching to the knuckles.

We sat down on a pair of leather armchairs and sipped at our large sherries.

"So, I'm dying to hear how it went during your coffin adventure," Thackeray said. "Why don't you fill me in?" He took his own seat, removing three or four passing kittens so he had room.

I gave him the quick version of the night's events.

"Dear God," he said, when I got to the whole scalpel-in-the-chest bit. "Maybe you should let me take a look?"

I was caught between the awkward horns of embarrassment and a man's natural enthusiasm for being a drama queen. In the end I settled for sighing manfully but unbuttoning my shirt and hoping it looked terrible enough for me to seem Ever So Brave.

"Oh, it's nothing to worry about," he said after a quick look, the old bastard, "just a nick."

I glanced around, ensuring the waft of blood hadn't encouraged a tide of cats from the shadows, then buttoned my shirt back up.

Thackeray sat back down and took the sort of contemplative sip of his sherry that Tom wishes he could naturally affect.

"It certainly sounds suspicious," was the somewhat obvious result of his contemplation. An anti-climax really. "Let me take a look at the drugs you found."

I got up to hand them over, cursing as I noticed a tabby leap into my seat the very moment I'd left it.

"Oh, just tell Bartholomew to move, old chap," said Thackeray. "He must learn some manners."

I lifted the cat from my chair, trying to shake the feeling that it was looking at me with a mixture of disgust and pity. It sat at my feet, continuing to stare up at me.

"Well," Thackeray announced, after another perfectly theatrical sip of his drink, "the first drug is nothing but a simple adrenal complex. It would be used to revive someone – coma patients, diabetes sufferers, say.

"The second is not dissimilar to the chemical I prescribed to you, Tom; it's for preventing coagulation of the blood. Certainly not something you would expect to find in an undertakers, but nothing you could really pin a crime on."

My phone rang, making Bartholomew the cat flinch and fix me with another hateful glare. He and I really weren't getting off on the right foot.

"Sorry," I said and took the call while Thackeray refilled our glasses.

It was Charlie, a brimming cupful of smug having cracked the email address we'd given him. Dr Herbert Snowdon would never be releasing a book of his correspondence – he was no Philip Larkin. He had, however ordered a number of substances that might seem unconventional in the corpse business: liquid nitrogen and something called tetrodotoxin.

"Tetrodotoxin?" Thackeray asked.

"Apparently. Know anything about it?"

"Enough to know it's not something an undertaker should have in his medicine cabinet. Are either of you familiar with Wade Davis?"

"Isn't he the little guy from *Star Wars*?" I asked.

"Hardly. Ethnobotanist, something of an *enfant terrible* in the field actually. He did a lot of research into zombification in Haiti."

I twitched a little at the use of the "Z" word, but tried not to show it.

"Well," Thackeray said, "he called it research, but there was a lot of scientific opposition to his theories. He posited that the Haitian zombie was the product of a unique blend of mental stimuli and a chemical compound, the active ingredient of which he claims to be tetrodotoxin – a substance found naturally in pufferfish."

"Don't lots of Japanese people die every year from eating them?" Tom asked.

"Hardly lots, but yes it does happen. Pufferfish are something of a delicacy over there. Eating their flesh is supposed to cause one's lips and mouth to tingle and create a mild sense of euphoria. If prepared incorrectly though, it can be fatal. You have to be a specially certificated chef to serve it."

"What does this chemical do?" I asked.

"According to Davis, the whole process sends the subject into a condition simulating death. The person is then revived days later, appearing to rise from the grave."

"Been there done that," Tom said.

"Haven't we all? Awkwardly, a sample of the compound was tested on Davis' return and found not to have the requisite effect. He claimed that the preparation was extremely hit and miss, far from a strict science – sometimes they got the balance right and sometimes they didn't, causing at best, nothing, at worst, death."

"Perhaps Snowdon has hit upon the right mix?" I said.

"Is it just me or does the idea of an undertaker creating a drug capable of feigning death seem just a little worrying?" Tom asked.

"It certainly does," Thackeray said. "Especially when you consider the other item on his shopping list: liquid nitrogen."

"What use would he have for that?" I asked.

"As an undertaker? Nothing. But its main medical use is the transportation of living organs."

We sipped our sherries and tried not to freak out.

Tom didn't help.

"Remember that letter Charlie found on the disc? 'Sourcing options for the requisite component… concerns over compatibility'?"

"Yeah," I said, "I do."

Tom nodded and scratched at his beard for a bit.

"Am I the only one here who's added two and two together and come up with an illegal organ-trafficking operation?" he said eventually.

"No," Thackeray admitted, "but the notion of something

like that going on in this country is… well, startling to say
the least. It's rumoured to exist in certain areas of Europe,
particularly Serbia and the Czech Republic, but here?"

"Why so surprising?" Tom asked.

"Well, it's not so easy to make people vanish in this
country, not to the levels we're talking about anyway."

"What better job to enable you to get your hands on
bodies, though?" I asked.

"No, that won't do. Organ transplants must be carried
out swiftly after the donor's death – you can't just raid
corpses. Plus, as you alluded to in that letter, there's the
minefield of compatibility."

"Unless your 'corpses' aren't really dead," said Tom,
taking a big mouthful of his drink.

"And you're able to shop on demand," I added.

Even Bartholomew the cat looked concerned at that
thought.

"Surely we have to tell the police," I said. "Isn't this
enough to go on?"

Thackeray sighed. "Maybe I could try and organise a
raid of the place," he said. "Maybe. Though to be frank, it
would be stretching my influence to its very limit. And what
if there's no more evidence of their operation there? All we
would succeed in doing is alerting them. Forcing them to
cover their tracks even further and vanish into the shadows.
What if the undertakers isn't their base of operations? They
could have another base entirely. Maybe several. We have
no idea if our suspicions are even correct…"

"Oh come on!" I argued, "what with everything we've
heard tonight I think we can safely say these people are up
to something outside their remit as a company."

Thackeray shook his head. "It's just not enough. It's suggestive, yes, but it's not prosecutable evidence."

"Which leaves us in the same position we already were," said Tom, "knowing they're up to no good but not having the first idea what to do about it."

3.

We took our leave of Thackeray.

"You realise," I said to Max, "that if we're right, Natalie Campbell is likely now nothing but a stew of parts, shipped off to the highest bidder."

"I do," he said.

We were walking along the road, both of us wanting the fresh air in order to think. Either side of us, luxury homes hid behind their privet and their high brick walls, a world away from the dark, terrifying thoughts that were bubbling up between us. Could their residents even imagine such a thing imposing on their delicate lives?

"If we had stopped them straight away," I said, "run up to the van and demanded to know what they were doing…"

"Then they would likely have tried to kill us and thrown our bodies in the back of the van with her. If these people are involved in something as terrible as organ-trafficking then they would hardly have been embarrassed into surrender."

He was right, of course. Still, the fate of Natalie Campbell weighed heavily on me. Our inactivity – or, more precisely, the failure of our activities – had achieved absolutely nothing. Likely a woman was now dead and all we could claim to be were witnesses.

"I feel sick," I admitted.

"You and me both."

"So what do we do now?"

He thought for a while, gazing down at his feet and kicking absently at the pavement like a child lost in their thoughts as they made their slow way to school.

"I don't want to give up," he said finally. "Maybe that's stupid. We're out of our depth and we're sticking our necks out. The last thing people like us should ever do."

I understood what he meant by that. People with our condition really should lead quiet lives. This was hardly the first time we'd broken that rule, but there was a difference between being boisterous in public and getting involved in a criminal investigation. We were drawing the attention of people who would spare no thought in killing us. Or attempting to, before they discovered that such a thing was impossible and that they'd stumbled upon something life-changing.

"We've gone this far," Tom continued. "Maybe it was too late to save Natalie Campbell, but who comes next? Right now nobody but us seems to know about them. If we don't do something, the next death is most certainly on us."

And that was something neither of us could bear on our conscience.

"All right," I agreed. "We keep digging. We should try and find this Dr Snowdon. Presumably he works out of a surgery somewhere. Or we could beat up that drunk priest at the church until he gives us more to go on."

Tom nodded. "Tomorrow. For now, we rest and we think."

I called a taxi and got it to stop off at my place on the way to taking Tom back to the club. Tom and I spent a lot of the journey in silence, trying to get our heads around it all.

I got out at my place and promised to meet Tom in the morning.

Pushing past the overgrown hedge that lined my path, I shoved the key into my front door – only to have it swing open.

Alarm bells rang for a moment, then I decided Charlie had likely arrived ahead of me. Picking the lock rather than waiting for a few minutes was Charlie to a tee, and I expected to see him sat, impatiently, in my front room, primed to deliver a lecture on home security, tardiness and the unsanitary drawbacks of keeping an animal in the home.

Jamie. Where was Jamie? He would normally be leaping on me the minute I stepped through the door. Maybe Charlie had let him out when he'd opened the door and the silly bugger was now running around the streets chasing people's cats and foraging in their dustbins.

I stepped into the hallway and flicked the light switch on.

There was blood on the carpet. A big fat trail of it leading towards the stairs.

I subconsciously pushed my house keys through the gaps in my fingers, forming a knuckle-duster of sorts, and made my way along the hallway.

"Charlie?" I said, not expecting an answer.

Somewhere, Jamie began to bark, alerted by the sound of my voice.

"Oh fuck." I saw what lay in the shadows at the foot of the stairs.

It was a mass of meat, limbs splayed, ribs exposed. The damn thing was in pieces. There was an arm wedged through the banister, severed at the shoulder. A couple of fingers congealed in the thick blood soaked into the carpet. Viscera were strewn everywhere like the contents of a party popper. His head hung at the end of a slick string of nerves and muscle, dangling loosely from the top of his spinal column.

"Oh fuck, Charlie."

I pulled my phone out of my pocket and called Tom.

Tom answered.

"Max? What is it?"

"It's Charlie…"

"What, he trying to interest you in an all-night *Star Trek* marathon or something?"

"Shut up, Tom. He's…"

Charlie's eyes blinked and I dropped the phone.

He was still alive. They couldn't kill him, the poor fucker was still aware. He was spread all over my stair carpet and he was aware.

"Max? Max?" Tom was shouting from the phone receiver.

The penny dropped.

I picked up the phone.

"You silly arse, you used my address. They picked the coffin up from this address."

There was a creak of floorboards from behind me; I barely registered it.

"Oh you stupid bastard, Tom, they know where I live!"

Something struck the back of my head and that was…

PART FOUR

‖‖‖ 12

1.

Natalie Campbell had a slight headache. Soon it would be the death of her.

"You should definitely see someone," said her husband, Laurence, more to bring the subject to a close than through any deep opinion. He was halfway through building his own Lotus Seven in the garage, and he rarely raised his attention from it out of choice.

"I don't like to make a fuss," she said, placing her knife and fork neatly across the back of a barely eaten dinner. It was a child's action, trying to hide the unpalatable under spread cutlery.

"No fuss," he replied, "just sensible. Better to be safe than sorry, eh?" He cleared away the dinner plates, running out of momentum at the sink. He gazed out of the kitchen window into the darkness and idly thought of machine parts.

"You're probably right," Natalie replied. She had been finding it harder and harder to get through her job as a teacher's assistant the last couple of days, the sound of the kids was bouncing off the school corridors before coming to a crash inside her pained skull. Something had to be done. "I'll make an appointment tomorrow morning."

2.

And so she did, though it would be a couple more days before she got through the door, by which time the headache had got much worse.

Sat in the waiting room, she could have imagined the environment was designed to be an endurance test. Tatty wall posters seemed to hem her in, pinned one over the other, like geological sediment bringing in the walls a thickness of A4 at a time. "Do the best by your breasts!" one advised, alongside a colourful cartoon of a blonde rummaging in her bra as if she expected to find gold in there. "You can't hold a cold!" said another. "All you do by visiting your GP is spread the germs – think of others!" This one was homemade, a whinge couched in cheerful terms, scribbled with a marker pen so neon pink it increased her headache.

"A little prick is all it takes!" shouted another, and Natalie might have assumed it was promoting birth control were it not for the childish illustration of a syringe that clarified the sentiment. "Don't forget to check about inoculations before you fly."

When the walls weren't shouting at her, two young boys were. They showed such exuberance as they chased one another around the magazine table she couldn't imagine what ailed them. Perhaps nothing, perhaps it was the mother that was suffering; she certainly seemed unable to match the effort of controlling them.

"Let's go fishing!" one of the boys cried, dragging a chair over to the fish tank in the corner and climbing onto it so he could loom over the false aquatic world of treasure chests and plastic pirate skulls.

His brother tapped on the glass while the elevated boy looked for a way past the lid of the tank to be able to plunge his fists inside. Natalie looked to the other people in the waiting room. The only other person to have apparently noticed the boys' behaviour was an old man who worked his false teeth as if they were a giant boiled sweet. He looked at the boys, then at Natalie. He smiled, as if pleased that they had both been able to share a happy moment.

By the time the child was unfastening the catches, Natalie felt she had to involve herself.

"He'll hurt the fish in a minute," she said, "or himself."

The mother looked up from her tired gossip magazine, looked at the boys and nodded.

"You're right. Still they have to learn, I suppose."

Who, Natalie wondered, *the fish?*

"Probably best to tell him to come away though, isn't it?" She struggled to think of a reason the woman might actually relate to. "I mean, won't someone complain?"

"Seems to me they are already." The mother sighed and shouted at the two boys. "Leave the fish alone, you daft buggers, you're not in the park now."

Natalie could only wonder what they might get up to there.

The boys stared at her, only too aware who it was that had brought their game to an end. The mother went back to gazing at the oiled torso of a soap actor as he tried to convince the readers that "Marriage has saved my life".

A door opened and her GP shuffled out, not lifting his eyes from her medical notes.

"Mrs Campbell?"

Rather than wait for her response, he did a U-turn and blindly shuffled back into his consulting room.

She stood up and followed him inside, absurdly embarrassed at having to do so in front of everyone else. It made her think of visiting the teacher's desk at the front of the class, the walk of shame past sniggering fellow pupils. The boys certainly shared the snide looks she remembered from her childhood, staring at her with amused contempt as she walked past them.

Inside the GP's consulting room the doctor was still being shy. He kept his face towards her notes as she sat down opposite him, looking at the photo of a child on the desk and a pen tidy that was brimming with brightly coloured biros, stationery that looked like sweets.

"So, Mrs Campbell," he said eventually, offering her tired eyes at last, "how are the shingles?"

"Shingles?"

He looked at the notes again and sighed. "Wrong Mrs Campbell. I'll fire that woman one day."

There was an awkward silence which she decided she should fill with her actual complaint.

"It's just a headache," she said, in the timeworn manner of an English person embarrassed by their illness, "but it's been going on for nearly a week now and seems to be getting worse."

"Hmm." He was still looking at the notes, clearly angry about the mistake. "Unbelievable."

"Really?" She felt a burst of panic that set the pounding off even harder behind her eyes.

He suddenly gave her his attention. "Oh not the headaches, sorry. I was still thinking about the notes." He leaned back in his chair and looked contemplative. "Whereabouts is the pain?"

"Behind my eyes."

"Any particular side?"

"More to the left," she admitted, but then a surge bubbled up on the right as if to prove her a liar, "but it varies."

"Any impairment of vision?"

"No."

"Nausea?"

"Sometimes. It gets so painful, you see."

"Yes." Though he gave no sign that he did see, rather that he had discerned all he could from his position behind the desk. "We'd better send you for some tests to be on the safe side, but it's likely nothing to worry about. Migraines can be a symptom of shifting hormones, or stress… Would you say you were stressed?"

"Not really, well… only about this."

"Naturally. I'll have you sent to the Batley," he said, referring to the local hospital, "and they'll give you a once-over. In the meantime I'll write you out a script for some stronger painkillers."

Silence returned and she realised this was her cue to leave. "Will I get a call?"

"No, you can collect it this afternoon."

"I meant about the hospital."

"Oh, yes, they'll send you a letter in a few weeks. I'm afraid that's not much to do with us, depends on their waiting times. It shouldn't be more than a couple of months."

That was hardly much relief. She could only hope the painkillers would be.

"Thank you," she said, though for what exactly she would spend the rest of the afternoon wondering.

3.

Her doctor's prediction proved accurate when the hospital letter came through and she read it twice through bleary eyes.

"I can't wait that long," she told her husband, who stood in the kitchen wearing old oil like warpaint. "If there is something wrong that would be too late."

"Maybe the insurance will cover it?" he suggested. He had taken out a policy a year or so ago, a prerequisite of their mortgage now that he was self-employed. "It's supposed to offer cover for dependants."

She felt she was one. At its worst, the pain made it hard to even stand. The painkillers were a mixed blessing; taking enough of them to help made her so spaced out she could barely function.

"I'll give them a call," he said, shuffling over to the kitchen drawer where they kept all their papers. He burrowed around and pulled out an A4 sheet, the company logo, a stylised sun, its rays pointing the way towards the name: "Sure Future".

Ten minutes later he wore the self-satisfied smile of a man who just hunted down a metaphorical wildebeest. "Relax, lass," he said, "you're covered. They're organising a private appointment for you."

4.

The experience could hardly have been more different. The appointment letter arrived within a couple of days and she was on a train to keep it by the end of the week. The journey was almost enough to rob her of her new-found hopefulness.

"I'm a pensioner," a lady insisted to Natalie while hovering over her. It was information she didn't know what to do with, looking the lady up and down in a hope that the answer could be found somewhere within the folds of the heavy overcoat she was wearing, despite the Indian-summer heat.

"Oh," Natalie replied, "can I help?" As soon as she'd said as much she realised how absurd an offer it was, though the lady didn't seem to think so.

"You'd hope you would," she replied, and looked at the seat Natalie was occupying, "my legs aren't what they were."

For a moment Natalie had the absurd vision of this elderly creature parting her overcoat to reveal glistening tentacles or maybe even cloven hooves. Then she understood she was simply being asked to vacate her seat. Her head was pounding. She hadn't taken any pills as she had wanted to keep her head clear enough to travel. She looked at the man sat opposite her, but his attention was suddenly occupied by the magazine he was reading.

"I'm not all I might be either," she said. "Is there any chance you could…?"

"I'm sure I won't beg for it," the lady replied loudly. "I would hope it was no great hardship."

"You and me both," said Natalie, but stood up anyway.

By the time the train arrived at her destination she was almost convinced she couldn't complete the journey to

the consultant's offices. The buffeting of the train had
turned the pain white hot behind her eyes. Deciding it
was more than worth the expense, she got in a taxi at the
station and offered the driver the address. Perhaps her
illness was clear, either that or the driver knew what lay
at the address. Either way, he drove in untroubled silence
and five minutes later she was outside an Edwardian
terrace, a heavy brass plaque advertising the presence of
Dr Herbert Snowdon.

Inside, she was disappointed by the functional corridor
and the curt secretary. No doubt her husband's ribbing had
led her to expect more. He had been acting like she had
made a royal appointment.

"Mrs Campbell," she explained. "I have an appointment
with Dr Snowdon." She glanced at the clock. "I'm a little
early."

The secretary seemed to feel this was irrelevant.
Looking at the empty waiting room, Natalie decided she
probably had a point.

"I'll tell him you're here," she said, and picked up the
telephone on her desk, gesturing for Natalie to take a seat.
She had only just done so when the secretary had her on
her feet again. "You can go right through."

Any misgivings were brushed away by the manner
of Herbert Snowdon. He could hardly have been more
enthusiastic to see her.

"Mrs Campbell!" he announced as if they were at a
cocktail party and she the special guest. "Do take a seat."
He tapped at the space bar of his desktop computer,
bringing it to life. "Do forgive me," he said, "just making
sure I have your notes to hand."

"I don't have shingles," she murmured.

He looked quizzically at her but she smiled and waved the comment away. "My old GP, it doesn't matter."

He nodded as if understanding the joke – though of course there was no way he could – and returned his eyes to the screen for a moment.

"It seems there's been a bit of a slip-up somewhere," he said after a moment, and she felt the dejection hit her even before he'd finished speaking. "You and your husband weren't booked in for your initial check-up."

"Initial check-up?"

"We insist on it with all our Sure Future clients – an MOT, if you like. We don't like to rely on the general medical notes, it's preferable to create a more exhaustive document of our own."

"Does that mean you can't treat me?" she asked, already quite convinced of the answer.

"My dear Mrs Campbell, it means nothing of the sort, please don't worry on that score. Though I would like to make a more thorough set of tests than I might otherwise have done, if that's all right?"

"Test all you like if you think you might be able to get rid of my bad head."

"We'll get rid of whatever we can, and that's a promise!" He got up and moved over to a cupboard on the far wall. "First we'll take a few drops of blood. Nobody likes needles so best to get it over and done with, don't you think?"

"Whatever you think best."

"Oh, Mrs Campbell, what a wonderful patient you're going to be. A doctor does love dealing with people that let them get on with what they do best."

"No point in seeing a specialist and then questioning their opinion," she said. "You know your job, I'm sure."

"Why have a dog then bark yourself, eh?" said Snowdon, laughing. "Quite right, Mrs Campbell, you just let me look after you."

Natalie actually felt relaxed for the first time in weeks, so much so that her headache lifted a little.

The good mood lasted all the week as she was tested, scanned, injected and dosed. For all the discomfort of Snowdon's attentions (and the other specialists he referred her to), there's nothing like a dose of heavy attention to help the sick feel a little better. It couldn't have been more different than the apathy she'd found from her own doctor; Snowdon treated her as if she was precious.

But then she got worse.

The first attack came while she was loading the washing machine, stuffing it with oil-covered overalls and sweat-drenched boxers. It was like a surge of white noise behind her eyes, and she toppled over, rolling on the cold concrete of the utility room floor, soap powder smeared against her cheek. It lasted no more than a few seconds, but when it faded, it left her feeling nauseous and afraid to move. Laurence found her there five minutes later and, after a typically ineffective panic, got her to her feet.

"I'm fine," she insisted. And actually, now that she was upright, she felt it. Her headache had all but lifted and there was no trace of the sudden pain that had come over her. "I probably just tried to get up too quickly."

It was a poor excuse but Laurence was grateful for it. She wasn't blind to the stupidity of the fact that she was consoling him when it was her that was ill, but he meant well. If she had been a faulty carburettor or oil filter he would have known how to deal with her; humans were a bit beyond him.

"You should call the doctor," he insisted.

"Maybe tomorrow," she replied, "there's no point in disturbing him out of hours."

5.

When the second attack came she wouldn't be so reluctant.

Everyday tasks had become intolerable hardships in recent weeks and there was nothing she dreaded more than a visit to the supermarket, squinting against the over-bright lights and the armies of shoppers. She made her cautious way up and down the aisles, hiding behind large sunglasses and drawing suspicious glances from those around her as she threw groceries into her trolley with haphazard abandon.

She found herself lost in indecision in the freezer section, leaning into the cool air and wishing she could just lie down.

"Excuse me ma'am?" someone asked, and she felt a solid hand grip the handle of her trolley.

She looked up into the comically stoic face of the supermarket's security guard. He had the earnestness of the worst pocket policeman, luxuriating in his meaningless uniform and brittle authority.

"Can I help you at all?" he asked.

"Not unless you have medical training," she muttered, and was pleased to see that made him back off a step.

"Aren't you supposed to wait until I try and leave to accuse me of stealing something?" she asked, feeling in a confrontational mood.

"Should I?"

"I'm not going to tell you your job." And the white noise returned, hitting her so suddenly and painfully that she screamed, flinging up her arms in a gesture the security guard mistook for an attack. He grabbed at her and they both went tumbling backwards, the trolley ricocheting off them and crashing into the side of the opposite freezer with such force it rebounded, wobbled and upturned, shedding its contents all over the floor.

After his initial over-exuberance, the security guard soon realised his mistake, clutching at her in a panic and shouting for someone to fetch a first aider.

Much good they'll do, Natalie thought, *when even the best private medical care can't make a difference*. And with that thought she passed out.

When she woke up it was to find herself propped up against the side of the freezer surrounded by faces altogether too eager to be termed caring.

"Will everyone please go about their business?" asked a red-faced man in a cheap suit. He was mopping at his forehead with his sleeve and she only caught sight of his name badge when he lowered his arm. She was now the problem of Barry Leatherhead, Store Manager, and he seemed horribly uncomfortable about the fact. "Can I help you?" was written beneath his name in a cosy comic sans font designed to make him seem the most approachable man you could imagine. It didn't work. "Has someone called for an ambulance?" he was asking, running through a barely remembered mental list of emergency training.

"That won't be necessary," she meant to say, but by the look on the gathered crowd's faces what came out of her mouth was nothing quite so distinct. The idea that she might have lost control of her speech was enough to make her panic and she struggled to stand up, bringing on another bolt of head pain.

"Sit still, love," suggested a kindly-looking woman beside her. "It'll be all right."

Natalie looked at her store uniform and wondered what made her qualified for such confidence, but restrained her anger – the woman was only trying to help.

She offered a glass of water. "'Bout the only thing I can give you these days," she said with clear regret, "everyone's terrified to crack open so much as a paracetamol now, in case you pop your clogs of it and your family sues."

What a relaxing thought.

"There's one on its way," someone shouted, and it took her a moment to realise they meant an ambulance.

"They don't hang about," the store manager said, looking down at a business card that Natalie realised he must have taken from her purse. She recognised the Sure Future logo on its reverse. Dr Snowdon had given her one at their first meeting, saying it was always best to carry it around in case she got into trouble. The thought of the store manager rummaging through her belongings made her feel wretched as she tried to think what might have been in her handbag or purse – what personal clutter had he waded past on the hunt for ID? The intrusion hurt almost as much as her head. Then it occurred to her what small fry some used tissues and a tampon were when compared to her current position. The urge to cry was almost more than she could bear.

"I just need to stand up," she said, and this time she must have been clearer as the attentive woman rested a hand on her shoulder.

"You just stay put until help comes," she said, "there's no need to put yourself through anything more."

If Natalie had felt sharper she might have pointed out that it was a member of supermarket staff that had helped to trigger her attack, though she supposed she could hardly be sure of the fact.

"I just want to go home," she said, though it was more a thought she hadn't managed to internalise than an actual request.

"Course you do, love," the woman replied. "I'm sure they'll have you tucked up in no time."

Natalie was sat there for another ten minutes before the ambulance arrived and people had long since dispersed. She had only been a momentary distraction from the mundanity of grocery shopping; now she had stopped making a scene the audience had quickly grown bored. The sight of two paramedics, crackling within the bright-yellow plastic of their high-visibility jackets as they wheeled an empty wheelchair past the row of tills, almost woke the spectators up again, but they were so casual in their business that their attraction was limited.

"Mrs Campbell?" one asked, unhooking a clipboard from the back of the wheelchair and reading it. A biro hung from the clipboard like a suicide victim.

"Yes." She made to nod but the movement of her head brought another wave of pain, and she gripped at her knees as if fearful that she might fall further than her already lowly position.

He scribbled at a form, hooked the clipboard back in place and gestured for his companion to help him lift Natalie into the chair.

"Don't worry, Mrs Campbell," he said as they dropped her onto the padded seat. "Mr Ackroyd and I will soon have you looked after."

She saw him share a glance with the store manager, and the look that passed across his face terrified her. It wasn't the confident look of a man assuring a bystander that everything was under control, it was a look that said things were worse than he had feared. Dear God! What did they think was happening to her? Had Dr Snowdon changed his confident diagnosis? Was she so ill?

They wheeled her out of the supermarket and over to a small van that looked far more commercial than medical. The sort of thing an affluent tradesman might use.

She began to panic.

"Can I see some ID?" she asked. "I really shouldn't just…" The pain returned and it was all she could do to keep from being sick into her lap.

"I'm Mr Lloyd and this is Mr Ackroyd," the paramedic said. "We're taking you to see Dr Snowdon, he'll soon have you at rest."

She might have wished for a better choice of words, but they loaded her into the back of the van before she could control her pain enough to say as much. Inside, it was somewhat more reassuring, an ambulance stretcher surrounded by the expected paraphernalia of stands and IV drip feeds. Fitted cabinets looked to contain pharmaceuticals and a pair of straps fixed her chair in place.

"This will help," said Lloyd, rolling up her sleeve and giving her an injection. She might have questioned what was in it but, given the pain, she didn't altogether care.

Suitably dosed, they closed her in and moved around to the front seats.

"Where is it we're going?" she asked. "The Batley?"

"We have our own facilities," Mr Lloyd insisted, before turning the ignition and reversing away from the disabled parking spaces he'd straddled outside the store. From the rear window, Natalie saw the concerned face of the store manager as he stared after the departing vehicle. He looked like he was attending a funeral procession.

"Can I call my husband?" she asked, suddenly aware of being very much alone.

"Dr Snowdon has already given him a shout," said Ackroyd, speaking for the first time. "He'll probably be there before we are."

They drove out onto the ring road and she lost all hope of conversation as the van built up speed on the dual carriageway. She began to feel isolated in a coffin of echoes, the hum of motors and the grind of tyres on tarmac. The pain in her head was receding, to be replaced by a dreamy sense of dislocation, no doubt the effect of the injection Lloyd had given her. Her head felt too heavy to lift and she let it drop forward, still conscious but lost in the thick mud of her own fractured thoughts.

She couldn't say how long it took for them to arrive at their destination. The awareness of the van slowing to a halt and the sound of the back doors opening seemed sudden, so she supposed she must have fallen asleep. She tried to lift her head to acknowledge her carers' presence, but it was more than she was capable of, and she just sat there as they unstrapped the chair and wheeled her back out into the light. Her eyes struggled to focus, but she was dimly aware of the sound of traffic and then was being lifted over a couple of shallow steps and taken inside a building. She squinted, trying to solidify the images around her. She thought she might be at Snowdon's office, or perhaps somewhere less relaxed, because she could certainly smell the tangy odour of chemicals. Wherever she was, Snowdon was certainly in attendance because she heard his voice, recognised the soft lilt of its Scottish accent.

"There you are, Mrs Campbell," he said. "We've been terribly worried about you."

"I already injected her," said Lloyd, "you don't have to worry."

"Oh." And here there was definite shift in his tone, that polite gentility replaced by something altogether more businesslike and cold. "Then we certainly don't have to worry."

She felt fingers on her face, her head being lifted. It felt like someone else's head, someone else's eyes that looked on the vague face of her private doctor.

"You're a very special woman, Mrs Campbell," he said, "and your legacy will live on."

"Aye," said Lloyd, "in our bank accounts."

Snowdon let go of her head and Natalie lost consciousness again.

6.

When she next awoke it was to hear her husband's sobs. She felt much more clear-headed but unable to move. Her eyes were closed and even the act of opening them was beyond her. She was, she thought, utterly detached from a body that she could feel but not control.

"We had no idea," her husband was saying, "we thought it was just something… I don't know… just…" His words petered out, to be replaced by more sobbing. What was he crying about? What did he know about her condition that she didn't? Was she in a coma? You heard about people who ended up stranded in their hospital beds, unable to move or communicate, yet still aware of everything that went on around them. Is that what had happened to her?

Apparently not.

"It was quick, Mr Campbell," Snowdon said. "She just slipped away."

Slipped away? What was he talking about? She was still here! Still hearing, still thinking, still alive!

"I just wish I had been able to help her," Snowdon continued, "but it's a sudden, progressive condition. Maybe if I had been consulted earlier…"

At this her husband's sobbing increased.

"But no," said Snowdon, "we mustn't think like that. It's a terrible fact of life that we can be struck down in our prime, thriving one moment and gone the next. It may be some consolation in the future to think that at least she didn't suffer. When it took her, it took her gently and quickly."

There was a pause as Snowdon allowed those shallow words to sink in.

"You leave everything to us," he said finally, "that's what we're here for. I'll handle the paperwork and the authorities. You just take a few moments to say goodbye and leave the rest to me."

Natalie felt Laurence take her hand with a gentleness he had never seemed to possess before.

"Oh, baby," he said, and she felt his hot, wet face press against her cheek, "I'm so sorry I let you down. I should have paid more attention, I should have done something… I should have…" He began to cry again and she found herself angry that he had only bothered to show such a depth of feeling when he thought there was nobody there to receive it. She'd remind him of this, she thought, once she was up and about again. If nothing else, it would have brought him out of himself a bit more.

Yes. When she was up and about again.

7.

They gave her another injection after Laurence left, and this time she blanked out for a long time. Maybe they renewed her dose while she slept, kept her under. Certainly they must have done something of the kind because days must have passed before she woke again. After all, funerals weren't arranged in a matter of hours, were they?

The sound was muffled and eventually she had to accept it was because she was sealed away inside a coffin. There was the distant sound of church music, like a classical station being played on a distant radio. Then the soft drone of a voice, its words indistinct, as dull and lifeless as the drone of a vacuum cleaner.

She tried to move, tried to make a sound, tried to do anything that might alert those outside as to what was going on. She felt sharper than ever, her senses acute, her mind clear. Yet still her body was detached. She tried to focus on it, to isolate the sensations of the coffin beneath her, the feel of the satin lining on the back of her hands, the pillow beneath her head. It was no use. The sensations were there, just, but they felt so faint, so indistinct, that she couldn't relate to them. Her head was a barrage of noise, a chaos of panic and non-coherent thought.

Then the coffin began to move, dropping down into the dull grind of hydraulics, and she knew that it was all far too late. Any moment now would come the flames, the heat and a slow fade into oblivion. With that thought came a sense of calm. While she had no wish to die – and most certainly not by that method – there seemed little she could do about the fact, and maybe the thing was not to fight the sense of dislocation but give in to it. She would no doubt have cause to be grateful once the gas-jets were lit if she wasn't altogether in touch with the sensation.

She wondered why Snowdon had done what he had done. And what Lloyd had meant about her improving their bank accounts. Then she pushed the questions away. She was about to die for real now, this absurd lie of an existence made solid by flames. She wasn't going to expire with a head full of mysteries she could never solve. Instead she thought of Laurence. As the coffin was lifted and set down once more, then slid into what she imagined must be the industrial oven, she fixed her mind on his stupid face, smudged with oil. She thought of his vague eyes, his thoughts always somewhere other than here. Then she thought of how his cheek had felt when pressed against hers. His words of apology, his tears and the realisation that he had felt much more for her than she had ever guessed. Yes, that was a thought to carry into an afterlife.

8.

She didn't die.

It took her a short while to realise it, so convinced had she been that she was experiencing her very last moments. The inside of the coffin remained cold, the flames didn't come and, having been so sure that she had experienced her last, she wasn't altogether sure what to do with herself.

Slowly her body became more sensitive, like chilled skin tingling at every sensation. With it, her mind began to think about what might come next. If they weren't going to cremate her, were they instead planning on burying her? Or had she missed something? Had something happened to alert them that she wasn't as dead as everyone seemed to think? That thought brought hope, and with it a determination to fight.

Her arms and legs still refused to move but her renewed determination wouldn't let her stop trying. It had been so long that what should have been automatic to her seemed a complex mental procedure. Her body felt removed from her and she tried to send her thoughts into her hands, tried to isolate the feelings in them, to own them and thereby control them. But nothing she did would bring her body back to her. She wanted to cry but even that was beyond her, stripped back to a terrible sense of panic, sadness and fear. In the end that fear felt like all she had, it felt like all she was. A terror given just enough thought to develop a sense of self.

Hours passed.

She became aware of voices and could only hope this might be someone coming to rescue her. She felt the coffin lift and she was carried away, rolling around inside the coffin as she was manhandled by men who seemed far too casual for the job. If they knew she was alive they would have opened the coffin. This could only be another reason for terror.

She shook and tumbled, the rough treatment actually waking her body up, if only a little. Just for a moment she felt a spasming in the fingers of her left hand, and she would have cried out if her mouth had been her own.

There was a shout and suddenly she was falling, the coffin tumbling, the lid snapping open. She fell to the ground, her face punched by cold gravel, a slight breeze tickling the hairs on her arms and legs. What had happened?

"Pick her up, you clumsy bastards!" someone shouted, and she was sure she recognised the voice – Mr Lloyd? "Come on!" he shouted again, and hands were tugging at her, throwing her back into the coffin as if she was nothing more than produce being delivered, something to be manhandled and dumped.

The coffin lid was closed and the whole lifted inside a vehicle, the sensation of being in the open air vanished, the grunts of the men carrying her echoed, their feet sounding out on metal, the creak of a vehicle's suspension. There was the sound of doors slamming shut, then an engine firing up.

She was on the move again, away from the church she had been sure would be her resting place. This didn't bring her a great deal of relief. The confusion of earlier was sharpening into a finer point. Snowdon and Lloyd knew she wasn't dead. She had suspected that but couldn't know for sure. Part of her had wondered if Snowdon had simply made a mistake, her illness giving the impression of death. But no, that couldn't be it. This wasn't a medical error, this was a definite plan. They had told everyone she was dead and now they were taking her away. But what could they want from her? What possible use was she? Thoughts of grotesque tabloid headlines flashed through her mind, stories of white slavery and prostitution. Surely that was for those younger than her? She was somebody you wouldn't recognise on the street, plain and too old to be a foreign fantasy… What the hell could they want from her?

Of course the fact that she was still alive kept a small fire of hope burning. The alternative was, after all, a finite problem. As long as she was still breathing – and she could feel her chest rising and falling, her body waking up more and more – then she had a chance of getting out of whatever situation she had got herself into.

Her face began to hurt, pieces of gravel embedded in her cheeks. She was glad of it – at this point even pain was good.

9.

Then the bright light.

"Ah, Mrs Campbell." Snowdon's face leaned down over her, and if only she had control of her hands she would have turned one into a fist and punched him with it. "You seem altogether more alert than I might have expected. Normally my special patients don't show any sign of revival until… well… until it's no longer an issue."

He stepped back out of her line of sight and spoke to the others: "Get her on the table, quick as you can."

She felt their hands on her, hoisting her out of the coffin and back out into the world. They were as rough as ever. She was aware of her shroud floating up around her face as the man holding her legs shrugged his shoulders and lifted her higher, trying to get a comfortable grip. Such indignity still had teeth, despite all she had been through, and she could only imagine how ridiculous she looked, how exposed.

Soon she had cause to think back on it fondly as she was dropped onto a metal table and one of the men tore the shroud off her so that she was naked, surrounded by these men who looked on her as nothing more than meat to be slung from one place to another. What did they want from her?

"Look at the state of her," Snowdon said, yanking her legs and arms straight. "What happened?"

"Lewis tripped," said Lloyd, "and they dropped the bloody coffin. Does it matter?"

"No," Snowdon admitted, brushing the gravel from her slack face. "She'll need to be scrubbed down anyway. Get yourself ready and we'll get right on with it. The clock's ticking on this one."

"Can't you just inject her again?"

"Too risky. It's unpredictable stuff as it is, and another dose might cause irreparable damage."

Too risky… another hopeful phrase. Whatever they were doing to her, they obviously needed her alive.

Her hands were tingling again and she could lift her index finger just a fraction. It was all she had to express her disapproval at the rough wash she received. Hard, scouring sponges reeking of disinfectant scraped across her torso so that it burned.

"That's enough," Snowdon said with a chuckle. "Or were you enjoying yourself?"

Natalie certainly wasn't, but nobody seemed inclined to care about that. Snowdon, when he once more appeared in her line of vision, was wearing a surgeon's cap and mask, and his lack of concern couldn't have been more evident.

"Right," he said, snapping plastic gloves into place, "let's get on with it."

With what? Natalie was desperate to know.

She did her best to shout and was surprised at a faint gurgle that crept over her slack lips. It was enough for him to notice.

"Oh dear," he said, "this would have been better for you had you stayed completely out of it. I can't add anaesthetic, not with the cocktail you already have running through your system."

"Anaesthetic?" she tried to ask.

"It's not a problem from my point of view," he continued. "It would be some time before you're awake enough to start thrashing around, even considering what I'm about to do. But if you're experiencing nerve sensation, you're not going to like this one bit."

He smiled, his face mask crumpling and his eyes sparkling. "There are most certainly better ways to die,

Mrs Campbell," he said, "but I have a lady in Belarus who has urgent need of your kidneys. I shall try not to hurt you more than absolutely necessary, I'm not a cruel man. Let us hope that shock kills you before the blood loss."

And with that he began to cut.

PART FIVE

ⅢⅡ⎮13

TOM
1.

Max's shouts were distorting so much through the earpiece of my phone that I had to hold it a few inches away. The grunt and sudden silence that immediately followed them had me squeezing it tight to my head, finger in the other ear.

"Max!" I shouted, making the cabbie jump and narrowly avoid driving us into a lamppost.

"Easy, pal," he said, throwing me what he no doubt thought of as a withering look via the rear-view mirror.

Nice try, I thought, but Tom Harris has been withered by the best.

"Just pull over for a minute, would you?" I said, forcing any trace of anger from my voice; the last thing I needed was to get in a row with a burly taxi driver. Especially the sort that saw baseball caps as acceptable dress away from an American sporting field.

There was the faint sound of people talking on the line, but it sounded like Max had dropped his phone again, and they were too far away to be heard clearly.

I took the phone from my ear and tried to fiddle with

the piddling little buttons, thinking there must be a way of turning the volume up.

It went dead; either Max's attackers had cut it off or I had.

"Change of plan," I told the driver. "Can you head back to where we just dropped off my friend?"

"Listen, pal, I'm supposed to have clocked off already. I'm not driving around all night 'cause you can't decide where you want to be."

Time for a bit of the famed Harris charm, I decided.

I reached into my wallet and pulled out a fifty-pound note, flashing it briefly in his direction then slipping it back into my pocket.

"I'll make it worth your while, old chap. Just open the taps, would you? I want to get there as quickly as possible."

He smiled and swung the car into a three-point turn.

We got to Max's house and I passed him a ten-pound note.

"Where's the bloody fifty?" he shouted as I stepped out of the car.

"I only showed it to you, I didn't say I'd give it to you."

Max's front door was wide open and I could see the blood on the carpet before I'd even cleared his front path.

"Max?" I shouted, slipping on the wet floor in my haste.

The body at the foot of the stairs made me swallow back the urge to throw up, but I could tell it wasn't Max so I dashed past the stairs and checked the other rooms. Jamie bounced at me from the kitchen where he had been shut in. He ran around searching for his master but coming up empty. He stared at the mess of blood and organs in the hallway and, with a realisation that he might see it as a source of food – something I couldn't even begin to bear –

I shoved him apologetically back into the kitchen.

I examined Charlie as closely as I dared. I saw his eyes move, and bit my lower lip to control the churning in my stomach.

I called Thackeray's number. It took him a few rings to answer.

"Jeffery," I said, "it's Tom. I need you over at Max's house right away. Bring your equipment. No, no... it's Charlie. Someone's really done a number on him, the poor man's been torn apart. Look, make it quick, would you? I don't know what... I don't..."

It was no good; I dashed to the door and threw up in Max's front garden.

After a few moments, I put the phone back to my ear.

"Sorry. Just get over here, would you?"

I cut off the call and leaned in the doorway for a minute, breathing in the fresh air and waiting for my stomach to settle.

Feeling a little better, I rang Len.

"Deadbeat Detective Agency, lost wine bottles a speciality – how may I help you?"

"Knock it off, Len, Max is in trouble."

"What's he done?"

"Nothing to my knowledge, it's what's being done to him that's worrying me."

I filled Len in on the potted history of the evening.

"Sounds to me like you should have stuck to propping up the bar."

"Damn right. Listen, can you call the boys in? I've a feeling we might be in need of a little muscle before the night's out."

"Of course, I'll make a few calls. I know Douggie's free, I don't know about Tony or Steve."

"Whoever, just get a few reliable bodies down to the club. I'll meet you there in a bit."

"Leave it to me."

"Thanks, Len."

"Forget it." There was a pause. "Look after yourself, Tom."

I couldn't help but chuckle.

"You sound like you almost care."

"Really?" I heard the smile in his voice. "There must be something wrong with the line."

He cut off the call. I stared at the dead phone in my hand, my head filling with nightmarish visions of what had happened to Max. They had taken him. Why? Because they wanted to know who we were, I guessed. They wanted to know who it was that had been poking their noses into their affairs. Yes… that made sense.

The phone rang in my hand. In my panic I nearly dropped it. It was Max's number.

"Max?"

"Don't be stupid," said the other voice on the line. "He's here, but he's not in a position to talk right now."

"Listen," I said, my teeth clenching as an anger the like of which I barely remembered began to bubble up inside me. I'm a calm chap, an affable sort, but when you press me then I can snap. "If you harm him, so much as a hair on his head, then I will come for you. I will finish you. Do you understand me?"

"That's the point," the voice said. "You will do nothing. You will speak to nobody. You will wait until we call you again. We have your friend here, and things could get painful for him at a moment's notice. Right now, you do exactly as we say or I start to make him bleed. Bleed more. Do you understand me?"

What could I say to that? "Of course I understand you," I replied, trying to bite back my fury, "but understand me too. I don't make empty threats either. His safety just became as important to you as it is to me. You harm him and we come for you."

The man on the phone gave a slight laugh. "We'll call you," he said, and hung up.

I burned with anger, the phone gripped so tightly in my hand that I realised I might break it unless I forced myself to let go. I have something of an issue with control, I will admit. The one species that can claim to have ridden roughshod over my sensibilities are the clan of wives I collected in my lifetime. Outside of those brutish yet delightful women, I have a single-minded hatred of being backed into a corner.

I am not a man who demands authority – you only have to look at my relationship with Len to see that – but there is a world of difference between handing over the reins of business to one better suited to them and having a cocksure little shit like this trying to force me into inaction.

Added to that, naturally, was the fate of Max. Like that noble hero of literature, Bertram Wooster, we Harrises have a code: you never let a pal down. If they hurt him they would find that I was not altogether the affable chap I see fit to present to the world.

At that moment I could have killed without my dull, inefficient heart skipping its hourly beat. I would not take this lying down.

2.

Thackeray got to the house in just under twenty minutes.

He paused in the doorway, looking at Charlie, and took a short breath. That was as much emotion as he showed; from there on in it was professionalism all the way.

He took a long-needled syringe from his doctor's kit and filled it up from a small jar.

"Anaesthetic," he explained. "Of sorts, anyway. It'll stop any signals he's still receiving from his nerve endings."

He popped the needle in through the corner of Charlie's eye and I had to look away.

"Sorry, but I can't guarantee another viable route. They've made too much of a mess of him."

"What chance is there?" I asked. From where I stood there seemed none whatsoever.

Thackeray sighed as he put away the syringe. I watched Charlie's eyes droop closed, a vaguely dreamy quality in them.

"Chance of what? The man's been reduced to a stew. I can patch him up a little, but he's never going to look himself. As for brain function, who knows? You don't need me to tell you I'm always working in the dark these days. Scientifically he should have been a vegetable long before this happened to him. We're resilient, supernaturally so..."

I raised my eyebrows at that. Thackeray, ever a man of science, was not one to use such words lightly.

"Oh, you know what I mean. Beyond science... I subscribe to the Clarke theory that everything unexplained will one day be taken for granted as scientific theory, but that doesn't help me in the present day. We're in uncharted waters and I sail them blind every day. I'll do the best I can for him, and that's all I can do."

He pulled on some rubber gloves, unfurled a waterproof body-bag and moved to gather Charlie's innards before, thankfully, pausing.

"Look," he said, digging into his coat pocket. "Do you want to open the boot of the car? As inhumane as it may sound, it's the least conspicuous way of getting him out of here."

I took the keys and moved to the door.

"Tom?"

I turned around.

"I'll be about five minutes, no rush," he said.

"Thanks."

I went out to wait by the car.

The night had turned chilly, but it didn't bother me. My anger was still stoked sufficiently to keep me warm.

I called Len again. I told him about the phone call.

"So that's the way they want to play it," he said. "Of course they can have no idea how many people they're dealing with. They need to know how much of a threat we are."

"'We'."

"Of course. Come on, Tom, you know me better than that. If someone's taking you on then they have me to deal with as well. And not just me. Douggie and Steve will fight your corner as well."

"I know." His loyalty didn't surprise me but it took the edge off the anger. "Thanks. Would you have one of the boys swing by Charlie's place and grab his computer? There might be some information on it worth having."

"No problem."

I cut off the call and tried to stop thinking about what might be happening to Max. Tried to convince myself that he was okay. After all, if they were going to do a repeat performance of their attack on Charlie, why bother taking him with them?

Because they wanted to do it in proper medical surroundings, that's why.

I mean, could you honestly think of a more likely response to finding a living corpse?

The first thing anyone with an even vaguely scientific bent would do is take it apart to see how it worked. I just had to hope that they would hold off doing anything drastic until they knew what they were facing. For now Max was useful to them. He was a bargaining chip. Only an idiot would cash that in until they knew the odds of the hand they were playing.

3.

I walked back into the house, hoping I'd allowed enough time for Charlie's body to be squared away.

"I hate to seem insensitive, Jeffery, but, for Max's sake, we need to be moving."

I told him about the phone call.

"Right, help me get Charlie stowed away then I'll drop you off at the club."

I screwed up my face and tried not to look at Charlie's body. Thackeray had done some rough stitching on the torso, but as far as I could tell it wasn't for healing purposes, purely a practical move to hold everything in.

"Sorry, old chap, but you're coming with us," I said to Thackeray, grimacing at the feel of Charlie's loose skin as I took as firm a hold as possible on his shoulders.

"Don't think me insensitive, Tom. I'd like to help, but it's not really my area of expertise, is it?"

We lifted the carcass into the bag.

"If Max has been hurt, he's going to need your help. The sooner you're able to give him that help, the better chance he's got. Sorry, but I'm really not open to negotiation."

Thackeray tugged the bag around Charlie and pulled up the zip. He looked at me and the fear in his eyes was tangible. I couldn't blame him.

Max was my first priority though, and to be frank... I really didn't care about Jeffery's feelings on the matter.

"Okay," he said. "I'm your man."

4.

We pulled up outside the club, and I nodded to Carl and Dave.

"Give us a hand, boys," I shouted. "You're both on overtime."

"S'all right, Mr 'Arris, Len filled us in," Carl replied in his usual monotone.

"Yeah," Dave piped up. "Who do you want us to whack?"

Dear Lord, where do I find them?

"Nobody for now, though it's very sweet of you to offer. To start off with, could you just take this body off the back seat and put it in my flat? Do be gentle, he's a friend."

Either through discretion or ignorance, they both nodded amiably and grabbed an end each.

"Go the back way, yes?" I said, before they manhandled a body-bag through my club.

"Of course," said Dave.

"Oh," Carl moaned, pausing. "We're not supposed to leave the door unattended when the club's open, Mr 'Arris."

"Don't worry," I said, pushing past them. "We're closed until further notice."

Len was there to greet me.

"Douggie's here, Tom. So's Steve. Apparently Tony's at his art class. Nobody can get hold of him."

"Art class?" I looked at my watch. "It's half eleven!"

"Perhaps he's a slow painter. I'll keep trying. Anyway, they're at the corner table. Carl and Dave are up for it."

"So they tell me. They seem to think murder's in the offing."

"Ah… the childish enthusiasm's infectious, isn't it? They've been cracking their knuckles like pop guns all evening."

"Bless. Listen, Len, I'm going to need you to clear the club."

"Not a problem, give me five minutes."

He strolled off towards the band, who were pumping out a syrupy New Orleans sound, beautiful and mournful all at the same time. Let 'em play, I thought, honey for the soul.

Douggie stood up as I approached the corner table. His shock of red hair still managed to alarm me, even after all these years.

"Now then, you mad Scots bastard, thanks for coming,"

I said, greeting him with the time-honoured crudity that only comes with real friendship.

"Nay worries, lad," he shouted, spreading his arms wide for a hug and a kiss, the camp old fruit. "You want to tell me what's goin' on, or shall we just hit everything you tell us to?"

"Oh, I think I can afford to fill you in a bit, Douggie. We've no secrets, have we?"

"Ain't that the truth, you sexy wee bastard, you!"

He grabbed me in his meatpacker's arms and planted a damp kiss on my forehead.

"Besides," he said, once he'd had his wicked way with my frontal lobe, "Steve's already had a look at your boy's wee laptop there, y'know?"

"Anything of interest?"

"Aye, beyond cut-and-paste pictures of Lieutenant Uhura with her thighs as wide as a five-bar gate, we've got a load of weird stuff about zombies and that."

He put his hand to his mouth in embarrassment.

"Christ, I'm sorry, I don't mean to be tactless, you know?"

"Don't worry about it, Douggie."

I nudged Thackeray towards a seat and took one myself.

"It's all about some guy called Wade Davis…"

Thackeray caught my eye. "We suspected as much."

"Then I'm probably not telling you anything you don't already know. But this bastard's doing things to folk that makes your scrotum shrink tighter than the grip of an angry bear on metal night. I tell you, I'm a hard man to shock, you know, but the more I think about this…"

"I know," I told him. "It doesn't bear thinking about."

But think about it we all did.

▐▌▌▌14

TOM
1.

Len strolled over.

"We've a few awkward sods but nothing I can't handle. The place will be empty in a couple of minutes."

"Thanks, Len."

"So," Steve said, closing the laptop, "we know what these bastards are up to but what are we going to do about it?"

"Our first priority is Max."

I placed his mobile in the middle of the bar table and told them about the brief threatening conversation I had endured.

"Of course," I said, gratefully accepting a glass of Merlot from Mandy behind the bar, "If they think we're just going to sit quietly and let them dictate our actions, they have another thing coming. I shall play their game for now, but we all know there's no way they're simply going to hand him back over and let us all walk away. We know too much. We're a threat. Our only advantage right now is that they don't know how big a threat."

"Naturally," said Len, "if they knew they were dealing with an aging jazz-club owner and a handful of his staff they would be quaking to the very Odor Eater-lined soles of their size twelves."

"Yes," I said, "we're not quite the formidable force they might imagine. That said, we're a tenacious bunch and, speaking for myself, they made a terrible mistake the day they threatened one of my friends. There is nothing I won't do to get him back safely. If I have to beat every single one of them so hard they will need centuries of evolution to recover, then I will do so with a happy heart."

"Oh good," said Dave, who had joined us. "That sounds like a laugh. Probably."

I have to say I rather agreed with him.

2.

I gave them the whistle-stop version of our adventure thus far (though I admit to a little dramatic showboating here and there – you can take the man out of the theatre but never the theatre out of the man).

We were a motley bunch, but well suited for the night ahead.

When I got to the grey area in our story of how Lloyd and Snowdon were selecting their victims, it was Steve that piped up with the answer, having shed some more light on the affair during his perusal of the laptop files.

"It's actually very simple," he said. "The undertakers is run as a subsidiary to the parent company, Sure Future, a health insurance company.

"It's a genuine firm, offices all over the country, and they offer an 'all-in-one' package that takes care of your burial arrangements in the event of death."

"Let me guess, the work is farmed out to Lloyd & Bryson."

"Sometimes. By running both as legitimate concerns, they pass enough genuine cases through the books to not raise any red flags on the odd occasion a crime is committed. Through his client list, Snowdon has an effective database of thousands of potential donors, with full medical history."

Thackeray leaned forward, enthused by the neatness of it all.

"So," he said, glad to be on his subject, "all he would have to do is match any organ request with the database and then make arrangements to harvest what he needed?"

Steve nodded.

"Precisely. Easy enough to carry out: dose the client with something – nothing life-threatening, of course, but enough for them to contact their doctor – via, as the policy dictates, Sure Future's emergency line. The doctor, no doubt in this instance Snowdon himself, who's been hanging around waiting for the call, will then make all the right sounds of it being too late while slipping the client a tetrodotoxin dose and then consoling the poor family members when they appear to pass away."

"So Sure Future then takes care of all the legal detail and Lloyd & Bryson organises the funeral," Thackeray concluded.

"Job's done," Steve said. "For a final theatrical twist they switch coffins at the funeral so that all concerned are convinced they've seen their loved ones buried or burned while, in actual fact, they've been whisked away by Lloyd and the boys."

"And Snowdon's left with a perfectly healthy human

body that legally no longer exists – to do with as he wishes," I added.

"Cunning little sod," said Thackeray.

"Sick wee fuck, more like," said Douggie.

"What's 'subsidiary' mean?" said Dave.

Luckily Mandy walked over to the table at that point to see if we wanted drinks, and the rest of us took advantage of Carl and Dave becoming completely distracted by the fact that she possessed breasts to move the conversation forward.

"As fascinating as all this is, it doesn't help Max," I said.

"True enough," Douggie replied. "We have to assume that their main base of operations is beneath the undertakers. We know there's a lift in your lad's office; it has to go somewhere."

Steve was tapping away on his laptop. "If I can access the council records there may be a map of the building," he said.

"Aye," Douggie replied, "because they're bound to have filed building regs for installing their super-villain's lift shaft."

"All right, maybe that's no use… What about a history of the building though?"

"I fail to see how that would help," I admitted.

He clapped his hands and turned the laptop towards us. "By telling us that it used to be a vintners. The site's bound to have extensive wine cellars."

"I wonder if it's for sale?" I joked, in that charming way I have of laughing in the face of danger.

"Well," said Thackeray, "that confirms there's space for them to operate there, but it hardly proves they're doing so."

"If you owned such a useful space, why would you not

use it?" I asked. "Besides, we have nothing else to go on. We have to start there and hope we get lucky."

"We have another problem," said Steve. "If the lift's the only access point then how are we going to get down there without someone noticing?"

"It can't be," I insisted, "surely there must be better access than that? What about deliveries? Supplies?"

"We can take a look," Douggie said. "You'd have thought there'd be vehicle access somewhere. Only way to find out is to have a good wee check over the place."

"Fine. What else do we know about Snowdon? Do we have an address for his surgery? Can we find out where he lives? We need to gain some kind of advantage over him."

At which point, Max's mobile began to ring, and with it came the first tingling of a truly lunatic idea.

▌▌▌ 15

SNOWDON
1.

I am a man who plans. Always have been. Planning is the route to getting what you want out of life. That and a healthy disregard for other people. The minute you realise that other people are nothing more than resources, building blocks in those plans, you will be a far happier and more successful individual.

It is obvious, therefore, how extremely irritating I found my current position. To have the work of some years – and extremely profitable work at that – threatened by the casual intervention of persons unknown was enough to make my fingers itch to reach for a violently wielded scalpel.

The metaphor is apt. I had to cut them out from the healthy, thriving body of my organisation like the potentially fatal, tumescent foreign body they were. But before a surgeon can even begin to cut he must isolate the problem. He must locate the tumour, account for its size and how far it may have spread, and work his operation accordingly.

That Mr Jackson and his friend Mr Harris were agents of the law was unthinkable. If they had any kind of legal footing we would already be feeling the heavy hands of the authorities on our shoulders. No. They were free agents. Why such people would choose to involve themselves in our business was a quandary. I struggle to believe they could be acting out of idle curiosity; one simply doesn't stick one's nose into a business that will likely see it hacked off with prejudice in order to quell boredom. Perhaps they were related to one of our previous clients (by which I mean the human resources that have been known to pass across my table, not the wealthy and largely anonymous donors who paid well to receive the goods)? That I could understand. While I had done my best to organise my business in as simple, yet watertight, a manner as possible, no plan can ever said to be perfect. Plans involve people and people are changeable and unreliable. They respond in ways that might run contrary to even the most careful predictions.

I confess I had concerns over our most recent acquisition. Mrs Campbell had been an opportunity dangled and then snatched. She had come to my attention through a genuine illness – albeit simply a matter of hormonal imbalance rather than the life-threatening condition it was later claimed to be. That she was an ideal candidate for a customer I had been struggling to fulfil was pure chance. The most joyful good fortune. Still, I had been aware that I was chancing my arm by using her, working so quickly, harvesting her mere weeks after she had been enrolled on my books. But if it was her absence that had triggered these enquirers then wouldn't the husband have been visible in their attack? I had taken the opportunity of treating him to a "follow-up" call and he showed no sign of suspicion, purely the usual, pathetic blubber of mourning.

I did not think they were friends of Mrs Campbell.
Perhaps someone else?

Even this didn't make sense. If they had been related to
one of the cattle, one would expect to receive more direct
enquiries. Quite simply: they would not have to break in
at night and sneak around my office. At least, not at first.
To begin with you would expect cautious phone calls,
thinly veiled accusations, enquiries through legitimate
channels. Once they had been successfully repelled then
perhaps more *outré* methods could be expected from those
tenacious enough to partake of them. But there had been
no such enquiries.

I had, of course, looked into their names. Neither
produced a viable trail of enquiry. I had no doubt they
were aliases.

Which made me think that what we were dealing with
was something altogether more worrying. Could they,
in fact, be part of a rival organisation? If so then things
were more serious, though the fact that their investigations
seemed so inept made me wonder even about that. Would
an organised gang really use their home address when
contacting us? That seemed so obviously stupid. I take
the opportunity of moving my office address once every
six months. That aside, it is little more than a shop-
front for my legitimate façade, a small office hired in a
building that offers a communal receptionist. Were it to be
investigated or searched, nothing would betray me. This is
simple common sense. And yet these people had used Mr
Jackson's home? Idiotic and slightly unbelievable.

And then the real shock: there was something about
them that was not altogether natural.

I had been willing to accept that I had somehow been mistaken in my cursory examination of Mr Jackson (pseudonym or not, we may as well continue to use the name). I am a medical man and I do not subscribe to the notion that dead men can fight back. Indeed, one might say that my organisation is built on the fact.

And yet the evidence of Mr Ackroyd was intriguing to say the least.

"He just wouldn't die!" he insisted, referring to the unconventionally dressed gentlemen he came into contact with at Mr Jackson's home. "I went at him over and over again, but the thing just kept ticking."

Mr Ackroyd is not a medical man. That said, he is not altogether an idiot, and if there is one subject he can claim to be an expert on it is that of violence. He is a man who knows how to kill. The fact that he seemed unable to do so makes me wonder about the nature of what we're dealing with. It makes me wonder a great deal.

None of these mysteries could be answered without further investigation. So I began to plan.

Then I made my phone call.

I naturally felt disinclined to allow myself to be exposed. And yet, I could trust nobody else to do the job. Frankly, our organisation is small and that night we were spreading ourselves thin as we worked to cover our tracks and ensure our future. The simple, distasteful fact of the matter was that we were going to have to retire for a while. Destroy evidence, tie up loose ends, vanish to the four winds and then regroup when we knew it was safe. A careful planner knows when retreat is the best option.

I arranged to meet Mr Harris in a suitably discreet

storage area a stone's throw from King's Cross. It felt perfectly clandestine for such a meeting. The ideal place to abandon bodies, should that be the way the night would unfold.

That done, I called Lloyd and Ackroyd to explain their duties.

2.

I waited for Mr Harris in the shadows of an empty storage shed, my mood growing more sour by the moment. I dearly hoped that this bump in the clear road of our industry was one that could be quickly smoothed over. The idea of having to abandon everything was wholly disgusting. The need to carefully eradicate any trail we may have left was no bad thing. A spring clean, in fact, a wiping clear of the slate. But if we had to abandon our premises entirely then that represented a financial loss and an irritation that fair made me boil with anger.

"Snowdon, I presume?"

I looked up to see a man walking towards me from where the rail tracks cut along this open space some hundred or so yards away.

He was not altogether what I had imagined. Lloyd's description had been irritatingly vague, as had that of the unreliable sot Father Gibbons, but the image of Mr Harris painted in my head was slightly at odds with the man facing me. Yes, he was a man in his late fifties but he had a steel, an authority, that Lloyd's description had failed to capture. This wasn't altogether surprising. The man I had spoken to on the phone was clearly not the slightly camp caricature that had been described to me. That mask was shed. Here was the real man, someone who might even present a tangible threat. But not for long.

"Mr Harris."

"I take it that's Max?" He pointed to the bound figure at my side, his mouth curling into a snarl as he took in the tightly cinched hood and the signs of abuse that had been heaped upon my prisoner. "I didn't think you'd bring him with you."

"He will prove useful. You came alone, as asked?" I replied.

He nodded. "So what happens now?"

"Well," I replied, "that is rather the thing, isn't it? I have to decide what manner of threat you present to my organisation. That done, I will be in an informed position as to know how to proceed. Of course, my easiest – and preferred – option is to simply kill you both. That would be ideal."

"But who's to say if there are more of us?"

"Precisely. This is the very hub of my problem. As you can imagine, while we are here my colleagues are doing their very best to ensure that all trace of our organisation is eradicated. My job is to ascertain whether that will be enough."

"And how do you plan on doing that?"

"Oh, simply by asking a few choice questions."

I have to admit I was beginning to enjoy this. The loss of control that had been so painful to me was slowly ebbing away.

"While you may have come alone," I said, "I, naturally,

did not. Currently one of my staff is sat a small distance away with a long-range rifle pointing straight at your head. If you take one more step towards me he will shoot. I am not a man who takes risks. I suggest that if you ignored my instructions and came in company anyway, you take this moment to explain to them the situation so that they're not so foolish as to threaten your continued existence."

"That won't be necessary."

"Which of course could mean one of two things. Either that you and Mr Jackson were acting alone or – and here we enter the realm of scientific fantasy – Mr Ackroyd is quite right in that you possess a state of being that would make you difficult to kill."

"Don't you know?"

Here he was treading close to an awkward subject. One that I could only avoid by keeping the conversational ball in my court.

"The only way to discover the truth in either case is to experiment," I said. "Mr Ackroyd found your colleague hard to kill, yes. That is not to say he was unable to cause him pain."

I held up the small revolver I had in my hand, ensured he had taken it in, then pointed the barrel towards the arm of the figure at my side and pulled the trigger.

"Max!" he shouted, fighting against a natural urge to move forward.

The bullet only wounded, naturally. The muffled screams more than proved that.

"So now we move on to a simple question-and-answer session," I explained. "How many of you are there involved in this?"

Harris thought about this for a moment. "More than I could easily count."

I was dissatisfied with this answer and proved as much by expending another bullet, this time into the shoulder.

"I trust you won't find the muffled quality of Mr Jackson's screams any less agonising?" I asked. "I felt it best to plan ahead in that regard. We could hardly continue our conversation for long if he screamed at full volume. As remote as this place seems you are never far away from life in London."

As if to prove my point, a train passed by on those distant tracks, full, no doubt, of late-night souls blissfully unaware of the dark business that sometimes consumes the working lives of others.

"I have done my best to ensure he will not choke," I continued, "though it's hard to guarantee it. I would sincerely recommend you stick to truthful responses. I have plenty of spare bullets in my pocket but I cannot swear to how many Mr Jackson can bear to have inside him."

"There are a few of us," he insisted, "mainly Max and I, but we have a little help. Eight of us in all."

"Eight?" That wasn't so bad. Certainly not the sort of numbers one would expect if dealing with a rival gang. "And what made you aware of our operation in the first place?"

"We saw your men carrying the body of Natalie Campbell. They dropped the coffin and I noticed she was still breathing."

"A condition that didn't trouble her for long. So it was pure coincidence?"

"We were… intrigued… decided to look into it." His sense of authority was crumbling, much to my pleasure, the truth being forced out of him. "So we broke into the undertakers and had a sniff around. In hindsight that was obviously something of a mistake."

"Certainly it was," I agreed. "Because it brought you here. And you know that you cannot hope to walk away from this, don't you?"

He shrugged. "The night will tell."

"I admire your optimism, naturally, but if you had any clear evidence you would have acted on it already. Eight awkward souls, less, of course, once this conversation is concluded, I can deal with." I raised my gun towards him. Deciding that the time had come to simply cut my losses. A period of retirement was irritating but manageable. What has been set up before can certainly be set up again.

Which is when a mobile phone began ringing in his pocket. This irritated me beyond words, having decided on my course of action.

"Would you mind?" he asked. "I really should take this." He reached into his jacket and pulled out the phone, answering it.

"Hello, Tony? Really? No, that's perfect. Absolutely." He looked at me and the damned man was smiling. Then a slight air of embarrassment crossed his face and he turned away slightly. "No," he continued, "I appreciate that, Tony, of course you can have time off in lieu. No. I appreciate that. Yes. Your art is important to you. Look… Yes. Tony, can we talk about this another time?" He hung up, sighed and rolled his eyes at me. "Staff," he said, "always a nightmare."

He dropped the phone in his pocket.

"A fact you'll empathise with, I'm sure," he continued, "when I mention that the useful gunman you mentioned earlier," he gestured vaguely in the air, "you know, the one with a rifle pointed at my head, is now sleeping the sleep of the unjust thanks to the fact that my man has finally found him."

"I don't believe you!" I insisted, unable to accept that the tables could have been turned so painlessly.

"Fair enough," he replied. "Now, Tony!" he shouted, and a rifle shot rang out, the dirt near my feet erupting as the bullet found its mark.

Instinctively I threw my gun to the floor, which was idiotic and childish, but I am not accustomed to being shot at.

"So," Harris said, "let's talk about your surrender, shall we?"

Naturally, I wasn't going to make it as easy for him as that.

"I think not. I am not so stupid as to put all my eggs in one basket. I shall be leaving you now and you will do nothing to stop me."

He raised an eyebrow. "Really?"

"Really. Because unless I make a telephone call in…" I checked my watch, "just over two minutes, your friend will be dead."

I tugged the hood off the bound man to reveal the idiot Gibbons, another loose end it had occurred to me to tie off. "This isn't Max Jackson."

"What a coincidence," he replied with a smile, "I'm not Tom Harris either."

‖‖‖ 16

TOM

1.

"He's never met me," I said as the phone buzzed on the table top. "That might be the only advantage we have."

"I fail to see how it helps us," said Jeffery, staring at the phone, only too aware of the possible consequences of our not answering it.

"He wants to draw us out," I said, thinking at a speed far beyond my comfort level. The phone rang again. How many before it cut to answer machine? "Keep us busy while he covers his tracks."

"But surely you met the undertakers that came to Max's house?" said Steve.

"Lloyd and Ackroyd," I said, "yes. That's a risk."

The phone rang again.

"You need to be quick, laddie," warned Douggie.

I grabbed the phone and threw it to Len. "You pretend to be me. Agree to whatever he says. He'll want to meet. That's fine. But you can be my stand-in."

"I'm used to that," Len admitted, quickly answering the call. "Harris," he said. "King's Cross, right… alone… I can be there in half an hour." He hung up.

"The meeting's arranged," he said, "so why don't you leave that to me while you get on with finding Max?"

"It's a plan!" I agreed. I looked to Jeffery. "You'd better follow us. He may need you if they've hurt him."

God help you, Max, I thought. We're coming.

2.

Douggie, Steve, Carl, Dave and I squeezed into Douggie's SUV and made our way towards Kentish Town and the undertakers. Jeffery followed on behind in his car.

My life has been filled with the sort of incidents that would blanche my younger self if he could only know what lay ahead. In all honesty, I've always been rather proud of the fact (the idea of a predictable existence is terrifying to me). Life is for riding, not enduring. There are those who would question some of the decisions I've made; certainly my hands are not clean. But I've never hurt someone who didn't deserve it and I've never broken a law worth preserving. That may be faint justification but it's all you're going to get. I've always done whatever seemed the right thing at the time. No doubt you would have seen things differently but, old loves, you weren't there, so Uncle Tom doesn't care to hear your opinion.

The one constant in life is the good friends. The ones who will not only help you pick up the pieces but will help you make the mess in the first place. While lovers and wives have come and gone, there are a number of people I can count on, point to and announce without a word of a lie: "Those people? They made life a whole lot better."

Of course, since my mid-life crisis (as I prefer to think of my unfortunate demise) I have had to leave the old friends behind and gather anew. I think I've done well. Len, Jeffery, Douggie and Max. The dry old wit, the wise medic, the clenched fist and the fool. All the food groups are represented. And heaven help anyone who lays a finger on them.

When we arrived at the undertakers, Douggie continued along the street a couple of hundred yards before pulling over. Jeffery parked across the street.

"No sense in advertising our presence," Douggie said as we all gathered around his SUV. "We should split up, take a quick recce and meet back here."

"What's a recky?" Carl asked.

"It means sitting in the back and keeping your gob shut, lad."

Both Carl and Dave nodded at that and did as he suggested.

"This is subtle business," said Douggie, "and not for adorable idiots."

"Agreed," I said. "How about you and Steve check out the front while Jeffery and I look at the back?"

"Aye, all right. Mind now, keep your head down. No disrespect but if I was looking to man a covert mission I wouldn't be looking to you two."

"We will be the very epitome of discretion," I assured him, "Last of the Summer Ninjas."

He smiled and shook his head. "Back here in five minutes."

We crossed the road and walked past the undertakers before crossing back over. It was the centre shop in a parade of four. The other three were a florist (what's the odds they took a look two doors down and rubbed their hands with glee?), a computer repair shop and a twee-looking spot that offered baby clothes from behind a frontage of ladybird spots and primary colours. A road carved through the street at that point and it was down that we headed, in the hope that we would find rear access. Things looked positive when we were able to take an almost immediate left. A high, orange-brick wall kept us from sneaking a peek but we soon came to a wooden gate in heavy, flaking blue paint. No doubt this was the access for the hearse. And hopefully for us.

"We need to get over there and take a look," I said. "Just to see what we're dealing with."

"If that's your way of asking for a leg up," said Jeffery, "then might I suggest we try the easy way first?" He pushed the gate. It wasn't locked.

We crept inside, finding ourselves in a yard big enough for about three cars, though it only needed to accommodate the one – the portentous black hearse I had loaded Max into so recently. My, but time flies when Jackson and Harris are on the slippery slope to hell.

At the rear of the building was a pair of heavy-looking double doors with a number pad to the side of it for entering the access key. It now began to make sense as to why the gate had been left unlocked: I'm not sure we could have opened them had we driven the damned hearse right at them. To make matters worse, the doors were visibly wired to a large alarm.

"Well," I whispered "on the one hand it's clearly impregnable, on the other: the fact that they have so much security suggests we're on the right track."

There were no windows, no other point of entry. It

seemed impossible, and I could only hope that Douggie would disagree.

We moved back to the front of the building, noting that the upper floors either side appeared to be occupied, so whatever we planned on doing we'd likely have an audience unless we kept extremely quiet.

Oh, Max, I don't mind admitting that I thought I might have to abandon you then.

Douggie and Steve were waiting by the SUV.

"Well," I said, "I hope you've got some good news because things are looking somewhat impossible from our end." I told them what we'd seen and Douggie nodded with a big grin.

"Bless you, lad," he said, "but did you expect we were going to get here and find a wooden gate left on the latch? This was always going to be a wee bit tricky. We've found the vehicle entrance to the cellar, but judging by the high-grade cabling leading through the wall we can assume it's also covered by the alarm. The front of the shop too. The front window was boarded up recently…"

"Very recently," I said, explaining to him how Max had escaped through it.

"He just loves being locked up in this place," said Douggie.

"His home from home," I agreed. "So what can we do?"

"Well, our best bet would obviously be to crack the alarm system. The less fuss we make when getting in, the greater advantage we'll have."

"And you can do that, can you?" Jeffery asked. "Crack the alarm?"

"Nope," Douggie admitted, "I haven't got a clue about anything made after ninety-six."

I chose not to ask.

"So," he continued, "let's think in the other direction. We can't disable the alarm, but there is one sure-fire time when an alarm cannot go off."

"Really?"

"Aye, when it's already ringing."

Douggie could be as theatrical as me at times. He stood there and smiled at his own as-yet un-clarified genius.

"Your point, you drama queen?" I asked.

With one final dramatic pause he explained it to us.

3.

"This is Jerome and Redz," announced Douggie.

The two lads were buried in the custom uniform of hoodies and baseball caps, as if terrified to show the night their skin. The faces that poked out from the narrow apertures, one black and one white, showed that they were no more than twelve years old. Frantic rhythms were leaking from somewhere within the folds of cotton; I believe it was the current *beat du jour* they call dubstep. (And yes, I do know what it is – just because I'm old doesn't mean my ears have stopped working... Music is my life... well, death... and I make a point of knowing my stuff. Though, for anyone taking notes, dubstep seems to be little more than security alarms and drum machines and should go away now.)

"Good evening, lads," I said, choosing to ignore the look of open mockery they gave me. "How would you like to earn twenty quid?"

They stared at me and I wondered if their headphones were jammed in too tight.

"Each?" asked Redz.

"Yes," I replied.

That woke them up.

"What do we have to do?" asked Jerome.

"Find two big bricks," I said, "then lose them again." I turned and pointed at the undertakers. "Through their window."

"What's the matter?" Jerome asked. "They bury a friend of yours?"

That might soon be true, though I was more struck by the impression he clearly had of what an undertaker did, roaming the country snatching people up and interring them whether they wanted it or not.

"Something like that. They just need a slap, and I'd like your help in giving them one."

Redz smiled at that. I took two twenties out of my wallet and handed them over.

"I'll even pay you up-front." They snatched the money out of my hands. "But do the job right or I'll send Douggie here to break your legs."

Douggie obliged by looming over the diminutive pair.

"No need," said Jerome, "we're professionals."

And with that they shuffled off to look for something to throw.

"Wait a minute," I said, "this is important: don't do it right away. Do it in…" I looked to Douggie. "… five minutes?"

He nodded.

"Didn't say we had to hang around all night," Jerome complained.

"We've got shit to do," agreed Redz.

"Five minutes," I repeated, "for twenty quid. You've got a good deal and you know it."

"And if you're early," said Douggie, "I will hunt you down and chew your fucking ears off."

They did their best to look casual but sauntered off in dutiful silence.

"Think they'll be all right?" I asked.

"They'll be fine," said Douggie, only too confident of the power of his intimidation.

He opened the boot of his SUV and brought out a large black canvas bag. It clearly weighed a great deal as even he strained to hoist it on to his shoulder.

"I suggest you wait in your car," he said to Jeffery. "We need someone on the outside in case this turns nasty, and there's nay point in wasting a good brain like yours by having it shot out all over the floor."

Jeffery gave a polite smile and looked to me. I nodded.

"Fine," he said. "If you silly fools don't come back out within five minutes I'll have the place swarming with uniforms."

"Good lad," said Douggie, patting him on the arm.

I took a moment to call Len.

"How's it going being me?" I asked.

"No different to usual," he replied. "Meeting's in five minutes. I planned on strolling over and boring him to death about Benny Goodman."

"Very funny. Just be careful."

"Of course I will. He's not going to do anything stupid for now. He needs to know who he's dealing with. Besides, with Tony's help I should get the upper hand soon enough."

"Such confidence."

"Comes from a lifetime of being the cleverest man in the room."

I left him to it and nodded to Douggie. "All is fine so far."

"There's time enough for the night to go tits up," he replied. "Come on, boys," he said to Carl and Dave. The two of them had been sat as if frozen, determined not to set a foot wrong. Carefully stored aggro, which we were now unpacking and preparing to set loose. As they climbed out, the SUV rose at least six inches. It must have been terribly relieved.

"Last one there's a nancy," Douggie said, and strolled away from the undertakers, cutting down the next road.

The rest of us followed and, catching our reflection in a shop window across the road, I was once again struck by the discrepancy among us. Douggie, Carl and Dave looked like they were taking part in a breakout from a butcher's locker. Giants among men, each wrapped up in tight black fabric that constantly surprised onlookers by its ability to stay un-torn with every flex of bicep or twitch of calf.

Then there was Steve, slight and bookish – should a man in glasses ever be involved in this sort of business? I had no doubt he could handle himself – without wishing to be crude, if he could survive a night of passion with Douggie he must be made of resilience and fortitude – but he seemed the sort of reserved gentleman that would tut if asked to stay out past half eleven. A caricature of prim respectability.

Finally, the old man bringing up the rear.

A few feet along the side road there was a single-lane ramp that descended below the buildings. Douggie held up a hand to stop us climbing down it.

"There's a camera," he explained, pointing towards the metal shutter that blocked access once you reached the end of the slope. "Limited focus, just there to check on who's coming in. But it means we have to wait before we can get close."

He looked around, checking to see how exposed we were. He waved us forward a couple of feet so we were just on the slope and covered by the walls either side. He put the bag on the floor and unzipped it.

"Right then, take your pick."

The thing was filled with guns.

Dave was like a kid at Christmas, grabbing one each for him and Carl.

"Where the bloody hell did all these come from?" I asked, my attempts to appear nonchalant in the face of a sack full of heavy artillery blown a touch by my red face and panicked voice.

"Ah, well, you know – here and there. I like to be prepared for unseen eventualities, y'know?"

"Full-scale war, that sort of thing?"

"Stop your moaning and take one, will ye? You might be able to intimidate awkward customers with that dry wit of yours, but you should never bring a pithy remark to a gunfight."

He had a point. Despite my somewhat chequered past I can at least say that I have never carried or fired a gun. Frankly, given how most practical tasks I attempt end up causing hospital visits and unscheduled demolition, I've never been tempted to lay a finger on one. Likely I'd only end up shooting myself. However, principles in a gunfight get you precisely nowhere if they aren't shared, and who knew what the night held in store? We all needed to watch each other's backs. Enough… we hadn't time for deliberation. I squatted down and picked out an automatic handgun.

"I presume I've seen enough movies to operate this?" I asked.

Douggie took it off me, checked the clip, re-inserted it and then pointed at the safety catch.

"When you want to shoot something, take that off and point the loud end at bastards."

I nodded. "That seems within my abilities."

"Well, let's hope we don't need to find out. If we look nasty and well armed enough, they should roll over. However much Snowdon's paying his thugs, I bet it's not enough to take a bullet."

"So that's the plan?" I asked. "Storm in there looking hostile and hope that everyone just backs down?"

"No point in complicating things," Douggie replied. "Two minutes after the alarm goes off we run at that gate, take out the camera, force the lock and run in. Hopefully the majority of them will be distracted by the damage at the front so we'll keep an element of surprise."

"Hopefully."

"This was always going to be difficult," said Douggie, addressing all of us. "We're taking our lives in our hands, and you need to know that there's a perfectly good chance we won't be walking back out. Now, for a nutter like me that's okay. I'm stupid enough to like a wee bit of danger and risk, and this isn't the first time I've made that sort of decision. Obviously, there's a fair chance it'll be the last. If so, to hell with it, it was still the right thing to do. For the rest of you… you have to decide.

"When we run in there, we do it with confidence, we do it with strength. This kind of thing is all about attitude. Half the time a fight is won before you throw the first punch. It's about presenting yourself as invulnerable, as something the other man can't hope to beat. We scare them. We intimidate them. We dominate them." He looked at me and his face was as gentle as I've ever seen it; Douggie only achieved serenity when faced with the worst.

"If you can't do that," he continued, "then nobody will think the worse of you. It's not weakness. It's not cowardice. It's plain common sense. But you should stay up here, watch our backs and be ready to call the police should things go sideways."

He looked around. "This is off the clock, this isn't overtime, this is private business. Whoever walks in there does it of their own free will."

None of us moved. We were committed.

Douggie nodded in approval. "One last thing, the minute someone fires a gun our time will draw short. Londoners let most things go, but even they draw the line at gunfire. There'll be an armed-response team on the way within minutes. So only pull the trigger if you have to."

There was the distant noise of breaking glass, and the night was filled with the sound of the alarm.

4.

Douggie checked his watch, counting out the two minutes he had decided would offer the optimum time for the distraction at the front to work.

We didn't get it.

The shuttered gate began to open.

"Shit," said Douggie. "Plan B."

The lower half of a Transit van was slowly being revealed.

"And that would be?" I asked.

"Improvise," he said and ran towards the van, his gun raised at the windscreen. "The rest of you get inside and remember, don't fire unless you have to."

Douggie, the mad fool, threw himself at the van, refusing to let the small matter of it being a large vehicle and him an eminently squashable Scotsman dampen his ardour.

The driver was quick. As soon as the shutter lifted high enough for him to see us, he pressed hard on the accelerator. He made one mistake: he had the window open, and as we ran either side of the vehicle towards the underground area it had vacated, I heard the sound of Douggie's fist connecting with the driver's head. I don't know many folk strong enough to endure that kind of treatment, but we were moving too fast for me to stop and check.

I had the most absurd sensation of being a boy in the schoolyard again, channelling John Wayne while in flannel shorts, a bent stick as a rifle, on the lookout for "injuns". I know it wasn't a childish matter, far from it; we were in deadly earnest, but fired up by Douggie's speech I was trying to get into the right frame of mind to pull it off. Has there ever been a better frame of mind for heroic violence than the Duke? It was all I could do not to shout "Fill your hand, you son of a bitch!" as I entered the basement area, the sound of running feet all around me.

The alarm ceased. Whether that was a good thing or not I couldn't tell.

We were in a small loading area, and Steve was the first to make it to a door at the end.

"We might still have the element of surprise," he whispered as we caught up with him. "So far the only person who knows we're here is the driver."

"And he won't be telling a soul," said Douggie, joining us. "He's asleep, dreaming about the days when he still had teeth."

"The van?" I asked.

"No sign of Max," he replied. "I was hoping as much too. The back was empty."

"Then we still have to hope he's on the other side of that door," I said, reaching for the handle.

"Cool your boots, laddie," he said, "let's be practical. We can only fit through single file and we don't want them picking us off one by one. Let's go through in stages." He looked to Carl and Dave. "You two come with me first, straight through the door, drop low moving to either side."

They looked confused so he helped them along a little.

"Carl, you go through keeping down, then move to the right and drop to the floor, keeping your gun up and your eyes open. Dave, you do the same thing but move to the left. All right?"

"No problem, Douggie," said Dave.

"Why do we get to go first?" asked Carl. "Is it because we're good at this sort of thing?"

"Aye, lad," Douggie replied, "and because someone would have to have an anti-tank missile to do any real damage to the pair of you daft buggers."

They laughed at that, God help them.

"You two hang back," he said to me and Steve, "then follow if it's clear."

He opened the door, waved the boys in and took the central path. We heard the sound of several kilos of bouncer hitting the ground then a good deal of shouting. Then there was a gunshot. Then there was silence.

5.

A pause. A terrible one, filled with confusion and indecision. Steve moved to push past me but I held out my hand. "If something's gone wrong we might be more help to them out here…"

Then a voice called out: "Drop your guns and step inside, single file, hands over your heads." We looked to one another. "Both of you," the voice continued. "Now. Or we start shooting your friends."

And with that, John Wayne left the building. I put my gun on the floor and stepped through the door, leading, as I should have done from the very start.

Inside was an open-plan room. One side was clearly fitted out for medical purposes with white tile and bright neon, a heavy plastic curtain drawn back that could presumably seal it off during operations. The other side was more of a control centre, a couple of large desks, computers and, most importantly, a bank of monitor screens showing feeds from various security cameras around the building.

"They saw us coming, lad," said Douggie, and I turned to look at him, on his knees in front of four armed men. Carl was kneeling next to him while Dave – poor "unstoppable" Dave – was lying on his back in a spreading pool of blood. "I'm a bloody idiot," Douggie continued, "sorry to let you down."

Looking to the security monitors, I saw the parking area on the other side of the door we'd just entered. These men had watched us run in and been only too prepared to deal with us the moment we walked through the door.

"They shot Dave," said Carl. I think he was crying.

"I know, Carl, mate, I know," I replied, not knowing what else to say.

"We'll shoot the rest of you in a minute too," one of the men said. I recognised the bastard: Ackroyd, Lloyd's "colleague" who'd collected the coffin. Out of his funereal costume he was just an oily little thug, leather jacket and hair gel, Jack the bloody Lad with a gun in his hand. I looked at the others and started to place their faces too, even the one who had dropped the keys outside the church, the one that had started this whole damn thing off.

I also noticed who was missing. There was no Max.

The whole reason we'd come here in the first place.

"On your knees," said Ackroyd.

We had little choice.

"Where's Max?" I asked.

"Who? Oh, you mean the other fella? Not here, mate, obviously. Think about it, why would we bring him here? We find out someone's on to the place, the last thing we're going to do is stick around, is it? Well, not all of us anyway." He picked casually at the corner of his mouth. "A few of us would hang about, just to see who turns up." He levelled the gun directly at me. "And deal with them accordingly."

Oh no, I thought, not again.

Ackroyd smiled. It was the sort of smile that made it clear we were unlikely to share the joke.

"Tell me," he said, just as soon as he'd stopped finding the situation so damned amusing. "I'm assuming that some of you share the same, rather unusual ability as that wanker in the flat I had such fun with." He nodded, almost amiably. "Quite threw me that did, take the bastard apart piece by piece and he's still clocking at the end of it."

"Prick," Douggie muttered under his breath.

"Oh you must do!" Ackroyd shouted, kicking Douggie in the gut. "You'd think twice before talking to me like that if you didn't."

He sighed and smoothed a strand of gelled hair back into place.

Douggie, for all his machismo, kept his mouth shut. It was obvious to all of us that Ackroyd was not someone to gamble with. He was getting too much pleasure out of this game; goading him wasn't worthwhile.

"So," he continued, "how shall we play this? I need to know who's who; to sort the normal from the freak."

We didn't move.

"How about a show of hands? That would be civilised, because I can be civilised."

He swung the barrel of his gun towards Douggie's temple, and I felt Steve tense up next to me.

"Or I can just pop a bullet in each of you and see who walks."

Douggie kept his face utterly still. He wasn't going to give the game away, not on any level.

"I'd rather not go that route if I don't have to," Ackroyd was saying. "I'm no scientist – for all I know I may damage the goods. But, and let me make this perfectly clear…" His finger tensed on the trigger. "I will do whatever I have to, to get the job done."

What happened next was fast. Time appearing to shift…

Dave screams and sits up.

Ackroyd jumps back, changing his aim.

Steve drops to the ground, reaches behind him and pulls two more handguns from the belt of his jeans. One is thrown to Douggie (who catches it without breaking the beat), the other is turned on Ackroyd.

Two gunshots. Ackroyd is falling, blood and grey matter fanning behind him. Dave's chest blossoms a second time.

Douggie shoots twice, both finding the mark before the mark knows what's happening – there's blood on the tiles even as the gunshot echo fades.

Steve fires again, low this time – the knee of the last man splintering as he falls.

Dave shouts: "He shot me again!"

Then falls back to the floor.

It was the best jazz I'd ever heard, wild, frenetic and life-changing.

Time went back to normal.

I ran over to Dave and started to check for vital signs. It didn't look good.

Douggie and Steve went straight for the one they'd left alive, Steve skidding the man's dropped gun across the tiles with his foot.

"He's dead," I said, putting my hand on Dave's shoulder.

Carl really began to cry now and, God, but there was something truly pitiful about that sound coming from such a giant of a man. Massive, child-like sobs.

Dave twitched again.

"Dear God," I whispered, shock making me invoke a name I had had little truck with for years. What was happening was utterly impossible. For once I was lost for words.

Dave opened his eyes and tried to speak. All that came out was a mournful wail.

"He's alive!" Carl shouted, grabbing his brother's arm. I stared at them, the ghost of a memory bubbling up from inside me. This wasn't possible. It just wasn't...

As I had said to Max all those years ago, a constant in our condition is that it takes time to reanimate. Ignoring the odds against the fact that Dave, one of our select number, might have the ability, he should never have been able to exercise it so quickly. It flew in the face of everything we knew.

But he had been dead and now he was moving. That was inarguable. It was also terrifying.

You might think I would be glad. Better this than that he was dead for good, but you have to understand, we know so little about what has happened to us. The idea that one of the inarguable rules was breaking right in front of me chilled me more than I can express.

"Where are they?" Douggie was shouting, pointing his gun at the man on the floor.

The man was shaking his head, tears in his eyes. He thought he was in pain – he wasn't, not really. Douggie pressed his boot down on the man's shattered knee and the scream bounced off the walls as if it would never stop.

Now he was in pain.

"For God's sake, stop!" the man shouted.

"When you let me," Douggie replied. "We have a matter of minutes before this place fills with police. We need answers now."

Then a phone started ringing and we all fell quiet.

"It's in his pocket," Steve said, dashing over to Ackroyd's body. Turning his face away from the bloody mess on the floor, he ferreted in the corpse's jacket for the phone. He pulled it out and checked the number. "Says it's Lloyd." He handed it to Douggie.

"Save your life," Douggie said to the man on the floor. "Tell them everything's fine and you'll call them back when it's done."

"I… I can't."

"Oh yes you can, because you want to live. Now do it." Douggie pressed the receive button and held it to the man's head, gun pressed square against his temple.

"H-hello?" There was a pause as the person on the other end spoke.

The man looked confused and not a little bit frightened. Then he nodded towards me. "It's for you."

I placed the phone to my ear and cautiously spoke. "Yes?"

||||17

LEN
1.

"What a coincidence," I said, "I'm not Tom Harris either."

I was, of course, thoroughly pleased to see the confusion that caused. I'm sure Snowdon had his worthy qualities. He was a fully trained surgeon so no doubt there had been a time in his life when he had made the bosom of a mother swell with pride. Intellectual achievements aside, he was a limp prick of the highest order and my palms itched to slap him pink.

"Of course," I added, "don't let that stop you making the phone call. It is, after all, the only thing currently keeping you alive."

He pulled his phone out of his pocket. "I intend it to stay that way." He held the phone aloft. "I'm going to walk away, and once I get clear I will make the phone call that allows your friend to live. For now. I shall decide what to do with him in the long term once I have vanished into secure obscurity. The minute I feel one of you close to me I will split him open and dance in the cavity, be warned."

How I longed to punch him in the throat.

I watched as he continued to move towards the train tracks, keeping one eye on us and the other on where he was going. As far as I could tell, we had one hope of turning things back in our favour, and that was if Tom had already found Max and they were both safe.

I could still follow him as he crossed the tracks and made along them, heading back towards the station. The moon was high and my eyesight is trained to that of a hawk's from supervising a club full of people and being ready for trouble.

He raised the phone to his ear and I watched carefully. Boom! He stopped dead in his tracks. That was not the call he was expecting and that was enough for me.

"Come on, Tony!" I shouted, "get after him!"

We ran towards Snowdon who, on hearing me shout, had given up his careful walk for a panicked sprint.

I knew where he had to be heading, if he could get as far as the station he would have a solid advantage. Railway stations are rarely empty. Late-night departures to airports, sleeper trains, the interminable, drunken slog back to the commuter belt. Once we were somewhere more public our options would be severely limited.

Tony was trying to cut him off, running at an angle across the open tracks. I could see he would never reach him in time. Snowdon wasn't fast – for that matter neither was I – but the panic from the phone call had given him a little extra pep.

My phone rang. Hoping for good news, I answered it. It was Tom. He seemed to be making his usual mess of things. Not that I could exactly claim our little mission had been a complete success.

I filled him in as best I could with the little breath I had and then hung up.

We were at the rear of the station, Snowdon running along the tracks to get inside the building. Where was the 1.03 to Crewe when you needed one?

Tony came alongside me. "He'll go for a train," he said, as if the idea had yet to occur to me. Tony's a lovely chap, with a savage bent towards watercolour that seems to dominate his every waking hour, but he does love giving breath to the obvious.

"He'll have a limited choice at this time of day," I said. "But he'll want to be heading as far afield as he can manage."

Snowdon had mounted one of the platforms, and was running towards the main concourse.

"The ticket barriers," I huffed, having well and truly had enough of running.

"This time of night?" said Tony, "they usually leave 'em open. They confuse the drunks too much."

I sighed, well and truly out of sorts with my evening.

Tony and I climbed onto the platform. I was looking around for sign of security, but if we were about to be pounced on by train cops there was a good chance Snowdon would be too so it might not be the end of the world. At least he wouldn't be able to make a getaway.

We ran the length of the platform, sailing through the open ticket barriers and then found ourselves without our target in sight.

People were shuffling around, tired, drunk and wanting to get home to their beds.

"Miss your train?" a young woman asked, laughing with her friend to see an old man so out of breath.

"As a metaphor for my life," I replied, "you're not far wrong."

I turned to Tony. "Where is the bastard?"

"I don't know," he admitted. "I can't see him."

Suddenly there erupted a roar of laughter from a group of drunks on the far side of the concourse. Looking over, we saw them gathered around a man who had clearly fallen over.

"Charming clientele at this time of night," I muttered. Then I noticed the man they were laughing at was Snowdon, pulling himself up and making a break for another platform.

"Got you!" I said, Tony and I giving chase.

18

MAX
1.

I told you I'd just stop in the middle of a sentence, didn't I? Say what you like about Max Jackson (people do, damn them) but he has never lost his sense of the dramatic.

I don't know what they hit me with but the pain was more than I have the words for, a searing heat that burned the thoughts right out of me. I heard the voices of the men who had attacked me. My brain couldn't make sense of them. It was just noise and the sensation of falling through the world. Then a solid bastard of a floor smacked me hard and my eyes grabbed a snapshot of bright light, the dangling forty-watt bulb in my hallway as bright as a star, all flame and heat and rage. Then there was darkness. And in the darkness, as always, came the car horn and the certainty that any moment now a wall of cold water would sweep me away from myself, punch me right out of my body and into dissipation.

The oblivion was unmercifully brief. The next thing I knew, hands were lifting me and dragging me back along the hallway and out of the front door.

The air outside brought a little relief. I hadn't been aware of the heat and the smell of what was left of Charlie until I had been removed from its influence.

The back of my head was leaking, the slight breeze chilling wet hair and my shirt collar. Until then the vaguest of thoughts had been about the promise of danger, that things were bad and that any minute now I could be in real trouble. That was the point that it occurred to me that I already was. Brain trauma was not something easily fixed; I might be in a better position than Charlie but that wasn't saying much. How wonderful that Tom and I had decided to get mixed up in this – would I ever stop making the stupid decisions in life?

I heard the sound of van doors opening but couldn't bear to open my eyes, even as I was thrown in the back, curled uselessly on the hard floor, surrounded by the smell of chemicals and petrol fumes.

"What about the other one?" someone asked. "We just going to leave him?"

"Why not?" said the man who had hit me, and the voice was familiar as one of the men who had carried me away in a coffin earlier. He just loved taking me places, that one. "He's a message."

And one that had been received loud and clear. This was not a fun game, a diversion from boredom, this was deep shit, and I for one was sinking below the surface of it.

They got in the driving cab and I rolled onto my back as the van pulled away from the kerb and onto the road. Slowly, consciousness slipped away from me again and the rest of the journey was lost to blackness.

It sometimes occurs to me that death is something

that never really goes away, however much it may seem
to have done so. Yes, unlike most, it was something I had
experienced and walked away from, but its presence still
hung around me.

You have to wonder if it resents me for avoiding it.
In those first few hours of reanimation, at the mercy of
Farmer, it had worked hard to snatch me back. I know… I
said I didn't want to talk about that, and I don't, not really,
but what happened clings to me and however much I try
and shake it off I end up stood there in that kitchen, naked,
looking down the barrels of a shotgun.

Do you really want to know? Is it that important to you?
The story unfinished?

Surely you can guess?

2.

"Now get up," Farmer said and, in the absence of anything
approaching a better option, I did as I was told.

Powerlessness is an all-consuming thing. I was naked,
confused and anticipating what it would feel like were
those shotgun barrels to bark into life. Would I see the shot
as it came towards me or would it just be noise and the
brief sensation of a head rupturing? Perhaps it wouldn't
even hurt, not at this range. Perhaps it would just be an
explosion followed by the vacuum of non-existence.
Maybe that wouldn't be so bad.

But we humans cling to life, even those who don't
possess sufficient of it to count.

"I could do anything to you," he said, standing as

close to me as the long barrels would allow. "And there's absolutely nothing you could do about it."

That was his thrill of course. It wasn't about sex, it was about power. This stupid, broken man had lost his and wanted to take some back. What had brought him to this point, what twist of the knife had reduced him to this empty, vicious creature, I could never know. Possibly, if he had just told me rather than enact his stupid little games, I would have even sympathised. As it was I hated him, and, in that moment, the powerlessness was gone. I raged. To be forced into this, to be used liked this, threatened and intimidated. Whatever had made him who he was, it was nothing to me, he deserved every bit of it, every bad night, every bottle drunk, every empty moment in his hollow home. What is more, I would bring him lower because I, for one, was not going to be treated that way. I was not going to just accept.

His mistake was getting so close. People are stupid with guns, they think they make them invincible. He was particularly dumb. He kept the advantage as long as he maintained a good distance between us; as soon as the barrels were pressed against my lips, I realised there was a very good chance I could beat him. He was drunk, both on brandy and power. All I had to do was turn, move my face to the side, swing my arm up and…

BOOM the shotgun emptied its load over my shoulder. The noise was deafening – still now I can't hear properly on my left side – but the sound couldn't kill me. And what doesn't kill you just makes you stronger.

I kept hold of the barrels, pulling them towards me and bringing up my foot to kick him as hard as I could in the groin.

Farmer screamed, more in panic than pain, and let go of the shotgun.

At that point I had won. I had beaten him. I had turned the tables and was now safe.

But I couldn't leave it, and that's why I never talk about this, that's why it's the secret I never share. Because I terrified myself. The anger that shook my entire body at that moment, the rage that had been building for longer than I could even remember, a rage that had continued to burn through death. I screamed, an animal sound, as solid a proof as any that I had lost all humanity in that moment.

Holding the shotgun barrels with both hands I swung it at him, again and again and again…

I can't remember it clearly, the anger was too strong. But it's the other noise that haunts me, just like that fucking car horn. The sound of a man I didn't even know, screaming, and another begging, until the heavy stock of the gun robs him of the ability to beg any more.

I killed him.

I beat at him so hard, so mindlessly, that the thing I looked down on, when finally my mind was back inside my own head, was nothing but a bloody, misshapen mess.

That is what I did. That is what I am capable of.

Maybe we all are. Maybe I'm stupid to deny it, to hide it, to bury it inside. But at that moment I had never been so terrified, so utterly consumed with horror. Horror at myself.

I dropped the shotgun and tried to back away. My bare feet slipped in the spreading pool of blood and I fell on my back, mirroring Farmer's splayed position, a Rorschach painting viewed from above.

I think I blacked out for a while. The passage of time

throughout those few hours is loose and impossible to pin down.

At some point it got dark and I was grateful for that, because as I stood up and walked out of the room I could pretend there was nothing in it I needed to see.

I showered again but still couldn't get clean.

My arms ached so much I could barely lift them. The knowledge of what I had done to strain the muscles haunted every move I made, and lifting the soap to my face was agony for both reasons.

I thought I was going to be sick, but my stomach was empty. Instead, I leaned against the cold tiles, retching.

I knew I should just leave. I was probably safe from visitors, Farmer clearly lived alone, fatally so, and I didn't imagine he had many friends who might come enquiring. Still, to stay there after what I had just done seemed madness – the justification never occurred to me, at that point I was little but torn muscles and guilt. But I needed to think. And after that I needed to deal with what I had done. Because for all the shock, self-disgust and guilt, I was already accepting that I needed to hide my involvement.

I got out of the shower, found there were no more towels and stood there, lost for a moment, as I remembered where they were.

I dripped my way across the bathroom and out onto the landing.

I had forgotten about his dog. It was sat there, looking quizzically at me, confused by my presence. And that broke me. I just started to sob. Squatting down against the wall, my whole body shaking as I wailed my guts out. After a moment the dog walked over, licked my wet arm and sat next to me, resting against my body, which just made it worse somehow. I held on to him and waited until there was nothing left to cry. Just me and the dog. Two abandoned animals with no place left in the world.

3.

I found a spare bedroom and shut myself and the dog up in it until morning. We shared the bed, both subdued and only too happy to content ourselves with unconsciousness.

The dog woke me at dawn, scratching at the door to be let out. Cautiously I let him go. I grabbed a dressing gown from the back of the door – pushing away the thought of who it must have belonged to – then followed in case the dog wanted to go into the kitchen.

I needn't have worried. He went straight to the front door and I let him out so he could run around in the unkempt front garden, emptying his bladder with unrestrained joy. He kept a cautious eye on me as he hunted around the bushes and grass, fearful I guess that I might shut him out and abandon him. Which of course I was going to have to do soon enough. But not for now.

It was the most atrociously beautiful morning. The world doesn't care what we do on it, the sun shines or it doesn't. It has higher concerns than our stupid problems. I drew all the pleasure from it I could and, at some point, my mood shifted. My memory was still a mess but I was still here, against the odds, and I saw no sense in not making the best of it. Once the dog had come back in I shut him away in the bedroom and decided to deal with the kitchen.

After all, as soon as it was done I could walk away from the place.

I had my hand on the door when another thought occurred to me: my clothes. He had claimed that he had put them in the wash and it depended on when he decided on what he was going to do as to how true that was. If he had always planned on attacking me then likely they had been dumped in a bin somewhere. If he had taken his time to build up the courage – and I was instinctively sure that was the case – then he may have been telling the truth.

There hadn't been a washing machine in the kitchen; no doubt it was kept in an out-house or utility room. I went back outside and walked around the house. There was a garage to the side but that was empty bar the usual collection of rusting tools and garden equipment. Moving around the back, I passed the kitchen window and couldn't help glancing inside, momentarily sure that his body would have gone, that I had made a mistake in thinking him dead and that he would leap out at me at any minute. Perhaps there was even a little hope in the thought; after all, I had handled danger. It was being a murderer I struggled with. I would continue to struggle: his body was clearly visible, a dark twisted shape peering out from beneath the kitchen table.

I looked away.

Just past the kitchen was a relatively new extension with an outside door. I looked inside. There was the washing machine, a tumble dryer and several loaded shelves and plastic storage boxes.

I stooped down to check the washing machine. I had been right, my clothes were in it.

I fished them out, a pair of jeans, a shirt and a light canvas jacket I liked to wear because it had as many pockets as I had things to shove in them. A typical man, he'd shoved the lot in together with no regard for whether it was safe to wash them. No doubt his thoughts had been on other things. My impending rape and/or execution, for example. Still, if they could handle a few days floating down the river they could certainly handle a lukewarm spin cycle.

I shoved them all in the tumble dryer and spent a minute figuring out how the arcane dials and switches might come together to form a useful drying programme. It occurred to me that maybe I would be leaving more evidence by doing this, but I couldn't see what the police would find. I turned it on then wiped everything with a convenient tea-towel. My memory being what it was, I couldn't swear that my prints weren't on record somewhere.

I left the utility room – wiping down the door handle as I went past. Then the absurdity of this hit me. I had been all over the house, there was more trace of me than a simple wipe-down could achieve. Whatever I was going to do to cover my tracks needed to be more thorough than that.

I headed back around the house. No more delays, it was time to deal with the kitchen.

4.

Farmer had gone stiff, his limbs slightly constricted so it appeared he had been trying to push himself up into a crab position. The blood was thick and dark, congealed and glutinous, feeding troughs for flies. I watched a particularly bloated bluebottle make its skittish way out of his half-open mouth and come to rest on his cheek. It moved like speeded-up film footage, appearing here and there on the corpse's face with no obvious transition. There was a quiet buzzing sound and I couldn't decide whether it was the heating system responding to the lit AGA oven in the corner or a sign of insects breeding in Farmer's cold meat. I decided it was the central heating. I mean, fuck it, when you've got the option, why go for the one that makes you want to throw up your lungs?

As hard as I tried, I couldn't see any way around dealing with his body. I could spend a few hours burying it but that wouldn't fool anyone that actually went looking, and did I want to risk further chance of being seen? I could chop him up and throw him in the AGA… except I couldn't; that sort of business was beyond me, which was a shame as at least fire would help destroy any physical evidence I might have left on the body.

Fire. It was the obvious solution really. We were miles away from anywhere, and if I was lucky, the whole place would burn to the ground before anyone had a chance to deal with it. All evidence of my having been here gone up in smoke. I wasn't naive enough to think the authorities would dismiss the idea of foul play, but as long as I ensured the kitchen went up they'd have little practical evidence and reason to suspect my involvement. I hadn't known him and had no traceable link to him.

You see who you're dealing with? Pragmatic little bastard when I want to be, aren't I?

I went to look in the garage. There was a five-litre fuel can, no doubt for topping up the chainsaw and lawnmower, both of which were petrol-fuelled. That would be enough. I needed to set a fire strong enough to get right out of hand but also slow enough in the first instance that I could get away before it really took hold. I couldn't speak from experience, but I was pretty sure that when it came to arson with petrol, a little was enough.

So, that decided, all I had to do was wait for my clothes to be ready.

I was going to have to walk out of here. I could have driven Farmer's car but the risk seemed too great. Either I would get caught in it, a vehicle easily identified as belonging to him, or I would be tipping off the authorities to my presence by having it turn up miles away. It was another thing that could link me to him, and I wasn't going through all this just to leave a trail.

I didn't know how far I was going to have to walk but I had nothing, no money or food, and that was stupid. As uncomfortable as it felt to dig through a dead man's house, I needed all the advantages I could get. So, while my clothes dried I went on the hunt for anything that could be useful. I thought my luck had turned when I found his wallet. If it had been in his trouser pocket I'm not sure I could have stomached retrieving it, but it was sat on his bedside table. My luck proved to be on form however, when I opened it and found nothing but a twenty-pound note and a couple of bank cards. I put the twenty in the pocket of the dressing gown and carried on hunting. There was an expensive-looking watch which I also pocketed. I needed to be able to tell the time and, if need be, I could always try and sell it if I really needed the money.

I sat on the end of his bed and wondered if it was possible to sink any lower. I was a murderer, and one with so little remorse I was picking through the dead man's things in the hope of finding something worth a few quid.

I looked over to my reflection in the dressing table mirror, the face of a man I still didn't altogether know. I wasn't sure I wanted to know him either. Perhaps this wasn't the first time? Maybe Farmer was just the last in a line of people I had hurt or killed?

Deep down I didn't believe that. The rage I had felt yesterday had been so terrifying that I couldn't believe, amnesiac or not, that it was a regular occurrence. I had snapped, through fear, and now I was just doing what I could to survive. Was that so wrong?

I'm still wondering about that.

I stood up and there was a crumpling noise from beneath me. Turning around, I could see that the mattress wasn't quite flat on the corner I'd been sitting. Lifting it, I found a padded brown envelope stuffed with cash. Seriously. You have to wonder about a god sometimes; if he does exist he's got a very twisted sense of humour.

I counted it roughly: there looked to be about ten grand there. What had a man like Farmer been doing with that amount of money stashed away? A man like Farmer. What a stupid thing to think, after all I had no idea really what sort of man he was. Who had he known? What family had he got? What did he do for a living?

That last thought suddenly brought me up cold. He must have had a job, and if he didn't turn up for it, wouldn't someone very soon be on the hunt for him? I pulled the watch out of my pocket and looked at it again. The little window on the dial said it was a Sunday. If that was true then I probably had twenty-four hours to worry about it. And to think I had been bemoaning my luck.

I tucked the envelope into the waistband of my trousers and went back to the kitchen. It was the last room I wanted to be in, but if I had to be walking for hours I would eventually need food. It occurred to me as strange that I hadn't yet felt hungry but I put it down to shock. I know better now, of course. We reanimates need very little in the way of food; bodily functions being what they are, an occasional top-up keeps us going just fine. It's just another of those medical impossibilities that keeps Thackeray awake at night while he tries to understand.

I did my best to avoid looking at Farmer's body as I loaded some bread and cheese into a carrier bag. There was an unopened bottle of mineral water so I threw that in as well. That would have to do. Picking through a dead man's shopping was somehow the worst thing of all, looking at the things in his fridge that he liked. A bar of chocolate, some fruit yoghurts, things you buy to treat yourself. Happy food that would never be enjoyed.

There was a big box of cook's matches on the worktop. I dropped those in my pocket too – I'd need them soon.

I went to check on my clothes. They were dry enough and I couldn't bear to wait any longer.

Dressed, I stuffed the money into the inside pocket of my jacket and put the watch on my wrist. Rubbing down the utility room again in case the fire didn't reach that far, I went back to the garage and fetched the can of petrol.

Time to leave.

I doused the kitchen, paying particular attention to

Farmer's body. As the petrol hit him his wounds sizzled and a handful of flies flew skywards.

I poured a trail of petrol out of the door then threw the more-or-less empty can back into the room. I lit a match, paused for breath, then lit the petrol.

The flame ran into the room, and the whole place was glowing and crackling in seconds. I've never seen anything so eager as that fire, chasing around like a child at play, desperate to burn.

I ran out of the front door and began to jog up his front drive.

Which is when I remembered the bloody dog.

I looked back at the house. How long did I have? How long before the whole place was ablaze? It was madness to go back.

But I just couldn't leave the dog.

I put my bag of provisions down and ran back to the front door, black smoke already beginning to pour out of it. The kitchen was to the left and the sound of the fire was low and angry. The stairs were to the right, the flames already licking the banisters. If I was quick...

I ran up them, the dog barking either because it heard me coming or because it smelled the smoke and knew something was amiss. As soon as I opened the door it bolted past me and ran back downstairs.

"Dog!" I shouted, not being able to remember its name. Surely it wouldn't run towards the fire?

I chased after it, and in the few seconds I had been gone the flames had already crept across the entrance hall, beginning to cut off my escape. The dog was barking at them, hopping around, staring towards the kitchen, clearly desperate to get past the fire and find its master. At least something had loved him.

I grabbed it, doing my best to keep hold as it struggled in my arms, and ran through the flames towards the door.

Outside, the smoke was rising and I knew it would soon be visible for miles. Who knew how long it would be then before someone called the authorities?

The dog continued to struggle but I ran to the back of Farmer's car, opened the door and hit lucky for the third time: its leash was on the back seat. I clipped it to its collar and dragged it back up the front drive, stopping to grab my bag before making a run for the open, dragging the dog all the way behind me.

5.

After about ten minutes, out of breath and sickened by the fumes of smoke, I slowed down to a walk. The dog seemed to have forgotten its master for now, trotting along next to me as if only too happy to be out for its morning constitutional.

I squatted down to him, and checked his collar for a tag. "Dudley" it said, followed by what I assumed was Farmer's phone number. I pulled the tag off and threw it into the long grass.

Behind us, Farmer's house was visible as a pillar of smoke. I decided we'd be best keeping off the main road as much as possible, at least until that was out of sight.

"Come on, Jamie," I said, it being the first name that popped into my head. "Let's go and find some signs of life."

6.

Some would say I never found any.

So that's who you're dealing with. That's the kind of man I am. Still want to know me?

Maybe now you'll think I deserved what I had coming…

‖‖‖19

MAX

1.

"Get up, Mr Jackson."

Somebody was invading my frequently inhabited, knocked out, sleep of the just.

"Mr Jackson, I know you're awake."

Which is more than I did.

"Mr Jackson, I shan't tell you again. Get up."

They obviously didn't know how crabby I could get in the mornings.

Well, sod them. There was an order to such things – strong coffee, strong cigarettes and lithe and curvaceous women on tap. This last is optional, of course. In fact, it's been optional for most of my life, so much so that I'm giving serious consideration to knocking it off the list altogether. That excluded, there was still a patented Jackson way of starting the day. No exceptions.

There was the sound of a gun being cocked.

This would, I decided on reflection, fit under Sub Clause 4 – Section B. "Acceptable Exceptions".

I got up.

Then fell back down again as nobody had had the foresight to tell me the ceiling was so low. I was getting heartily sick of head-butting things; I seemed to have spent the last twenty-four hours constantly having my head whacked.

"I'd move out of there first, if I were you."

I appeared to by lying in a stone alcove, the kind where people stored bodies in a crypt. I glanced to my left to see one of the undertakers sat on a sarcophagus, big, cold and grey it was, the sort of thing you'd expect to see in a tomb... or crypt. He was pointing the gun I'd heard cocking directly at me, which was to be expected. It had a long silencer screwed into place, which worried me: it showed he was only too willing to use it. The room was tatty red brick, cobwebs, with a stone staircase in one corner. It was airless and yet cold at the same time. Rather crypt-like, you could say.

I put my detective brain to work, collating all the data to hand.

"I'm in a crypt," I said.

"Oh but you're good," he replied, rather too sarcastically I felt.

"Mr Lloyd?"

"Right again."

"I'm positively on fire. I'd give up now, if I were you. You haven't got a chance." I slipped my legs out first then dropped to the ground.

"Forgive me if I hang on in there for a bit longer," he replied, gesturing for me to stay still.

"You're sure? If you knocked it on the head now, we could all make last orders."

"Oh do shut up."

"Probably good advice, but I'm feeling a touch nervous and I tend to say lots of silly things when I'm nervous." I shrugged. "Nerves, I expect."

"Ah," he said, "and that's the interesting thing, isn't it? Yours really shouldn't be working, should they?"

"Shouldn't they? Why? Have I got nothing to be worried about?"

"Don't be obtuse, Mr Jackson. You know damn well they shouldn't. Along with any of your bodily functions."

"What are you talking about?" I blustered.

"You're dead."

"Oh." He had me there. "Yes, well there is that."

"My colleague, Ackroyd, was rather surprised when he dealt with your friend at the flat. I'm sure Dr Snowdon will be equally intrigued, once he finishes dealing with the rest of your friends. A dead man walking... You see why I might find that a little curious?"

"What, as a professional in death?"

"If you like."

"But I don't like!" I shouted, my nerve finally snapping. "Sitting there wafting your sense of superiority about the place. Chopping up innocent people and hiking out their organs to the highest bidder. All that makes you is a pathetic little hack, a butcher, a vampire..."

"An incredibly rich man."

"Oh, well, that's all right then, isn't it? As long as you've got a few quid in the bank."

"As far as I'm concerned, yes, it is. This little... sideline of ours is, by necessity, quite a modest affair. A cottage industry, if you will." He grinned. "Although would you care to hazard a guess as to how much it's made me over the last couple of years?"

"I couldn't care less."

He laughed and shook his head. "Such a sanctimonious young man. We have had over a hundred donors pass through our hands since Snowdon struck upon Wade Davis' mythic formula, all of them a potential goldmine. For merely one of their kidneys we can get anything up to eighty thousand pounds. You do the maths."

"Am I supposed to be impressed?"

I was, but I would hardly tell him that.

"You certainly should be. Regardless, it might give you an idea how seriously we take our trade, and, of course, the lengths we would go to in order to maintain it."

He put his hands in his pockets and paced a little.

"Of course, that could potentially be nothing compared with an alternative commodity," he said, looking directly at me. "The secret of immortality, for example."

So, here we had it. This was the crux of the matter. Naive of me not to think about it really, but, then, I knew immortality wasn't all it cracked up to be.

"Trust me, my existence isn't worth paying for."

"I disagree, as I imagine would most of our clients."

He stepped up close and took hold of my face. "You have no idea the problems you've caused us. Forcing us to destroy everything, prepare to go into hiding. But all of that might end up proving worthwhile with you. Maybe we could end up going into a new line of business altogether?"

I wasn't sure what was worse, having his baby-soft hand touch my face or his breath. Finally I plumped for breath. It smelled of garlic, a fine bulb going down, but a bitch second-hand.

"I've never had a head for business," I said, giving him a sample of it by slamming my forehead into the bridge of his nose.

I gave him a colossal shove that sent him back onto the sarcophagus lid, the gun dropping from his hand. I picked it up and gave him a pleasing punch to the face. He rolled off the sarcophagus and landed on the floor, dazed. Keeping the gun pointed at him, I took the opportunity to rifle through his pockets. I found a mobile phone. Perfect. I whacked him on the back of the head with the butt of the gun and ran up the stars out of the crypt.

Coming out into the main body of the church, I wasn't in the least surprised to find I was in the church where this mess had first started.

Main door, main door…

There it was, just behind that man with a gun.

Bugger.

I raised my stolen gun to fire but found the trigger wouldn't pull. Safety catch. Now where did they put the safety catches on guns?

I dived behind a pew as a sharp bang told me a horrid bastard was shooting at me. The gun was knocked out of my hand, skittering out of sight beneath the pews. I think we can all accept I am not much cop as a man of action.

There was another door right by me. I shuffled along on my hands and knees to the end of the pew and darted for it as another shot splintered the door frame.

I found myself next to a large bookcase of Bibles and hymnbooks. I grabbed a sizeable tome and waited on one side of the door. As the man appeared, I smacked him in the face with the Good Book and gave a hallelujah, turning on my heels and running up yet more stairs.

All in all it's a general rule that, if you want to leave a building, running upstairs is not the best way to do it. At that point I had very little choice; I could only hope that I would be able to hole up somewhere long enough for rescue.

At that point the mobile phone started ringing. I saw no need to be rude so I answered it.

"Lloyd?" asked the voice on the end, "things are falling apart. You need to kill Jackson and get out of there."

"I don't think that's the best idea," I replied. "Jackson's lovely and we've really hit it off. We're thinking of holidaying in Crete next year."

There was a pause.

"Jackson?"

"The actual. Lovely to finally chat to you. Sorry to hear things aren't going well though, naturally. Do make sure you don't fall under a bus or anything, won't you?" I hung up and tried to remember Tom's number. I couldn't. It's programmed into my phone, what's the point in doing that and then going to the effort of remembering it? Fuck. Arse. Balls. I was pretty sure it had some sevens in it. Maybe a three.

He would probably be doing something brilliant like trying to rescue me by now but it wasn't working terribly well because he wasn't here. I imagine he'd gone to the undertakers where this lot would have left someone nice and violent to do something horrible to them. Someone Lloyd would likely have talked to recently… It was worth a try. If all else failed I could pass the time chatting to his mum and telling him what a prick I thought her son was. I went to the dialled call menu, 'SnowdonMob' was at the top followed by 'AckMob'. In for a penny… I called the number.

"H-hello?" a nervous-sounding voice answered. I hoped he was nervous for all the right reasons.

"Hi." I said, "Erm… is Tom there? Can't miss him, he's the beardy little dead bloke."

A gunshot echoed up the stairway as I reached the balcony, Lloyd's voice chasing after it.

"Will you stop firing at him! I want his body intact!"

All the times I've wanted to hear someone say that, and it has to come from a psycho with designs on my liver.

The stairway brought me to the musician's gallery. The door was so small I had to crouch down to get through, which seemed an ideal place to try and slow them down. The organ wasn't original, an electric behemoth standing in front of the old wall-mounted pipes. Sad for organ purists perhaps, but damned convenient for me.

"Hello?" Tom said on the other end of the phone.

Bingo! I'd call myself lucky but, you know, given all the being dead and shot at I was experiencing, that would have been an exaggeration.

"Hi, Tom. Let me tell you I'm having a really shitty evening. Bear with me." I slapped the phone on top of the organ and shoved the thing towards the doorway. It took some shoving, but nothing stokes the fires of strength like a handful of evil buggers wanting you dead.

I sent it crashing against the small wooden door just as someone pushed against it.

I leant on the keyboard a moment to get my breath back before picking up the phone again.

"Sorry, mate, caught me mid manual labour."

"Where the hell are you?" Tom shouted.

"You'll never guess!" I started playing "Chopsticks" on the organ; I always get fidgety when I'm on the phone.

"Where?"

"The church where we first bumped into Lloyd and the gang."

"What are you doing there?"

"Oh you know, bit of quiet reflection, some brass rubbing…" A bullet flew past my head and clanged off one of the organ pipes. Someone was taking pot shots from ground level – Lloyd had some unruly staff, that was for sure.

"He told you not to shoot!" I shouted.

"What was that?" asked Tom.

"An irate choir boy, what do you think?" I ducked low and moved back against the wall as far as I could.

"Sarcasm's the lowest form of wit, Max."

Someone was kicking at the door. I couldn't stay where I was.

"No, Tom, that would be you after a few drinks."

Time to go up again, then. A set of spiral steps led from the gallery – presumably to the bell tower.

I was backing myself into a tighter corner with every step.

"Listen, Tom, do you think you could drop by? I'm having the odd bit of trouble this end."

"We've been having a bit of trouble too." It sounded like he was running and, after a moment, I heard the ignition of a car.

"Pleased to hear it," I said, running up the staircase.

"You deserve it for getting us into this in the first place."

"Oh, so it's all my fault now?"

"You know it is! Now get over here!"

"We're already on our way."

"Good. Put your foot down, would you?"

I came out into fresh air with nowhere left to run. I looked over the edge of the bell tower, a wide chunk of London spread out waiting for the coming dawn. My God, what a night.

There was a loud, and faintly musical, crash from below, which I took to be the organ giving up the ghost.

"I'd better be going, Tom, things are about to get a bit hairy." I cut off the call, put the phone in my pocket and was trying to think of a really good plan of action when Lloyd appeared in the doorway, gun in hand.

In the absence of any better ideas I ran at him screaming, grabbing his gun hand and smacking it against the wall. The gun fell from his grip but he brought his knee up into my stomach and I let go of him. He caught me a good solid punch on the jaw, and I was rolling back against the parapet. I grabbed him again as he came at me, but I've never been much cop in a fair fight and it was all I could do to stop him from hitting me, let alone getting any worthwhile licks in myself.

We ended up wrestling, neither of us giving each other room to swing a blow. Then there was a blinding pain in my eyes as he smacked his forehead into the bridge of my nose. I let go of him on reflex and, with a roar, he dealt an uppercut that sent me toppling right over the edge of the parapet.

Which would be just about where you came in, if memory serves.

||||/20

TOM
1.

Obviously I couldn't have been more relieved to hear the sound of Max's voice, though I took some care not to show it. After all, if Max knew my heart could melt so easily he'd be getting himself kidnapped on a nightly basis.

I held my hand over the mouthpiece. "It's Max, we need to get out of here now."

"Max?" said Douggie. "He okay?"

I nodded and waved for everybody to move back outside.

The police were bound to make themselves felt at any moment and Max was clearly in need of us.

Douggie ran around, collecting the guns that had been dropped – I began to see how he had managed to build such an impressive collection – and ensured the one surviving gang member would still be in attendance when the law came by giving him a solid clout to the side of the head. Steve went for the evidence. Ackroyd and his thugs had clearly been in the process of gathering everything together. There were several of those stackable plastic boxes, filled with papers and equipment.

"Give me a hand, Carl," he said, "we need to grab as much of this as will fit in the boot."

Carl looked to his brother, who was still covered in his own blood but otherwise disturbingly well. Again, I pulled my thoughts away from him; there would be time later to worry about what had happened to Dave.

"He'll be all right," said Steve, "won't you, Dave?"

"I'm fine," Dave replied, getting up and wafting his crimson T-shirt, "just a bit gooey, that's all."

Throughout all of this I kept talking to Max. He's a chatty bugger when nervous, and given the recent events, it was only too pleasant to catch up.

Once we were outside I waved to Thackeray, who leaped out of his car as if it were on fire.

"What happened?" he asked, staring at Dave.

"Something we'll need to talk about later," I said, covering the mouthpiece of the phone, "Dave died. Then came back."

"Don't be ridic–" He saw the look on my face and stopped speaking.

"Later," I insisted. "Max is in trouble right now and we need to move fast. Follow us."

Douggie and Steve loaded their ill-gotten gains into the boot of the SUV while Carl, Dave and I climbed into the back seat.

Within seconds, we were on our way, pushing out into the Camden night, men high on continued survival and determined to win the day.

Max hung up.

"How's he doing?" asked Douggie.

"Badly," I admitted, "though facing it with the usual

inane jollity. Say what you like about Max, he doesn't go down quietly."

"My kind of man," said Douggie with a grin. He put a heavy hand on my shoulder. "It's not far, we'll make it in time."

"We'd better," I replied. "Take your next left, straight on till the lights and then right."

I called Len. He sounded out of breath.

"You all right?"

"Running around King's Cross – not my preferred way of starting a new day. We've got Snowdon on the run. You found Max?"

"Not yet, but we know where he is. He's causing trouble in a church."

"As long as he's enjoying himself."

He gave me a shorthand version of his meeting with Snowdon, and I began to get a real sense that we were fast achieving the upper hand.

"Stay safe," I told him, "but get that bastard. We can't let him get away."

"I would never have thought of that," he said. "Thank you for making it clear."

With that he hung up.

I watched the clock: it was just past one in the morning. All of this had happened so quickly. One long night of panic, chasing and crazy decisions. Perhaps that had been for the best; like John Coltrane I'm always best when winging it. Give me an elaborate plan and I'll only have forgotten it five minutes in. Head down and push forward, it's the only way to get through life.

The roads were completely empty by now and we were

making good time. If Max could only hang in there for another five minutes we'd be there to save him.

MAX
2.

"Jackson!" Lloyd shouted, "get back up here now!"

"Bit busy at the moment I'm afraid, can we get together later? Have a coffee, perhaps?"

A frame of those metal spikes they use to discourage pigeons surrounded the bell tower. It was wearing loose in places but it had been enough to stop me falling. I was hanging from one of the support rails, having earned a torn sleeve and a throbbing shoulder for my efforts but still beating the odds. The old iron was creaking as I tried to pull myself into a secure position. Lucky for me I had taken hold of the next rail along, as the first snapped with a pathetic crunch of rust and age, leaving my feet swinging in the air.

The whole structure was a bit of a cowboy job, if you asked me. The pigeons obviously thought so too; they were sat on the lengthwise struts looking perfectly comfortable, if a little baffled as to what the bloke without wings was doing out there.

Looking up, I could see Lloyd peering over the edge at me.

I tried to get a stronger grip on the railing but the damn things were so slippery with pigeon shit I was fighting a losing battle. I tried to swing my legs up to hook on to another rail, but that kept putting more pressure on the one I was holding. I could hear it creaking and knew it would likely snap at any moment. If only I could distribute my – admittedly considerable – weight more easily, then I might stand a chance of being able to lodge there a while. My constant hope was that Tom and the cavalry would arrive any minute. If I could just hold on long enough for them to arrive…

"Come on, Mr Jackson," said Lloyd, trying to sound reasonable, "what have you got to gain from falling off there? I would rather you were in one piece I admit, but I'm sure there'll be something of worth left whatever happens. Why not save yourself unnecessary pain?"

Unnecessary pain. The story of my life and death.

"Why not make my life easier, you mean?" I shouted.

"Precisely. There's no reason we can't do everything possible to make this as tolerable as possible for you."

"That's very kind. Under the circumstances there is something you could do for me," I replied, scrabbling at the brickwork with my toes.

"But of course. Come up here and we can discuss it."

"Well, actually I was wondering if you'd mind awfully throwing yourself off face first. If I have to go through all of this, it would make me feel considerably better. You're just so ugly, you see. It's quite putting me off my stroke. I'm sure between gravity and a well-placed tombstone we could turn you into something more appealing."

I can be so childish at times.

"Have it your way then, Jackson. I can be patient for a few more minutes. I'll see you at the bottom."

"Race you!" I shouted, but I think he'd already gone.

My arms were beginning to shake under the strain; I certainly wasn't going to be able to stay there much longer.

I tried various tricks, altering my grip, shifting my body weight just to flex my cramping muscles a bit – anything to buy a bit more time.

The strut I was holding on to gave another terrible creak.

I tried to reach out my hand to the next one along, but my arms were straining too much as it was and I needed both to support me.

Why is it only times like this when you truly appreciate the benefits of being fit?

Lloyd was back. I gave a quick glance upwards as saw him leaning over towards me. Did he plan on pulling me back in? He would have to be a damn sight stronger than he looked.

My left hand slipped off the railing…

TOM

3.

Douggie swung the SUV into the church drive with a spray of gravel.

"Look!" he shouted. "Top of the tower!"

Max was hanging there by one arm, lit by the floodlights on the roof. I'm ashamed to say my first thought was: *Silly bastard, he'll hurt himself if he's not careful.* All he had to do was keep safe for five minutes, and he ended up dangling off tall buildings.

Someone appeared above him and, though it could hardly be a friendly face, it did at least seem that someone was coming to his rescue. But no. The figure swung over the edge of the tower, extended a leg and kicked at Max's hand.

I subconsciously grabbed at Douggie's arm and watched my friend fall.

Other people were appearing at the doorway of the church, not many of them – three or four perhaps – my attention was elsewhere. I didn't even notice the guns, oblivious to the danger of bullets as I jumped out of the SUV and ran over to where Max had fallen.

I just wanted to see him. Part of me, naively I suppose, thinking he'd be fine. We couldn't have gone through all this, to have come so close, only to have him lost to us after all.

Obviously, he would survive, but if you know anything about us now you'll know that that might be no blessing at all. A ruined cripple, as physically broken as poor Charlie… All I could think was that my stupid bloody enthusiasm had reduced my best friend to a life of agony and fracture.

I have never been one for regrets, but just then, running across the grass towards the bushes where he had landed, I had nothing but. I would have done anything to turn the clock back, anything to avoid this one, stupid night.

MAX
4.

Lying on my back in the recently trimmed grass of the graveyard, I looked up at the sky and took in the stars. Nothing monumental, nothing evangelical, just the appreciation of random lights. *It's a big old universe*, I thought, aware on some detached level that I couldn't move my legs. The smell of the grass made my nose tickle, I've always been a little susceptible to hay fever. I wondered what sandwiches the gardener would bring with him tomorrow.

"Max?"

Tom's face came into view above me. He looked ever so worried about something.

"Hi, Tom, how's it going?" I said.

He was looking at me funny, almost tearful. I wondered what I might have done to upset him. Not that he didn't deserve it nine times out of ten, but I'd never want to cause him the sort of pain I saw on his face just then.

"Sorry, Tom."

"What for, you silly sod?" He was crying, I could hear it in his voice.

"I don't really remember, to be honest. You just looked upset about something so, you know, sorry."

Tom laughed but I didn't really believe the sound; it seemed forced.

"You just fell off a bell tower, you idiot. I'm upset because I'm worried about you."

"Oh." That's right, falling; I remembered that. "That's what it is, I wondered why I couldn't move."

I looked up at the sky. "I thought it was just the usual symptoms of a good night out." I looked at him. "We do do them rather well."

DOUGGIE
5.

I drew the car to a halt and watched Tom running off through the graveyard.

We'd seen Max fall, and with it felt the bastard sense that it had all been for nothing. Not that I was surprised: you don't go through life like those two without taking a tumble now and then. It was only a matter of time before one of those tumbles was too big to pick yourself up from.

"Was that Mr Jackson?" said Dave from the back seat.

"Aye, lad," I replied, "I'm afraid it was."

"What's he doing jumping off a church?"

What can ye say when faced with such an inquiring mind?

"Nothing good." I looked at Steve, pulling my gun out of my pocket. "Ready?"

He nodded. We climbed out, Thackeray running past us having seen Max fall.

A wee twat in a morning coat was bearing down on me. I stepped to one side and brought down the handle of the gun on the back of his head. One nice, dull crunch and the bampot was kissing gravel.

Two shots at the doorway, one from me and one from my sexy wee lad, and the opposition was down to one. He showed good sense, turning on his heels and running back inside.

TOM

6.

I was holding Max's hand when Jeffery came rushing over.

"How many times?" he said. "You need to take better care of yourself, I can't keep patching you up!"

"Yes, doctor," said Max. "Sorry, doctor. If it's any consolation I did hit quite a lot of foliage on the way down.

The gardener's going to have his work cut out trimming that rhododendron back into shape, what with the Jackson-shaped hole I've just put in it."

"Can you move?" he asked.

"Not right now," Max admitted, "but that's probably just because I'm tired, it's been a hell of a long night."

"You look a right state."

"I'll have you know this suit is hand tailored," Max replied, and I couldn't resist squeezing his hand. That was my boy!

"Could someone find my cigarettes for me?" he said. "They should be in one of my pockets."

"The last thing you need is a cigarette," said Jeffery. "If ever I needed proof of your apparent death wish…"

"I know every smoker thinks this," said Max, "but I really don't think they're going to kill me."

I had a quick hunt in his pockets and pulled out a flattened pack.

"And a light."

I hunted again but couldn't find one.

"Sorry, old chap, you must have dropped it."

"Oh for fuck's sake, this night just keeps getting worse!" he shouted. "What's going on inside?"

"Douggie and Steve are hunting down the rest of the gang," I said. "Soon be over."

"Good," Max said. "Do me a favour though, would you?"

"What's that?" I asked.

"Go and give that Lloyd's arse a damn good kicking. It's the only thing that might put a shine on the day so far."

I looked down at him. He was in a dreadful mess; I didn't like to leave him.

"What about you?" I asked.

"Oh, I'll just hang about here if that's all right. I'm not really in the mood for running about."

I had to laugh.

His face turned serious. "He knows, Tom," he said, "he knows about what we are."

"Understood," I said.

I looked to Jeffery. "We need to be getting out of here before the authorities arrive."

"I don't think it's safe to move him," said Jeffery.

"Probably not, but it's certainly not safe to leave him here either."

Carl and Dave had joined us. It was turning into a perfect staff picnic.

"You all right, Mr Jackson?" asked Dave, the colossal bloodstain on his chest making his concern for someone else all the more touching.

"I've been better, to be honest, boys," Max admitted. "What happened to you?"

"Dave got shot and killed," said Carl with obvious pride. "Nothing puts him down!"

Max glanced at me and I shook my head; there was time enough for explanations about that.

"The lot of you, get Max back to the club and the rest of us will follow on after."

I squatted down next to Max. "I'm trusting you to get better," I said, "understood?"

"Yes, Uncle Tom," he replied, "now go and make yourself useful for once."

"Do my best."

TOM

7.

Inside the church there was nobody in sight but I could hear the sound of fighting coming from the far end, just beyond the altar, so I followed the noise.

There was a door leading off to the vestry and, sure enough, that's where I found Douggie and Steve. They had cornered Lloyd. He was cowering with his back against the wall, arms held out.

"All right, all right…" he shouted. "Let's be sensible now, shall we?"

There was another body on the floor; the smell of cordite in the air and the gun in Douggie's hand left me in no doubt as to how it had got there.

"What's that?" Douggie said. "'It's a fair cop'? 'I'll come quietly, officer'?"

"Problem is," I said from behind them, "we're not police, are we, Douggie?"

"You're not wrong there, lad. Kinda operating outside the law here, are we not?"

The look of fear in Lloyd's eyes grew deeper.

"We are indeed, Douggie, but, please, give me the gun, I don't want you to shoot him."

"Thank you!" The pathetic little man was almost crying.

"Don't thank me," I said as Douggie handed the gun over. "I just didn't think it was fair that he had to do it."

With that I shot him, quickly and efficiently. I took no pleasure in it; it was a simple matter of self-preservation. We couldn't have him talking about us.

Given the business he had been involved in, I can't

say it troubled me much.

I rang Len, one more to go…

"Where is he?" I asked. On hearing the answer I led Douggie and Steve back out into the cool air and towards the final part of our night.

||||| 21

SNOWDON

1.

What a mess. What a ridiculous, sickening, idiotic mess. To have built up so much and watch it fall apart, piece by piece, thanks to the interference of these meddling idiots.

I was feeling distinctly homicidal as the train pulled out of the station, my hands throttling the plastic armrests of my seat.

At least I was safe. Or soon would be. I had enough money put away to lose myself on the continent somewhere. I would spend a few quiet months ensuring that Dr Herbert Snowdon vanished from the world. The advantage of working with the sort of people I had been of late was that I had gathered enough connections to help that process move smoother. I thought of one of my recent clients, a Russian gentleman who I was quite sure would have the wherewithal to give me a new name and legal identity in return for some of the money he had paid me for his wife's new kidney.

It would be fine. I tried to reassure myself of that as the lights of the station passed behind me and the train made its way towards Peterborough. I had yet to decide where I was going to get off; for now I was happy just to put as many miles between myself and the chaos I had left behind. I would soon be able to regroup, I decided, make plans to start again.

Start again. The idea was infuriating.

But lessons had been learned. I would be even more careful next time. Even more cautious.

Closing my eyes, I allowed myself to doze off, the relief at having got out of London washing over me as the train shook my anger away.

I woke up with a start. I was not alone. Sat opposite me was a small man in his late fifties. He was smiling at me.

"Dr Snowdon, I presume?" he said.

I jumped to my feet but found myself facing the man who had claimed to be Tom Harris back at King's Cross. Behind him was a large man with a violent shock of red hair.

"Sit down, laddie," he said. Not seeing much choice in the matter, I did as he suggested.

"Tom Harris," the man sat opposite me said. "Sorry not to have been able to meet you earlier, I was rather busy. It's been a hell of a night actually, not least sat in the back seat while Douggie back there drove to Stevenage like a maniac."

"Got you there in time though, didn't I?" he said.

"Indeed you did, my friend, indeed you did. I would have hated to miss my train."

I began to panic. I am not proud to admit it but I did.

"Look," I said, "if it's money you're after I have plenty of money. We can come to some sort of arrangement."

He shook his head. "You need to calm down, Dr Snowdon." He reached into his pocket and pulled out a small vial and a syringe. "Luckily I have something for that."

He held it up so I could recognise it: a tetrodotoxin preparation, taken, no doubt, from my supply at the undertakers. Could I not even trust those idiots to tidy up properly?

"You wouldn't," I said as he filled the syringe from the vial.

The other two men came and sat down, the one with ginger hair putting his arms around my shoulders, as if he were no more than an old friend.

"For Natalie?" said Mr Harris. "For Laurence? For Charlie? For Dave? For Max? For every poor bastard who has ever ended up on your accounting ledger?" He leaned forward, grabbed my wrist and, as much as I tried to fight back, slipped the needle into a vein. "I assure you I would."

The drug began its slow creep through my system, the lights above me flaring and the sound of the train's movement becoming more and more raucous.

"You never know," said Mr Harris' voice, a terrible, roaring noise in my heightened brain. "You might get lucky. It all depends on how long it takes you to wake up, doesn't it?"

And with that, the blackness descended.

2.

And then the light. And the relief was such that I would surely have cried if only my tear ducts were my own. The drug lingers you see, thought returns before physical control. For now, at least, I was alive.

There were voices:

"… found on a train," one said, "dead as a dodo."

"Heart attack?" asked another.

"Time will tell," said the first voice, "that is, after all, why they pay our wage."

What could he mean by that? My dazed mind wondered.

Then I felt the scalpel slide its neat way along my torso as the pathologists made their first cut.

║║║22

MAX
1.

Let's be honest, I've had my fair share of lousy times. Still, the months that followed did not see me at my finest.

Thackeray was at constant pains to tell me how lucky I was, and no doubt he was right, but I had a hard time believing it what with the pain and being stuck in a wheelchair for eight weeks. No doubt the fact that I managed to beat up so much plant life on the way down made the difference, but there was no lasting spinal damage. Both legs were broken, my left forearm shattered and I have bruises that still show now. Maybe, given my unusual biology, they'll always be there, great purple and green tattoos to remind me of my night of adventures. I'm up and about now, walking with a limp that's probably here to stay, but it doesn't really slow me up, and let's be frank, I am a man only too used to crawling home at the end of a night.

But yes, I was lucky, I know that really. And if I ever doubt it then all I have to do is look at Charlie to see how bad things could have been.

Thackeray did his best to give him some kind of physical

existence, but it's no life. Not really. The corruption of his body was one thing, he might even have been able to move on from that, but Charlie has always been a man of the mind and his mind is no longer the thing it once was.

I saw him the other day while at Thackeray's for one of my interminable physiotherapy sessions. He's moved Charlie in there full time – there's just no way that he could fend for himself – but I wonder how Thackeray manages with the extra strain. He's given him his own room on the ground floor and he just about gets around in an electric wheelchair, a considerable effort having afforded him the use of one of his arms.

"What does he do all day?" I asked, watching Charlie stare out of the window showing no sign of registering a thing beyond the glass.

"Not much," Thackeray admitted. "And I can't tell if it's physiological or psychological. He's either so brain damaged it's all beyond him or so depressed he just doesn't care."

Which marked him out as being a world away from Dave, who has taken to his new existence with all the enthusiasm of a randy bull.

"The man's a bloody menace," Thackeray admitted. "We're supposed to be living a secret existence, and yet the other day he threw himself off Tower Bridge 'just for fun'."

"He always did think he was indestructible," I said.

"Well, he's not. Now more so than ever. A fact I really need to get through his dull head."

Thackeray is still at a loss to explain how Dave was able to reanimate so quickly and I know the fact terrifies him. To be honest I couldn't see the big deal. After all, what real difference did it make?

"He shouldn't exist," he insisted, "and until I understand why he does I won't rest easy."

"Surely that goes for all of us, though," I said. "We're all glitches."

He just shook his head and refused to be drawn. Something that worries me more than anything else: there's nothing Thackeray likes more than talking about his theories; if something scares him enough to keep quiet, you can bet it will one day come back to bite us on the arse.

"We really screwed up, didn't we?" I said. "Sticking our noses in where they didn't belong."

Thackeray was actually angered by that. "You helped put a stop to an ongoing crime that it still sickens me to contemplate. We'll never know how many fell victim to Snowdon and his disgusting operation, but we can at least assure ourselves that it won't happen again."

He was certainly right there, and in no small part down to his enviable connections within the police force. The newspapers had been filled with their usual gleeful outcry the day after, stories of gang warfare having broken out in a church. "SHOCKING EXECUTIONS ON HOLY GROUND" insisted one of the more hateful tabloids before descending into a purple rant about possible witchcraft, and, of course, "the ever-present threat of immigrants bringing their culture to our shores". All trash. Beyond all the hyperbole and sabre-rattling, Thackeray had made sure that enough evidence had been placed in the right hands for an investigation to be conducted and eventually concluded. As he rightly pointed out, we could never know how many of the people on the books of Sure Future insurance died of unnatural causes. Given that the majority of people associated with the crime were in no fit state to see trial, it was decided there was little to be gained from exhumation orders and tissue sampling but bringing further distress to the families. Sometimes it is best to draw a line under these things and move on.

Of course, the one man that could have clarified matters was far beyond questioning. Dr Herbert Snowdon, found dead on a train to Peterborough, had endured a post-mortem. The results of that hadn't helped the investigation. I don't imagine it helped Snowdon much either.

"I didn't kill him," Tom insisted, "though he might wish I had."

I didn't press him on the point. After all, if there was one thing I understood, it was the shame of acts committed in the heat of the moment.

Though, in the unlikely event that you care, I seem to be getting beyond that.

Perhaps it just took experiencing worse to wipe it from my mind. You see, life (and death) is full of bad things. It's full of pain, regret, disgust, horror, injustice, recrimination and disaster. But that's okay, because without all that you wouldn't appreciate the brilliant stuff that's left.

A wise – but deeply annoying – club owner once tried to show me that, staring out over a field of tombstones, but it's taken a while for the lesson to sink in. I am what I am and I'm bloody lucky to be it. Whatever the world throws at me, and however much I may rail against it at the time, I'm still here and I'm going nowhere. You know what they say…

What doesn't kill you just makes you stronger.

READ ON FOR AN EXTRACT FROM:

DEADBEA†

DOGS OF WAUGH

GUY ADAMS

COMING SOON FROM TITAN BOOKS

1

MAX

1.

After hours, and the traffic lights bleed onto wet tarmac. Neon bounces reflections everywhere you turn and somewhere in the distance drunks laugh at the jiggle of cellulite buttocks sliced through by glitter spandex. This isn't the hustle and bustle of daylight hours: this is the flip-side, the kingdom of shadows which comes out to play when the streetlamps begin to glow. The wolves hunt on street corners, guzzling their cans of lager and whistling at hookers; the lost and wounded huddle in doorways, praying for just one more dawn; and bleary-eyed taxi drivers tune out to late-night radio, hoping for the one more fare that'll get them the hell out of there.

Yes, that's right, it's me: Max Jackson, suburban poet and habitual barfly, lost in the backstreets of Soho and high as a hamster in a snow pile of crack.

I do seem to get myself in some pickles, don't I?

In fact I'm thinking of having my name changed to "Max Pickles" just to simplify matters. Or maybe "Pickles Jackson" – what do you think?

Forgive me, not thinking straight at the moment. Pulse racing, I can hear my heart thudding in my ears, sweat pouring off me. Every part of me is twitching, every nerve, every muscle, *every bloody hair follicle*. I want to be sick, but there's nothing to throw up. Besides I haven't the time, because I can hear it behind me and it's gaining. I don't know where I'm running to. I have no plan of action: this is basic "fight or flight" stuff.

And "fight" really isn't an option. Trust me.

"Excuse me, pal."

Shit…

He shuffles in front of me, stained blanket round his shoulders and the dregs of a Special Brew in his pink and chapped fist.

"Spare some change, mate?"

Not now! I haven't got the time or energy. I move to run past him but he follows and we're dancing like footballers.

"C'mon, pal, just a couple of quid for God's sake!"

He's getting angry and – looking into his dilated eyes – I realise I'm face to face with a brother space cadet, so there'll be no space for reason in our negotiations. My trip was force-fed, but this guy's got a monkey on his back the size of King Kong and I just bet it's horny for a banana.

"Out of the way!" I shout, and make to shove him to one side, which, considering his mental state, is something of a mistake. He screams at me and clouts the side of my head with his fist. That's all it takes to knock what little physical control I have into touch: I'm on my arse in the gutter within seconds, with no clear idea of how I could ever get back up again.

Then I see it.

He'd called it a "dog" – the bastard who had set it on me in the first place – but, drug-addled brain or not, I couldn't quite accept the description. There was a touch of the canine to it sure enough, but only enough to highlight quite how *un*-dog-like the rest of it was. If a rabid buffalo had decided to go to a fancy-dress party in dog disguise, then this was how I imagine it would look as it loitered by the canapés waiting to strike. A sinewy ripple of muscle and teeth, froth at the mouth, and nothing you could relate to in the eyes. If their owner had given it exercise, I imagine it would be more likely located in a war zone than a park.

"All I wanted was a couple of quid!" the addict shouts, completely blind to the creature that is standing no more than a few feet away from him. I'd got used to that by now; there was something about these beasts that just slipped off the eyes. Maybe they were just too much for a rational mind to take, or maybe there was some kind of hocus-pocus going on. Whichever it was, when these things ran free on the night-time streets, nobody seemed to notice but me.

The homeless guy could certainly feel it though. I could tell that by the short scream he gave as it pounced on him and gently tore off his face with a wet, tearing sound like Velcro.

Then the beast turns – with fresh meat hanging from its mouth – to look at me.

ABOUT THE AUTHOR

Guy Adams is the author of over twenty books, from *The World House* and its sequel *Restoration*, to the weird western series *The Heaven's Gate Chronicles* from Solaris. He has written original novels featuring Sherlock Holmes for Titan Books – *The Breath of God* and *The Army of Dr Moreau* – adapted classic horror titles for Hammer Books and is currently working on a new horror/espionage series forthcoming from Del Rey UK, *The Clown Service*. He has also worked with comic artist Jimmy Broxton on *The Engine* for Madefire, as well as their creator-owned series *Goldtiger*.

SHERLOCK HOLMES
GUY ADAMS

THE BREATH OF GOD

A body is found crushed to death in the London snow.
There are no footprints anywhere near. It is almost as if
the man was killed by the air itself. This is the first in a
series of attacks that sees a handful of London's most
prominent occultists murdered. While pursuing the
case, Holmes and Watson have to travel to Scotland to
meet with the one person they have been told can help:
Aleister Crowley.

THE ARMY OF DR MOREAU

Dead bodies are found on the streets of London with
wounds that can only be explained as the work of
ferocious creatures not native to the city. Sherlock
Holmes is visited by his brother, Mycroft, who is only
too aware that the bodies are the calling card of the
infamous vivisectionist, Dr Moreau. Mycroft charges
his brother with tracking the rogue scientist down,
before its too late.

HOT LEAD, COLD IRON

ARI MARMELL

Chicago, 1932. Mick Oberon may look like just another private detective, but beneath the fedora and the overcoat, he's got pointy ears and he's packing a wand. Oberon's used to solving supernatural crimes, but the latest one's extra weird. A mobster's daughter was kidnapped sixteen years ago, replaced with a changeling, and Mick's been hired to find the real child. The trail's gone cold, but what there is leads Sideways, to the world of the Fae, where the Seelie Court rules. And Mick's not really welcome in the Seelie Court any more. He'll have to wade through Fae politics and mob power struggles to find the kidnapper—and of course it's the last person he expected.

"Ari Marmell has a remarkable flair for the sinister."
Scott Lynch, author of *The Lies of Locke Lamora*

AVAILABLE MAY 2014

NO HERO

JONATHAN WOOD

"What would Kurt Russell do?" Oxford police detective Arthur Wallace asks himself that question a lot. Because Arthur is no hero. He's a good cop, but prefers that action and heroics remain on the screen, safely performed by professionals. But then, secretive government agency MI37 comes calling, hoping to recruit Arthur in their struggle against the tentacled horrors from another dimension known as the Progeny. But Arthur is no hero, can an everyman stand against sanity-ripping cosmic horrors?

"Wood creates vivid, intensely human characters... A funny, dark, rip-roaring adventure with a lot of heart, highly recommended for urban fantasy and light science fiction readers alike." *Publishers Weekly*

AVAILABLE MARCH 2014

For more fantastic fiction from Titan Books in the areas of sci-fi, fantasy, horror, steampunk, alternate history, mystery and crime, as well as tie-ins to hit movies, TV shows and video games:

VISIT OUR WEBSITE
TITANBOOKS.COM

FOLLOW US ON TWITTER
@**TITAN**BOOKS